SHAMELESS

A Morning Star Institute Novel: Book 2

Alissa T. Hunter

MuseItUp Publishing
Canada

MuseItUp Publishing
https://museituppublishing.com

Cover Art © 2016 by SuzieDesigns
Layout and Book Production by Lea Schizas
Print ISBN: 978-1-77127-866-9
eBook ISBN: 978-1-77127-789-1
First eBook Edition *March 2016

Dedicated to my best friend and husband, Frederick.
Love you to the moon and back babe.

I would like to thank my group of cheerful readers, for without them this book would not be what it is: Callie Hoeman, Jaime Loeppky, Natalie Trouten, Kris Ford, Katrina Best, and Reyanna Hubbard. A thanks to Alex Hayes for your encouragement, and Shane Morse for his enthusiasm. My mother and father for their love, and instilling creativeness into my life. My wonderful husband for his unswerving belief in me, and enduring my many moods from one character to the next. Grandma Kaye for sharing all of her stories, Nana for her quilts which keep me warm. An extra thank you to my dad, Kit, for encouraging me to be silly, and enjoy life to its fullest. Mom, you have been my rock no matter the hour, rain or shine, angel or demon! My talented editors, Christine I. Speakman, and Lea Schizas for making it sparkle, and everyone else living through this book with me. An extra special thank you to my wonderful publisher, Lea Schizas. Without you none of this would have been possible. And perhaps most importantly, a big thank you to all M.S.I fans!

Preface

I don't like the dark. I never have. It's not because I'm scared of the dark or anything, it's because there's so much that gets overlooked in the dark. Believe me, I know firsthand how those creatures in your nightmares are all too real.

I'm one of them.

Of course, there's another reason why all should fear the dark; when you are sleeping, the darkness often uses your mind as a gateway for otherworldly creatures to go from one realm to another.

Even with this knowledge, I could not escape the heavy cloak of the dream from slowly pressing over me like a black veil at a funeral, before finally holding me captive, vulnerable to all the creatures who prey upon dreamers. My mind had no choice but to surrender.

Soon, I was lost within a horrible, nightmarish world, susceptible to all influences beyond my control.

When I entered down into the tombs of the cathedral, he who had beckoned me was standing on a raised dais at the other end of the candelabra-lit room, putting him several steps higher than the rest of the room. His back was to me, preventing me from putting a name to his face quite yet. Even so, there was something oddly familiar about the way waves of golden hair curled around his neck and shoulders. He heard my entrance and turned around, magnificent wings unfurling behind him. I sucked in a sharp gasp, and took an involuntary step back, both because I was surprised at who stood before me, and because of the glorious sight of his wings. My heart thumped painfully inside my chest. I knew this person all too well, and most importantly, hated him beyond a comparison. "Kione," I whispered, watching my breath curl out of my mouth and soar upward. The stone walls and marble flooring only seemed to make the tomb, placed deep within the earth, seem dreadfully colder. Seeing him now sparked the memory of an old dream I'd had, also involving Kione. It didn't take long for my groggy mind to make the connection. This was not the first time he held me captive while I lay sleeping in my bed helpless to his persuasion.

"I've been expecting you, little Starr," Kione said. His wings, the color of a charcoal-gray sky stuck somewhere in-between dusk and a moonless night, were stretched out in full at his sides. Their vastness was breathtaking. Reaching an arm out in front of me, something within me felt eager to touch his glorious wings despite the distance between us, or my hatred for him.

"What it would be like to touch just one feather?" I found myself wondering out loud. It was the only thought swirling around my mind while standing frozen for an immeasurable amount of time. At last remembering whose wings they were, I'd somehow resisted the urge. Finally gathering enough strength, my arm fell back down by my side, with it an intense feeling of regret and want. The smile on his face spoke legions of both his desire for me and of his approval at my reaction to him. My hatred for this person outweighed any desire; Kione had betrayed my brother, Abaddon; it was because of him my brother was wrongfully accused, and taken from me! Tearing my eyes away from him was the only way to keep me from throwing myself at him in an attempt to claw his eyes out. The darker part of me was awakened when in Kione's presence. As though the mere thought alone had summoned it, I could already feel the sinister, snake-like creature begin to make its way up my spine. It took all of my control to will the thorny creature back in its place by telling myself, attacking Kione wouldn't do any good anyway, seeing as this was only a dream. I looked away from his taunting smile, focusing on the marble flooring and the way bright flames burned up through the cracks. Even with the fire, the atmosphere still felt ice cold. Once certain the beast of my anger was concealed, for now, I gazed back up at Kione, determined to not show him any weakness. "What are we doing here?"

"Why are you here?" he echoed my question, his smile never wavering. When he smiled, it was easy to mistake him for anything other than the spiteful and traitorous creature he could truly be. The chiseled lines of his face dominated his smile, making him mimic a Roman god in all his magnificent form. "You're here because you want to be."

"Sorry to tell you, but you're mistaken. I'd never wish to be anywhere near you, not even in my dreams."

Kione opened his arms wide out in front of him, making a grand gesture, "It is true. In order for us to be here it was rather simple. You see all it entailed was for me to accept your cordial invite—when you unknowing put it out into the atmosphere by having me in your thoughts already; this place would not exist if not for your deepest desires to be near me. No need to be ashamed, little Starr, I too have yearnings and dirty little secrets."

Every nerve and muscle in my body tensed before, relaxing, as a feeling of contentment washed over me. Hearing him say he had yearnings, without the need to clarify to what, or whom he was speaking about, excited me. It was all wrong, though, and my mind knew these feeling—whatever they were, weren't organic. They were being forced upon me. It reminded me of the first time Kione ever used his charismatic powers to try and sway me on the beach during a celebration bonfire. I'd been so close to giving in to him then as well.

I swallowed away any feelings he gave me, whatever I was feeling couldn't be real; they were only what he wanted me to feel—it was the way Kione toyed with his prey.

"Don't play games with me Kione," I warned, hands coming to my hips. It was then I noticed my dress for the first time. Glancing downward over my body, it confused me to see an iridescent gown scarcely covering me, and leaving me mostly exposed to pleased, watchful eyes. It was beautiful and felt softer than anything I'd ever had against my skin before; it temporarily distracted me from my current situation.

"It's Victorian satin. Do you like it?" Kione asked, but did not wait for a response when he said, "I must say it looks even better on you than I imagined it would." He stepped down the dais, and began to slowly walk toward me. "Seeing you here now, looking as you should—as a Dark Princess, proves you are more glorious than anyone gives you credit for. But not me, I've also known there was more to you. With you owning the part, you shall stand famously beside me." His voice sounded as smooth and alluring as the fabric did against my skin. He was standing directly in front of me now, and reached one hand to gently trail down one arm before reaching my hips, where he went back up in the *opposite direction, this time trailing the side of my waist, the side of my breast, before resting his hand on my collarbone. Even though this was only a dream, I could feel his touch as if he'd really been there. That was all it took before I fell beneath his spell once more, and had to jerk myself back from his compliments and tricks.*

Furious at how easily he got to me colored me angry-hot from the inside out, and a new understanding about when people say that if anger could be a color it would be red...made since that's all I was seeing at that moment. "The only part I'll play in your demented delusion is to be as far away from you as possible," I said venomously.

"It is the truth. Though I do enjoy the chase, I'm not the one playing games here, little Starr, and as soon as you stop fighting, you will find pleasures beyond your deepest imaginings. You could be the most powerful creature in all the worlds: Heaven, Earth, Hell, and beyond if you let me help you, I can show you the way. We could get there together. All you have to do is take my hand," he said, offering me his hand, with a river of desires flowing through the gleam in his eyes.

My head felt dizzy as it filled with the promises Kione made. Part of me wanted it, wanted it all to be true. The other part of me kept reminding me how Kione fed off what others desired; he toyed with people's minds in order to get what he wanted and to sway people in his favor.

Mustering up all the strength within me, I stepped back and away from Kione. It surprised me as much as it did him. Sounding breathless from having to work so hard to get the words out, I said, "You disgust me. The only pleasure I'll find with you is when I prove to the entire Morning Star Institute what a liar you are, and then have you fed to the Devoraks."

Kione spoke fiercely, ignoring all threats, "As soon as you stop resisting me, you'll realize how impeccable we could be if together."

"Never—I'll never stop resisting you, even if it kills me!"

All traces of humor vanished from Kione's face, and in its place was a look so cold, fear took over, freezing all motion so I could not move.

"And so death shall find the eager," Kione said, and took a step toward me.

"This is it," I thought, before a feather the color of smoldering ashes, pierced my heart.

CHAPTER ONE

Warnings and Lies

I've never been good with taking direct orders. Probably because I thought I could do it better my own way and seized the opportunity every given chance. It didn't help that the person giving orders at the moment was insanely hot, and all I could think about was the way his muscles stirred beneath his shirt with each movement.

That's how the game is played; to see who can get close enough to our opponent and make the winning move. I was losing, considerably.

He may have been my opponent for the time being, but he's also my exceptionally hot, extremely irritating boyfriend who also happened to be the top shape-shifting Hellhound-in-training in our entire Institute…Alcander, Ace. Or at least I thought he was my boyfriend— honestly it's hard to say since he was particularly moody lately, that and we hadn't officially put a name to what we were yet and I was terrified to ask.

It's still all so confusing, especially since it was only a few months ago we had both hated each other with a passion. I'm talking full-blown drive each other crazy, can't stand to be in the same room without wanting to rip someone's throat out, crazy.

Things changed between us when my dad, Apollyon, made Ace my personal Hellhound-guardian when these really horrible, really disgusting creatures called Lamia demons, were obsessed with trying to torture and or kill me. Ace had saved my life and almost got his soul ripped out of him in the process. We both had a hard time lying to ourselves about our feelings, and we ended up letting go of all our reservations and giving into each other fully, and like that, all of our past hatred turned into something else—something fiery and exciting, and nothing I'd ever felt before. It was the most amazing night of my life. Now I'm not sure if I hadn't dreamed the whole thing.

It's hard to say what's real anymore since my mind was running on practically no sleep, and after the disturbing dream I'd had last night, well, my mind was capable of conjuring up anything at this point. One thing was clear though, his standing in front of me looking the way he did: sweating, yelling, combating—all of it was torturing me! And man was he swift. I'd given a half-ass attempt to stop a blow with his foot to my thigh, and ended up taking the hit before stumbling back. I shot Ace a haughty look, one he impressively ignored.

"No, you have to move faster, Dessi! Remember, a moving target is hard to catch. Keep a sword in both of your hands; every strike has the potential to be the fatal blow—wrong again," he said when I tried correcting form. "Put your whole arm into the movement." Ace barked out commands oblivious to the internal war waging through my mind, managing to block every one of my miserable attempts at attacking.

"I'm trying!" I yelled back.

Ace disregarded my outburst and continued to bark out orders. "You hit like my grandmother, now come on and hit me!"

"Isn't your grandmother dead?" I asked, every word dripping sarcasm.

"Exactly. Now, hit me like you mean it." He sounded as frustrated as I felt. It's been two weeks of non-stop training—two-weeks since the Lamia attacks and since my brother was taken, and we were running in circles, and both equally frustrated.

"Why can't I summon some hellfire, or dark magic—something at least?" I asked, again. Despite Ace's strong opinions about how he wanted me to be well trained physically in case there were times when magic wasn't accessible to me, I thought this was a complete waste of both our time.

"No dark magic, no fire-balls. Use your strength. It's got to be in there, somewhere."

"It'll only be a little fire-ball, nothing over the top, swear!"

"No." His answer was short and final.

"Fine," I said, still unhappy. We could be out looking for my brother, Abaddon, and stopping Kione (Abaddon's backstabbing, lying friend) from whatever he was up to.

Kione started this personal vendetta when he framed Abaddon for conspiring with Angels against the Devil by unleashing demons through the Fountain of the Lost. Apollyon who is Abaddon's father and mine, didn't waste any time buying into Kione's bullshit. Apollyon had Abaddon chained and dragged away from the Morning Star Institute. He was probably being held somewhere horrible, maybe getting tortured each day that we hadn't rescued him yet.

He could be starved, or beaten to near death!

My mind conjured up the most awful scenarios it could, in turn making me sick. I had to take a deep breath and force myself not to think of what could be happening to Abaddon right now.

Ace was standing back, giving me space while watching me struggle with my thoughts, a concerned look on his face. It was the first indication in days (other than the trainings), he cared about me at all.

"Are you ready, or do you need another break?" he asked, more of the same concern bubbling up to the surface.

If I said yes, would you keep looking at me like that?

Every day during these past few weeks we practiced sparring in every condition Ace could think of. We would take turns choosing different simulation settings to practice my skills in, we could make our entire training barrack turn into anything we wanted—to go anywhere we wanted to go. That was the cool part of our day. We both had a common dream about seeing the world someday.

Today it was Ace's turn, and he chose for us to be on top of a sky-rise building with an amazing view of a city-jungle in the backdrop. It was identical to the poster he had hanging in his room over his bed.

I eyed Ace heatedly, thinking about the place where Ace slept at night, dreaming about traveling the world. *If he wanted me to fight him and give it my all, I'd do exactly as he wished!* An all new kind of determination fueled me.

I strode forward with a smile tugging up the corners of my mouth. While walking forward, I noted how the sunset splayed out behind Ace and made his usual mossy-green colored eyes look more ocean-blue. Pair the eyes with his dark hair and tall muscular physique, and it was understandable why my concentration slacked.

"Be careful what you wish for," and "prepared to be amazed," were two cliché remarks getting ready to slide off my tongue, annotations I bit back, preferring to show instead of talk.

"Oh I'm ready, are you?" is what I actually said.

Ace detected the challenge in my tone and awarded me with a winning smile. He put some distance between us before gesturing at me with his hand in a wide-sweep of motion to his side. "Let's see what you got, little Starr," he said, calling me by the nickname he'd given me. For a brief regrettable moment my mind flashed back to the dream I'd had of Kione, and how he'd called me by the same name, before shaking the thoughts free.

Stay focused, Ace already doesn't think you're serious enough, I thought, trying hard to hold onto my earlier bravado. With hands on my hips, I studied my surroundings carefully, calculating how far Ace stood from me and the roof's edge. Within seconds I knew exactly what to do. *Now if I could only pull it off.*

Using my strong legs as leverage, they gave me the speed I needed to charge forward off the balls of my feet into a sprint. Loose gravel shot up and stung my calves as a result. I didn't care though. I needed all the speed I could manage to get this right. Ace braced himself, ready to defend my attack. With less than five feet away, I surprised him by spinning in a full one-eighty degree circle to my left, before catching my footing on the ledge of the building, pushing off into the air, my muscles screaming in pain with the exertion. I was only on the ledge of the roof for a split second in order to push myself up even higher, soaring over Ace's form. I looked down long enough to see a look of sheer surprise on his face before landing a solid blow to his shoulder with perfect warrior-grace. Ace would have approved if he had time to get a word in edgewise. My kicking his ass sort of prevented further commentary on his end.

He swayed backward from the force of the blow, but it wasn't enough to take him down. If he had been a demon—like the one Ace and I fought off together a month ago when we accidently opened the portal to the *Fountain of the Lost*—I would have gone for the arm, severing it. Of course *that* particular Demon we'd fought had had six arms, but that's beside the point. It wasn't until landing behind Ace in a kneeling position with a sword poised and ready, waiting for Ace to turn around for me to strike. He was met with the tip of my knife aiming at his chest.

I did it, I actually did it! I couldn't believe it worked. How do you like me now? I thought, unsure of why all these corny sayings kept popping in my mind. Judging by the look on Ace's face, he couldn't believe I'd gotten away with it either.

"Who's your grandma now?" I admit, it was a cheesy line, but effectual, and not a phrase I'd ever heard used before. The pleased, if not slightly amused look on his face matched mine.

"Better," Ace said, his words of encouragement short-lived when he followed by saying, "but you won't always be given time to figure out your next move. You need to be able to act swiftly without pause. Your adversaries won't allow you time for calculation. "

My smile vanished.

Why was he being so hard on me?

Standing, it took a lot of energy not to cry tears of frustration. "Next time when I'm fighting an opponent, they wouldn't already know all my moves," I said, between clenched teeth, letting some anger resurface. Of course, I didn't really mean it—Ace was the best here at the Morning Star Institute—well, except for Abaddon but he wasn't around right now.

Ace's face fell as though I'd slapped him. "That's not fair, Dess, you know I have to be tough on you. I want you to be prepared—to be able to protect yourself. If anything happened to you…" he trailed off, making my heart give a little squeeze inside my chest. Wounded pride won out over the way Ace melted my insides, and more biting commentary began pouring out.

"I did fine when the Lamia-demon had you pinned down, and no one else was around," I said, unable to quit hitting him with my words—they were my only weapon. Ace was only taken by the Lamia in the first place because he was trying to protect me. Gods I make the lousiest girlfriend ever!

I watched as the muscles in Ace's jaw tensed reflexively. "If a new instructor is what you want, I'll see what I can do," he finally said after an agonizing moment of silence.

"If you think it'll help, chief," I said, and immediately guilt and regret began sinking in.

In truth, I didn't want to do this, any of it without Ace. Unable to tell him as much, he continued. "We're done here and you must be tired." He turned away, gathering our training supplies before stuffing them into an oversized duffle bag.

I looked around at the simulation still set in New York and my shoulders dropped. I was doing it again, what the old me—the one who still hated Ace—would have done a month ago—putting up a wall of defense and lashing out irrationally as a built-in defense mechanism to keep from getting hurt, something I didn't need to do anymore. Behind Ace's hard shell of a mask that he wore to keep people away, was really this caring, selfless person. I'd seen the goodness of his heart enough times by now to know him for his true self. Deep down his soul was one of the good ones.

You're such a jerk, Dess! It was too late to take back the words once they were in the tension-filled air.

I sighed and called after him when he turned and started to walk away. "No, Ace, wait." Ace stopped in his tracks, and slowly turned around with a guarded expression on his face.

He looked so vulnerable, like *he* was the one trying to protect himself from getting hurt. It made him seem more complicated, deeper somehow, and made me realize I still had a lot to learn about him.

"What?" he asked, barely louder than whisper.

This time it was my turn to flinch; if we weren't careful with the way we were throwing around our words, someone was bound to lose an eye or something. "Look, I don't want you to find someone else to train me, okay?"

Ace let out a heavy breath. "Dess, I think you were right," he started to say, but I went on like he never spoke.

"I'm trying here, it's just…ever since that whole council meeting disaster I've sort of lost myself—a small piece of me each day it seems. I can be better, but only if you're willing to stay. Will you, Ace, stay? I can't do it without you." I was promptly interrupted by the sound of applause.

Ace and I both whipped our heads in the direction of the clapping intruder who was standing near the roof's entrance.

Kione.

Of course who should we find other than the one person to be blamed for everything going bad in my life right now, not to mention hated more than words could possibly explain—though I wouldn't mind trying; Gods know I had plenty to tell him. Ignoring Kione's attempts at getting under my skin by not dignifying his efforts seemed best.

"Having a lovers' quarrel?" Kione asked, looking thrilled to have walked in on what was painfully obvious going on between Ace and me.

"What are you doing here, Kione? I thought you were smart enough to keep your distance," I said, concentrating on not getting distracted by his striking appearance. It seemed cruel those looks had to be wasted on someone like him. Don't get me wrong, Ace placed higher on the sexiness scale, but Kione sure knew how to make a grand entrance. I'd forgotten how tall and strong he was—in a carefree surfer-hunk kind of way: complete with shaggy blond hair, and strong bronzed muscles that were easy to identify even through his clothing.

Up until now I hadn't seen Kione around, not since he stuck the putative knife in my brother's back weeks ago. We all assumed he had fled the Institute true to his nature. Once a drifter always a drifter, I thought, still troubled by the fact I couldn't get a good reading on him since he had some kind of block on his soul, not allowing others to assess his identity.

That's another thing about me, I'm a soul-reader. Meaning I can pretty much see a person's true capabilities and get a feel on what kind of person they really are by peering deep into their eyes or with a quick reading of their soul aura. The name a person is given at their time of birth is branded onto their soul and forever molded into their character. It is a gift I actually enjoy; it's not everyone who gets to see what kind of mark each person will leave on the world, or worlds. I can tell if someone has wrongful objectives or not; it's sort of my own personality, or mood gauge. And by not being able to get even the slightest glimpse of Kione's brand, I had no way of seeing through to his true intentions. The allure of the unknown was what drew me to him in the first.

Kione's timing was spot on with the end of our training simulations. It slowly began to fade away before our eyes, leaving the three of us standing back in the middle of the training grounds: a cold, dull landscape of boring gray walls, and plain cement floors. I was already missing the city view.

"Why, I came to see my favorite little Starr, of course," he said.

"Don't call me that," I said, and went to take a step forward, my hands balled into fists down by my sides. I guess keeping my thoughts to myself wasn't going to be so easy after all.

Luckily, Ace's hand reached out and prevented me from unleashing my full rage on Kione. I turned my stormy gaze on Ace who kept a similar stare locked on Kione. He must have not appreciated Kione using the name he'd given me either. "Don't, he's baiting you," Ace said, being the more rational one, a rarity when it came to Ace who normally acted on pure impulse ninety-nine percent of the time.

"He's delusional!" I shouted, angrily eyeing Kione who watched my reaction as though I were every bit as entertaining as he'd hoped.

"You're probably right, but don't give him the kind of response he seeks here," Ace spat venomously at Kione.

The only thing that may have stopped me from going after Kione right then and there, was when I took a second glance at Ace and had seen how every muscle in Ace's body was rigid, and shaking with anger. He wanted to give Kione a piece of his mind, and maybe his fists too. I didn't blame him; after Abaddon brought Kione to the Institute to help thwart off the demon attacks, Kione accused Abaddon of working with the two Angels, Ethan and Lain, to bring down Apollyon and his precious Institute of Hellions.

"Fine," I said, and when Ace was sure I wasn't just saying what he wanted to hear as some trick for me to go off and make good on my promise to kill Kione, he released his hold on me.

"Hmm," Kione hummed while making disappointed clicking sounds with his tongue, regarding the two of us.

"What are you going on about?" I asked annoyed, though it was against my better judgment.

"Oh nothing really, I just find it funny when remembering a more gracious welcome the last time I paid visit to the Morning Star. Does a moonlit walk on the beach ring any bells?" Kione asked, eyes shining in delight at having baffled me. It was only then did I realize my mouth was hanging slightly open in disgust as Kione spoke of the night he'd used his persuasion on me, and long story short, we ended up kissing. The worst part of the story is I'd liked it. "No matter, I can conjure them up here,"—he tapped the side of his head—"in my memory when the mood strikes. Now to deliver the news I'd come here too. Apollyon asks for his daughter to be present during his announcement, which he'll be making momentarily."

"What announcement?" Ace beat me to asking Kione.

"Telling you would take all the fun out of it. I could, however, escort you there myself if you prefer?" Kione said, putting the full weight of those startling, stormy-gray eyes on me. Despite my best efforts, I felt myself sway under his gaze.

Ace put an arm around me protectively. "No need. We'll be there," he all but growled at Kione.

"Very well." Kione gave me a significant smile knowing exactly how he affected me. He turned then and left the training grounds, a chipper stride to his step.

"Man, I hate that guy," Ace said, once we were alone again.

All I could do was nod my head, still affected by the residual air of odium Kione awakened in me. I'd have to watch my self-control around him. It was all too easy for me to fall under Kione's charismatic powers. Chills spread over my body with the memory of how easily swayed I'd been by Kione on the beach only weeks ago when I'd wanted nothing more than to please him. The feeling of weakness tangled within Kione's marionette strings as he toyed with me however he liked, would never happen again.

"He might be staying for a while this time," Ace said, voicing the same fear I'd been thinking at precisely the same moment.

If that's true, and Kione is planning on staying a while, I can't be left alone with him. I can't trust myself around him and his compelling influences.

"Yeah," I said, letting Ace lead me out of the training grounds with one arm wrapped around my shoulders while his other arm carried the bag with all our training equipment. It was nice to have him here to help carry some of this weight bearing down on my shoulders, figuratively and literally.

We were silent as we walked down the narrow stone stairwell, and the rest of the way through the school to drop our bag back off at the training ground before heading over to the dining-hall to hear Apollyon's big announcement.

* * * *

The dining-hall was located in the main part of the Institute. Instead of resembling a typical luncheon area for teenagers to eat, as you might expect from watching high school dramas on TV, ours matches the rest of the Institute's gothic, Romanesque architecture, boasting detailed gold paintings on the ceilings, intricate stone carvings, and arched stonework used in doorways and window areas. By the time we got there the room managed to become packed with Hellions of every size, shape, and color. A constant buzz of chatter floated around us in curiosity as to what the announcement would be. I recognized a certain peach-skinned Pixie who wore her blonde hair in a stylish jaw-length bob. Her name was Ebony, or Pixie-girl; a name given to her by yours truly. Our friendship started off rocky, until we learned how both of us have psychotic dads who were both kings of their domains, hers being a glitter-loving Pixie King, and mine a sinister bastard truly living up to his title as the fallen Angel, making one fricken-fantastic Devil, and winning the lousy father of the year award repeatedly. Nothing like daddy issues to bring two people together.

Pixie-girl saw the two of us and waved us over. She was standing next to a familiar tall and goofy, though handsome, Hellhound-guardian-in-training, Blake, my best friend. The two of us had been inseparable since before I could practically remember. Which is why it felt strange to not be spending as much time together lately, and seeing him spend more of it with Ebony, since they were pretty much dating now. Plus, ever since Blake announced he had feelings for me, feelings I could not return, things had been more than awkward between us.

"There," I told Ace, pointing to where Pixie-girl and Blake stood, meaning for us to make our way over to them. Ace and I squeezed through the crowd, "This is crazy," I said to Ace nearly shouting over the noise. Every Hellion must have been in there.

"Hey," Blake said as we took our seats next to him and Pixie-girl. Once I was able to get a closer look at Blake, I had to choke back a laugh upon seeing his muddy-brown hair disheveled every way, suspecting he'd styled it to look messy on purpose. It suited him.

Blake caught me staring and blushed, his cheeks turning a shade of red, making him cuter still.

"Do you know what the big news is?" Ace asked Blake, leaning over me in the process. Maybe sitting in-between Ace and Blake wasn't such a good idea after all.

"Um, I'm not sure, and actually, I was about to ask you," Blake told Ace.

"Must be something big, why else have a full audience?" Ace observed.

"True," Blake agreed.

"Or we could be quiet and pay attention, it looks like they're about to get started," Pixie-girl said, reminding me of the bossy librarian's assistant she was, similar to the first day we'd met. I've come to appreciate her no-nonsense attitude of late.

Finally, someone stepped up to the large makeshift podium set up in the front of the room.

Aeglaeca, or Aeg, as we referred to the old demon, motioned for the noisy group of Hellions to be silent by raising both arms in the air. The black cloak he always wore looked two sizes too big for his bone-skinny frame, drooped low around his arms appearing to be black appendages resembling bat wings. A bat was a fitting comparison when you threw in his beady eyes and milky skin that always looked like it was molting. What everyone else couldn't see that I could, was the black and olive-green colored aura tailing Aeg, branding the old demon as a creature who could befriend you one moment and as easily be your worst enemy in the next.

When he gestured, the room quieted immediately. Aeg showed indifference to the obedience shown to him, though it was hard to tell since Aeg used the same facial expression for every occasion. Even so, whatever he was about to announce, a feeling of dread came over me.

The feeling intensified the moment Kione walked up the few steps of the podium to come and stand silently behind Aeg. "This is not going to be good," I said under my breath while looking at Ace. He shook his head side to side as way of agreeing with me.

"When did he get back?" Blake said.

I felt bad for not having time to catch him up to speed beforehand.

Guilt must have been a prominent feature on my face, because it didn't take long for Blake to understand. "You knew he was back, didn't you?" he asked, this time leaning over Ace to speak to me.

Ebony, who was sitting on the other side of Blake, watched all of our exchanges with unease, not quite knowing what role she played or when to speak up within our dysfunctional group. Pixie-girl would have to get used to Blake caring about me, I thought taking some kind of messed up satisfaction in her discomfort.

Yeah and you might have to accept Pixie-girl sticking around too.

"Yes—but we just found out a little while ago. I'm sorry we didn't tell you," I rushed out.

"We?" Blake asked, glancing from me to Ace, and then back to me again, shaking his head when Kione stepped forward and addressed the room full of Hellions, ending our conversation.

"Many of you have heard the rumors spreading around the Institute faster than a swarm of flesh eating insects,"—Aeg waved his hand over the crowd of pupils distastefully, not hiding his dislike for teenage Hellions—"about a new mentor joining us. Apollyon, who could not be here today, sends his sanction in accepting this new mentor, Kione, another amiable Succubus, to the Dark Manor."

"Thank you, Aeg, for that gratifying introduction. Hello Morning Star pupils, it is an honor to be amongst what I believe will one day be some of the finest hell-sent creatures to ever exist."

Immediate applause and cheering broke out, filling the dining room. I was vaguely aware my mouth was hanging open as I watched Kione, who stood up there with his hands clasped out in front of him, smiling charismatically at a group of girls all of whom were swooning over him. No one swoons anymore, but that's what they were doing. It was sickening to witness.

"He's seriously trying to pass himself off as a Succubus!" I said, outraged. It was clever of him, but I wasn't buying any of it: not the Succubus thing, not the fake smiles, not the being-here-as-a-mentor-thing. There had to be more to explain Kione's abilities. For one, a

Succubus could never create the kind of fire-creature Kione had when we first met on the beach.

"I can't believe this is happening," I said.

"Me either," Ace said, and then thought to add, "Don't go and do anything stupid," while leering down at me sternly.

I was tempted to say, "He started it." but refrained.

"Succubus?" Blake asked suspiciously, joining in on the disbelief.

"Yeah, right? The position has already been filled. We don't need another Succubus thinking they run things around here," I said speaking of Scarlett, a Succubus and bitch set on making my life a living hell.

"So what, we have a new mentor, I mean what's the big deal?" Pixie-girl asked, completely clueless to why we were all responding the way we were. Blake obviously hadn't told her about the connection between Kione and Abaddon being imprisoned.

What did they talk about when they were alone? I wondered curiously. "The big deal is," I began to say, trying to remind myself it wasn't her fault for being just as naïve as the rest of the Institute obviously was, "Kione is a big, fat, fake and I'm going to show everyone the real him."

"Yep, it's too late. Let me guess. You've come up with some kind of crazy plan to expose Kione," Ace said, sounding exhausted by the notion.

"No," I said, and Ace looked relieved, right up until I said, "But I will,"—and hastily arose from my seat and made way to leave.

"Dess?" Ace questioned whether or not he should follow. I could see a similar expression on Blake's face. "No, I have to get out of here," I called over my shoulder before leaving.

Out of the corner of my eye, I could see I'd caught unwanted attention from Kione in the process. We held gazes for a moment, long enough for me to see the humored and slightly accomplished expression on his face. He was acting as though he'd reached the goal he had set out for today.

I couldn't care right then though because staying there in the dining hall and watching the satisfied smirk growing on Kione's face, was going to make me lose it. Kione was a reminder of the way Abaddon's face had twisted with shock and sadness as his friend openly betrayed him. He might as well have fed Abaddon to the wolves, because framing him before handing him over to the council, and worse, our father Apollyon, was the biggest betrayal of all. Thoughts of that night continued to cascade through my mind, and before I knew it, my legs and feet were running far away from there, from Kione.

I found myself outside the Institute's spear-tipped iron gates. My stomach felt like a million knots were forming at the bottom of it, and I wasn't sure if I was going to be sick or not. *Why, why come back? Was he purposefully trying to torture me?* If so, I hated how it was working.

All of a sudden I wasn't just feeling sick anymore. The world began to spin dizzily.

Oh, this was no good. It was happening again!

My mind panicked as the familiarity of change came over me. My knees buckled out from under me, landing in the sand hunched over in a feline position with my back arching up toward the sky. I held in a scream from the pain, not wanting to cause a scene and chance seeing *him* again, even though my upper back, the spot over my shoulder blades, felt as though there were a hundred scorpions stinging me, tearing my flesh open and exposing it to raw air.

My back was red-hot all over as the magic of an omen set on making my life more challenging than any teenage girl's should be, seized me. When it was done I sat drenched in sweat and too weak to move. When my body began to tremble, I knew that the part where I black-out—as I'd done the previous few times this had happened to me—was next.

I closed my eyes and wished there was an Angel out there who felt like saving me, again, and somehow miraculously make the pain go away.

But one would never come. Not for someone, who by very definition of their existence, was considered part of the damned—the unholy. It was still a nice thought to have as I drifted off to nothingness.

CHAPTER TWO

Bittersweet

His warm breath had a lingering smell of spicy-sweet cinnamon as our lips crushed together with an all-consuming urgency. His smell had become a familiarity to me, even so, breathing him in never got any less intoxicating.

There was an unforeseen hunger to the way Ace kissed me that could have sunk ships in the sea it was so substantial. It was the same with the way his hands played with the hem of my shirt, teasing me, and sending me over the edge.

I burned with the same curious desire. I kissed him back matching his hunger. We'd been holding back so long it seemed neither of us knew where to begin or how far to take it.

Wherever his lips touched skin, as they did on my jaw first, and then my neck, a trail of gooseflesh followed. All of the hate—or at least what I thought was hate at the time, melted away as our mouths eagerly explored one another's. And at last my world felt as though it had completely shattered.

We kissed for hours, while holding each other close. The glassy glare in his eyes showed how his world had also shattered for the better. I could have stayed right here forever memorizing the way his spicy yet sweet mouth tasted, and the way his hands felt on me.

"Hello, earth to Desdemona, anyone home?" I heard our mentor ask. What's he doing here? My mind wasn't thinking straight. *Was I daydreaming?*

"Um," I managed to say embarrassed and blushing. "Huh?" I asked, and felt my cheeks fill with heat thinking about the dream, or was it a memory? From a lifetime ago. Being around Ace all the time and not being able to talk about the night we shared was starting to mess with me.

To my left I noticed both Blake and Ace were watching me; Blake looking more guarded while Ace seeming curious to what could have possibly made me so flustered.

Seeing Ace watching so intensely sent heat all over my body again; the memory of us had felt so real, real enough I could still taste the sweet, spiciness of his mouth on mine.

Before anything had happened between us, we'd both been so wrapped up in trying to hate each other all the time, and now that we finally accepted our true feelings for each other, things were even more complicated.

Why did Ace have to be so damned difficult all the time?

I had to look away or else I'd probably cry; nothing more embarrassing as having a steamy daydream in the middle of a room full of Hellions.

When the mentor cleared his throat, I realized he was still waiting on an answer from me."Yes, here. Sorry," I said, scooting my chair back to stand, backing away from the table, careful to avoid direct eye contact with Ace. "Um, I need to be excused." Without giving the mentor a chance to ask why, my legs carried me out of the class. Being the daughter to the Devil had its perks sometimes.

I half expected to hear the sound of hurried footsteps following behind me. When I'd made it half way to the recovery bathing chambers and only the sounds of my own feet echoed down the hall, I knew no one was coming. The bathing chambers were a part of our training routine, and my muscles were unhappy from the change in schedule. It had been a matter of wanting to eat, or wanting to bathe, I'd chosen the first, food winning out over cleanliness.

It's just as well, I thought, and started to undress. *After all, if Ace was here, he'd demand to know what had gotten into me back there, and I didn't feel like explaining myself to him.*

After a few more seconds of being angry, I dropped my arms down by my sides, releasing them from where they were crossed tightly over my chest. Stressing over my relationship—or actually lack thereof on top of this whole Kione thing—was exhausting. And frankly I was too tired and sore to care.

I walked over to where a giant barrel-shaped bathtub sat in the middle of what pretty much looked like a locker room, and walked up the three steps to look down at the blue water.

Water ran out of the old bronze faucet and spilled up and over the edge before collecting in a basin at the bottom. It reminded me of a fountain more than a bathtub. I dipped the toes of one foot into the water to first gauge the temperature and had to quickly get down to adjust it. Once satisfied the water was perfect—hot to the point I could handle—I stepped in, and my whole body relaxed. *Now this was pure bliss.* The water worked wonders for my sore and fatigued muscles; training took its toll on my body.

Lifting my hand up out of the bath I examined the way the water beaded off my skin; the healing components in the bath, made from a combination of milk, honey, eucalyptus, and some other supernatural component, made it feel waxy.

I wasn't sure how long my eyes had been closed before the metal door to the healing room flew open, banging into the wall.

My eyes shot open and a small yelp of surprise bubbled up out of my mouth. Sitting up, alarm bells sounded in my mind.

"Ace! What are you doing in here?" I demanded, sinking into the water to conceal my body from him.

"You wanted to find out where Abaddon was being kept right?" he asked.

Asking me a question he knew I couldn't ignore…smart of him, I thought.

Momentarily forgetting I was naked, I moved closer to the edge of the bath, gripping the sides of the barrel with both hands eagerly. "You know where he is?"

"Not exactly," he said, regret showing on his face, "but, I know how we can find out," he quickly added.

"Oh, okay," I said, letting out a long, dejected sigh.

"Don't you want to ask me how?"

Sure, why not? "Okay, how?"

He gave me a contented smile and walked forward until he was about an arm's length away. It was then I remembered my nakedness, and sank further down into the water so only my head stuck out of the water, huddling my body as close to the edge of the tub as possible.

Not that it seemed to matter. Ace didn't appear affected one way or another. He spoke excitedly when he answered my question with another question. "Who do we know with a direct link to the council?"

Who did I know with ties to the council? The only creatures coming to mind were all higher-demons, all of whom we couldn't get close to, and even if we did they'd never agree to help us.

And then the answer hit me. "Pixie-girl." Her father, the Pixie King, happened to be a huge part of the council. *Of course, why didn't I think of that?*

Ace's head began to nod. "Uh-huh, and I think I know a way we can get her to help us," he said, smiling down at me. His eyes gazed down the length of my neck before falling to my collarbone where they stayed. I'd been thinking about Ace's question so intently I'd forgotten to stay fully immersed beneath the water.

As brilliant as this lead was, the difficulty of the task of getting Ebony to agree to help where her father was concerned wasn't lost on me. "How? And do you think Pixie-girl, err—Ebony would be willing to help?"

Ace shrugged unconcerned, "I figured we could ask Blake. I mean what could it hurt?"

Probably a lot. "Yeah I'm not so sure it's a good idea, Ace." In theory it was a great idea since Blake and Ebony were somewhat of an item. He could probably talk her into it.

"You can't avoid him forever, Dess, now's as good a time as any to start speaking again."

Another painful thought. "I know, and we talk, kind of," I said.

"Kind of is not the same as doing," he said, unimpressed with my answer.

I inhaled, there was one thing I could think of to change the topic, *and* deliver the payback he deserved for always walking around, looking so dammed smug and sexy all the time. In one smooth motion I stood, trying hard to remain unfazed by the rush of cold air that greeted me, a cool smile on my lips.

Ace, momentarily stunned, sucked in a quick gasp. When he finally did breathe again, he turned his head to the side slightly taking in my form in all its natural beauty. "Can you hand me a towel please?" I nodded my head in the direction behind him for emphasis since it didn't seem as though he could make sense of words, a novelty I enjoyed immensely.

Ace's response was to open and shut his mouth a few times before he could properly respond, "Um yeah, hang on," he sounded winded. Reluctantly he took his eyes from my body. Without needing to be in front of a mirror, I knew what he would be seeing: my long sculpted muscles that made me look strong and durable due to all the training. When he managed to recover, slightly, he turned from me and strode over to the bench where my towel was laid out and ready. Turning back around, he tried not to fumble nervously, failing when he handed me the towel and forgot to let go of it. He was in a daze, looking at me with hungry eyes; aqua and thoughtful. I reeled him in.

"Um, Ace," I said.

"Huh?"

"I'm kind of getting cold here," I told him.

"Oh, right. Here you go," he shook his head, letting go of the towel.

"Thanks," I said and began towel drying my hair.

"I'll-uh, wait outside," he spoke with effort. It was evident he needed to put some distance between us.

When the door closed him off from the healing chamber, I couldn't hold back a little victory dance, resisting the urge to laugh out loud in case he was standing near the door and hear me. Score one: Dessi, Ace, zero…I thought, smiling while getting dressed.

For times like this, I kept a spare pair of clean clothes in one of the lockers. I grabbed the black leggings and emerald-green tank top I had stowed away, and then had a hard time sliding into them since my skin was still damp from the bath. Reaching up and wiping away the fog covering the mirror, I gave myself a once over in the full-length mirror. Two charcoal outlines of wings stared back at me. I reached one hand back over my shoulder and glided my fingers across the raised edges studiously. I already stood out as Apollyon's daughter, but now with this marking branded into my skin, I felt like a freak among what the world already considered unnatural abominations. I wasn't sure if I'd ever get used to seeing it there, and not entirely understanding why it was there or what it stood for. All I know of it is it had something to do with being Apollyon's daughter, something he referred to as phasing, and how I would continue to do it until I blossomed into all my powers. Something to do with what the Angel, Lain, had once told me about needing to choose the right path before proclaiming he believed the good would outweigh the darkness in me.

Shaking those thoughts from my mind, I began finger-combing my wet hair with more vigor than necessary. My hair, naturally dark, looked even darker when wet, reminding me of the blue-black hue of a raven's wing. While straightening my hair out over to the side of one shoulder allowing me to gaze at the intricate lines on my upper back, thoughts of what Lain said to me flitted through my mind.

"Evil's purest light shall break through desire,
as Angels weep in fear and love, through flames of fire,
the pits of Hell quake before her,
even the strongest of the fallen shall fear her bending their knees in
fright of her power.
Creator of the darkness shan't bend the light, while Eve's Beloved,
shall conquer the night."

I still didn't know what it meant, not exactly. Lain had spoken those words to me as some kind of life raft meant to keep me from drowning.

Sighing it all away, I smoothed my long, dark hair back over my back and shoulders to conceal the outlined wings once again, and left to meet up with Ace who stood not so patiently, waiting.

"Took you long enough," he grumbled.

"Sorry," I said, though I really wasn't, and after, we both walked together, mostly silent, but a good comfortable kind of silence, toward the Hellhounds' living quarters of the Dark Manor, another name for Apollyon's lair. The Institute portion of the building took up most of the Manor's space, though the living quarters and the training quarters weren't small occupancies by any means. The whole Institute was adorned in rare art and lavish furnishings all while set around a Romanesque-gothic architecture including Cornish moldings, gold-painted ceilings, and candelabras hanging on the walls.

The Hellhounds' living quarters, where we were now, was located on one of the lower levels. To me, the living arrangements inside the Hellhound quarters resembled college-style dorm rooms. I could compare because once Blake and I had snuck onto the campus during what was supposed to be a field trip on pointing out other Hellions who blended into society without humans knowing. These rooms still integrated the same feel of gothic interior the rest of the Manor did, with rose-stained glass in every window, and more gray stone. All of these rooms were neatly crammed down both sides of the long hallway. The Hellhound quarters also sat closest to the training grounds where guardians-to-be spent most of their time. Even though I too spent a good deal of my time training there, my room was positioned near the center of the Manor in the highest possible corner, making me get a workout in before our trainings began for the day.

We finally found Blake in the recreation room after having first checked his bedroom. He was in the middle of a game of pool with Warren, a fellow Hellhound comrade.

Blake's head turned at our entrance. Our eyes locked briefly before he turned back to the game, giving it his full attention. Ignacio—a lively hound whose soul aura always appeared intense and fiery, resembling the neon-purple Mohawk he wore his hair—waved enthusiastically over at me.

It was nice to see Ig's happy face. Especially since every time I saw Blake he made me think of how I imagined it would be like to look into a soldier's wounded eyes: I could tell that he was trying to conceal the hurt he really felt. Blake was always one to carry his heart on his sleeve, including the broken fragments of his heart.

With a pretend indifferent flip of my hair, I strode forward giving a small laugh at Ignacio.

"Come. Sit. Play," Ignacio ordered.

Walking over to where Ignacio and the other Hellhounds sat gathered around a large felt-covered table playing cards, while Ace remained where he was leaning against the doorframe, I said, "Nah, I don't feel like hustling you all today with my amazing card skills. We came for Blake." Though I had a feeling he wouldn't go easily, and we might as well let him finish his game. I did a quick headcount, besides Ace, and Blake, there was also: Ignacio, Caleb, Braeden, Sheldon, Warren, Hunter, Jair, and Fergus…ten out of the thirteen were present. The only ones missing were Damarcus, Ralph, and Nass. From the sounds of the steady thrumming coming down the hallway, I'd bet they were next door playing basketball.

Ignacio kept playfully turning his head to me and then back to the game before turning back to me again, feigning nervous indecisiveness when it was his turn to play. I smiled. "Cute, Ig, you're such a dork. We all know you don't have anything worth laying down," I said, laughing.

"No way, was that actually a smile I saw? Look guys, Dessi Starr smiles!" Ignacio said, addressing the others who did not look impressed by his findings. They did, however, look to be waiting anxiously for Ignacio to call or check. "You better be careful with that,"—he pointed at my face—"or we'll start to think you care."

"Careful, Ignacio, you might hurt her feelings and she'll run off to tell her boyfriend," Sheldon teased, suggesting Ace as my boyfriend while elbow-nudging Hunter who was unfortunate enough to be sitting next to him.

Hunter didn't even blink. With so many different people in the room, my soul-reading gauge was running on overdrive, and it threatened to overwhelm me. I was usually pretty good at turning it off when needed, but for some reason today it struggled to close off to the rest of the world. Since Sheldon was the one I was looking directly at, his shone the brightest, his soul aura had hard lines around the edges, suggesting he often put walls up, not letting people in. Something I could relate to.

Resting one elbow on the table, I propped my head up to try and ward off a headache getting ready to make its debut. "Nah, I'll just play my *Dark Princess* Card and tell my dad, I think you know him as Apollyon, or the Devil—you know, big horns on his head, sharp, pointed tail, red all over." When every hound at the table looked at me with a different version of their own shocked expressions, I couldn't hold back the laugh that followed. "You should so see your faces." I laughed even harder.

Several of the hounds relaxed, some even chuckled along with me. "Big horns, that's funny," Ignacio said.

"You're right, I wouldn't do that. But, maybe this," I said, feeling the heat of hellfire lick at the palms of my hands. It formed instantly for me now, when only a month ago it took all of my concentration to create even a spark. I sent a dragon fire creature swooping over the poker-table, swarming in-between everyone. Ignacio was the first one to burst out laughing, and it wasn't long before everyone joined in, even Sheldon. Finding time to steal a glance over to Ace I saw him watching me in amusement, and there was something else there too; some undetected foreign emotion.

Whatever the look, it was doing funny things to my heart. When our eyes met, he held onto the look making the moment between us almost feel too private to be sharing it with a room full of Hellhounds. All too soon, it ended. Ace blinked it all away, and straightened up before walking over to where Blake stood. "Well this has been fun, but hey man, we need to talk with you, Blake. Now," he said, not wanting to waste any more time.

Blake turned to face Ace, clearly annoyed at being interrupted. While I didn't think of Blake as the angry, violent type, I decided it wouldn't hurt to keep an eye on the pool stick rack hanging on the wall right next to Blake. "That doesn't surprise me," Blake said, never taking his eyes off his cards in hand. "After I finish here."

Ace fixed stormy eyes on Blake, and strode over to him, "Sorry, we don't have time to wait," Ace said. Tension could be seen building between the two hound comrades. It wouldn't have been a surprise if the rest of the hounds pushed their chairs back and all started shouting, *fight fight fight*. Luckily they didn't.

Sometime during the stare down, I'd moved closer without realizing it, and had gone so far as to put one hand around Ace's arm, ready to pull him back if need be.

Blake bounced his gaze back and forth between Ace and me, eventually translating the urgency. Breathing out a heavy sigh, Blake set his cards down, pushed his chair back and then stood. "Okay. You have my attention. What's going on?" Relief flooded me.

"Let's take a walk," Ace suggested, after seeing eight curious Hellhounds-in-training watching our exchange hungrily.

"Good idea," I agreed.

After stepping out of the room, and walking down the hall until we were sure no one was around, I said, "Do you know where Ebony is at?"

Calling her Pixie-girl might not gain us any favors from Blake. "We actually need her for this."

"Tell me what's going on first," Blake said, crossing his arms tightly over his chest. His sudden skittishness annoyed me.

"Fine. You know how we're trying to figure out where Abe is being kept so we can break him out?" I asked, fiddling nervously with the hem on my shirt.

"I do now—though I suspected you were up to something," he said, voice peaking sounding interested now.

"You're right, which I guess you already knew either way."

"What she's trying to say is, we need to use Ebony and her valuable connection to the Pixie-King, since her father is part of the council of higher demons," Ace finished for me.

"Hey," I said, "I was getting there!"

"Yeah, maybe in ten years," Ace murmured.

"No. No way!" Blake complained, pacing back and forth while clenching his fists together.

"Whoa, what's with all the testosterone? You're not even going to ask her, not for Abaddon—for me, just like that?" *What happened to my friend from before? The one who would do anything to help me?*

"Yeah exactly like that," he told me. I could feel my eyes start to fill up with tears. It's the way my body responded to emotion I didn't know how to process. Turning a help-me-glare on Ace was his queue to step in again.

Ace stepped in front of me, putting himself directly in front of Blake and his unusual hostility. "Look, we wouldn't be asking if we had any other option here. Right now it is the only one we have," he told Blake.

"Sorry, but unlike some people, I don't like screwing with people's lives—I'm not going to use her," Blake said firmly.

"Nobody is screwing with anyone, we only want to talk to her, see if she might know anything, or if she can ask the Pixie King what he knows. I swear, Blake, I'm only trying help my brother." Blake could be mad at me all he wanted for asking, because Abaddon, wherever he may be, was the only one truly suffering here.

Blake watched my face for several long breaths. Eventually saying, "Fine, though you should know Ebony's a good person."

"Never said she wasn't," I said, with an afterthought of getting offended at what he implied.

"Peachy. Now that that's settled can we please go find her?" Ace asked the two of us.

"Fine. Come on, she's in my room. If she's still there," Blake said, reluctantly.

On our way to Pixie-girl, I asked Ace to give Blake and me some space so we could talk. He was happy to oblige, maybe a slight bit too happy.

Looking over at Blake, told me he didn't look especially happy to be cornered by me. "I get that I'm not your favorite person in the world right now, but you know we were going to have to do this eventually," I said, echoing Ace's words at Blake.

He made a huffing sound, turning his head in the opposite direction of me as though the wall was more interesting at the moment. "Right," I said. "It's been kind of a crazy year, hasn't it?" Jeez, he was making me feel more stupid by the second.

What I couldn't have guessed was how my saying this would make him open up to me, "Yes, you could say that it has, among other things?" Blake said.

"Most of all for you; Soul-sucking Demons, pissing off a cranky Banshee, no wait, forget the Banshee; pissing off a whole room of Arch Demons *and* taunting War…now that takes skill," he said, and I couldn't believe my ears when he actually laughed, sounding more like *my* Blake again.

"I'm glad my pain amuses you," I said dryly, feeling comforted.

"Well you've always had a knack for doing things the hard way," he agreed.

I huffed. "Yea well, what else can you expect from someone as badass as me?" This time Blake was the one to huff. We continued walking in silence, lost in our own thoughts for a minute.

Blake nearly tripped me when he grabbed my arm, making both of us stop in the middle of the hall. "Wait, Dess, I need to get something off my chest real fast, I was a jerk to you back there—"

"Yeah you were," I blurted, receiving an annoyed stare. "Sorry. Continue…"

"I was a jerk back there."

"I don't think I'm going to get tired of hearing it…nope, not tired of it," I said, unable to control myself.

"Will you shut up so I can finish!" he said angrily, though I could see the corner of his mouth tilt up slightly contradicting his tone. After making a motion of zipping up my lips, he continued uninterrupted. "It wasn't right for me to talk to you the way I did, and I'm sorry. Helping you find Abaddon is important to me. He didn't deserve any of this—you didn't deserve to have him taken from you when you'd only just gotten him back."

"Thank you, Blake."

Blake nodded. "If Ebony agrees to try and help, so will I."

"Really, Blake, you're amazing."

"Yes, really—but I meant it when I said she's a good person," he warned, pointing a long finger at me.

"Okay I believe you," I smiled, grateful for his efforts. I thought about hugging him, but decided it was probably still too soon.

"Glad the band's back together again and all, maybe we should actually go find Ebony so we can ask her," Ace said, after quietly watching our conversation from a distance.

"Ask me what?" a girl's soft voice asked. We all looked up to see a blonde figure approaching from down the hallway. She must have been on her way to Blake's, I realized, wishing this knowledge didn't bother me as much as it was.

"Ebony, hi," Blake replied, quickly walking around Ace and me to meet her. "We, uh, sort of had something we needed to ask you." He was blushing at either having been caught talking about her, or having been caught with me, while talking about her, I wasn't sure which.

The three of us decided it was better we talk in private somewhere and designated Blake's place to do it. After making it to his room, I could tell Pixie-girl was getting a little freaked out, and as soon as we entered through the door, she crossed her arms over her chest and demanded to know, "Okay I'm here now, so what were you going to ask?"

"Did you want to do the honors?" I asked Blake.

"Probably best," he agreed. Pixie-girl turned toward Blake before grabbing one of his hands in reassurance. I stared at her orange-tinted hand on his and felt guilty for not feeling too fondly about it, Blake's explanation bringing my attention back to their faces.

"There's a way we might be able to find Abaddon, or at least where he's being held."

"Okay." Pixie-girl nodded.

"We need your help though," Blake said, looking sheepish as though he were the bearer of bad news.

Pixie-girl shook her head, confused. "But I don't know where Abaddon's being held."

"No, but you know someone who does, or at least has the power to find out?" Blake hinted.

It didn't take long for understanding to flash across her face, turning her normally orange-tinted skin to a sickly shade of gray, looking horrified.

"No, Blake, I can't." She pulled away from him. Pixie-girl was withdrawing from us, backing up toward the door. We were making her frightened.

Blake looked helplessly over at me, "Maybe there's another way to find Abe without the Pixie King."

"There's not," Ace said brusquely. "This is the only way, and we're running out of time."

He looked from Ace and then back to me again, sighing and nodding before turning back to Pixie-girl. "I know it's unfair for us to ask this of you, and we wouldn't be if it wasn't serious. You don't have to be afraid, we'll protect you—I'll protect you," Blake spoke softly as though he were talking to a child.

Pixie-girl weighed his words for what felt like forever, when in all reality, it had only been several seconds before saying. "I'll do it. However he'll want something in return, you know he will."

"Then we'll deal with whatever it is when the time comes," Blake said, once again surprising me with his chivalry.

I stepped forward. "Please, Ebony, can you find him?"

"I can. You'll want to stand back though," she told us before calling out some strange word I'd never heard before. "Kaj!" Her voice filled the stuffy air in Blake's small room.

Blake stiffened beside her, while Pixie-girl looked paler than usual, her skin turning a sickly gray-hue. Kaj must have been something of importance. I was about to ask when Ace beat me to it.

"What's a Kaj?" Ace asked.

"I'm not really a what, I'm really more of a *who*."

Practically jumping to turn around, I let out a sharp gasp of surprise when spotting him sitting comfortably on the couch—his bare feet up on the coffee table in front of him. It was none other than the Pixie King himself.

CHAPTER THREE

Promises, Promises

"Miss me already, daughter?"

"Hello, dad," Ebony said, less than thrilled to see him. I wondered what could have happened to make her short with him. Having a rocky relationship with a father wasn't completely lost on me.

"That's the Pixie King?" Ace said in disbelief, sizing him up.

"I think so?" I said. His appearance was lacking something. He didn't fit in a stereotypical hierarchy set. Unlike the first time we met, he wasn't wearing his crown made of gold and thorns, or the clothing that had looked perfectly tailored to him during the council meeting. Before he had also been wearing a lot of jewelry; from gold to jewels of different colors and sizes. All of those nonessential things were gone now. It must have all been for show. His outfit also seemed pretty plain, consisting of casual, earth-toned clothing, suggesting he'd been working outside since there were patches of dirt and grass stains on them.

If I hadn't known any better and had met him randomly, let's say on the cobblestone streets of Santorini, I would have guessed he was a gardener, or at the very least, a florist of some kind.

Furthermore, instead of having his hair worn down as it had been during the council, it was secured into a ponytail at the nape of his neck. His hair resembled Pixie-girl's since they both had white-blond hair color making them both look years younger than I'm sure they actually were.

The only thing indicating he was a Pixie King at all was the way glitter fell every time he moved, even the slightest.

Like a rubber band expanding out in my mind, I opened myself up to the Pixie-King. My eyes widened with what lay hidden there.

"What do you see?" Ace leaned in and whispered, recognizing my soul-reading face.

29

Minds are a miraculous thing. No one ever thinks exactly alike. We all come up with our own interpretation of what we see and hear. It's for the same reason why no one else can really explain the significance of emotions felt when listening to a special song, or story from your childhood. It would be similar to trying to explain what the colors of a sunset looked like to a blind person—or a blind person telling you what it's like to see a sunset for the first time. Emotions are purely subjective for the beholder.

My reason for thinking this had something to do with the fact I'd been reading souls for a long time, practically my whole life. Soul-reading didn't seem strange when I was younger, since I had no idea it wasn't normal until the first time explaining the gruesome side of what I saw to a group of girls my age, and ended up scaring all of them practically to death. They ran off before telling our mentor. The mentor brought it up to Apollyon out of concern—or obedience, I wasn't sure which. After, Apollyon dragged me to several different seers, until finally someone explained how this was a gift and how it allowed me to glimpse into a person's true character. Apollyon had pretty much named me his special tool to use against friends and enemies alike whenever he wished, and ever since then has been pushing me to see what else I might be capable of.

"Nothing, weird," I told Ace. The Pixie King's soul aura looked vast with possibilities; it wasn't exactly good, but it wasn't bad either, and more somewhere in the middle. Most of all what I was picking up off him had an earthy feel to it, matching the colors his soul released into our world. His name meant *Earth,* making sense to me since the world as we know it is colossal, and sometimes an unpredictable thing.

It was almost *too* simple.

All this time the Pixie King remained silent, looking as though he enjoyed our uncertainty while we continued to whisper and contemplate. When he spoke, he did so with humor behind his voice, "Were you expecting someone else? Did you not speak my given name?" The Pixie King—or Kaj, moved forward, positioning himself closer to Ace. On instinct I also moved closer not completely trusting him, blaming our training tactics for the comrade alliance I felt toward Ace, or Blake— really any of the Hellhound-guardians.

It was true, Pixies were not claimed by either Heaven or Hell since nobody wanted to deal with them, and for good reason too, my mind added, since Pixies couldn't be trusted. They will do anything, no matter the costs if it benefited themselves.

Precisely the reason why I didn't trust this one. Who knew what he would do or say to spin things in his favor?

With remembering my Pixie facts came the realization he would want something in return. Depending on what he wanted, I wasn't feeling particularly hopeful about him being our ticket to finding my brother. I'd promised Blake not to let anything happen to Pixie-girl and if her dad wanted anything other than a fair trade…my mind started to picture the worst. I opened my mouth to speak, catching the eye of Pixie-girl, who must have seen the panic on my face, stepped forward, and quickly spoke first, "Father we—*I*, need to ask a favor of you."

A playful smile made his lips twitch; it was the only indicator he'd been taken by surprise. I had a feeling catching the Pixie King off guard wasn't an easy task.

Kaj's eyes lit up in excitement, his aura becoming light, making me imagine a strong gust of wind picking up a pile of leaves before scattering them all about. The earthy tones turned to more of a gold-tone shimmering all around the edges. *Well that's a big surprise*— feeling a cynical laugh somewhere within.

"Oh?" he asked intrigued. "Please, do go on."

"We need to know where Abaddon is being held prisoner," Pixie-girl said, straight to the point.

"Oh that *is* interesting," he said, and began tiptoeing around the room with his hands clasped gallantly behind his back as he spoke. "Let me first make sure I'd heard correctly—you want me to help Apollyon's daughter whom he covets as some prized possession, to help find the son whom he despises and regrets the day he was ever born?"

"That's one way to put it," I mumbled, irritated, while Pixie-girl didn't look amused, standing next to Blake with her arms folded over her chest.

"Oh this is going to be fun," Kaj said.

"Look, can you help or not?" Ace asked, growing impatient.

The Pixie King pointed his finger in Ace's direction, shaking it at him like a lecturing teacher who thought one of his students had said something adorable, "Indeed I can. First, a little deal needs to be made."

"I'll do it!" I blurted without thinking. My instinct screamed at me to not let Pixie-girl do it, that no good could come from giving the Pixie King what he wanted.

"Wait, what?" Blake asked stunned.

"I'll do it. I'll make the deal he needs. Abaddon is my brother, so I'll do whatever it is he wants." The Pixie King's eyes widened in happy surprise.

"No, Dess, are you crazy?" Ace grabbed me by the arm, dragging me closer to him, and out of the Pixie King's reach. Pixie-girl remained silent, possibly out of shock.

"You don't know what you're asking, Dess," Blake said, and there was fear in his voice.

"Great, now you two decide to agree for once and you're both wrong," I said, throwing an exasperated glare at both Blake and Ace.

That's when the Pixie King decided to throw his two cents into the mix. "Who I make the deal with is not important, so long as the deal gets made—and soon. My time is rather precious and my patience is growing thin," he warned, and then he did this weird glitch-thing; one moment he was standing in front of us, and in the next he was sitting on top of Blake's TV armoire, his legs crossed at the ankles and his hands gripped together tightly in his lap. By the expression on his face, I'd say he was getting bored with all this and would probably be leaving soon if we didn't hurry and make a decision.

"Me—the deal needs to be made with me, it's what he really wants anyway. Right, father?" Pixie-girl walked across the room to stand in front of the armoire and asked her father, scornfully.

"But Abaddon is *my* brother."

"And so we've all heard you say, many times. It doesn't matter. He wants me to make the deal," Pixie-girl said.

There was no arguing with her when her mind was set. It was sad news, I'd already broken my promise to Blake.

"Are you sure?" Blake asked her.

"Believe me, this is the only way," she told him. It was the way Pixie-girl worded it that made me think she needed to sort out some issues with her father.

If it were Apollyon sitting up there in front of us, I'd have done the same thing. "You're up," I told her.

Pixie-girl gave me a tight smile before turning toward her father. "Let's get this over with," she said.

In less than a second, the Pixie King flashed down off the armoire and stood in front of Ebony, holding her in a crippling embrace between his hands. Pixie-girl was motionless, not even a muscle in her face twitched as he took her shoulders tightly leaning her body down facing the ground. What he did next was frightening: he pushed his mouth against her ear, and began whispering in her ear. Whatever he was saying was indiscernible to the rest of us as we watched the gruesome display in morbid fascination. Pixie-girl remained in a trance-like state as he did so. We all watched as Pixie-girl's skin-tone began to change, becoming almost translucent—so translucent we could see the veins pressing up under her skin, the blood within them turning an ominous shade of black. That was right before the worst thing happened; we watched helplessly as Pixie-girl's mouth opened in a silent scream, only nothing came out. She was stuck inside herself, motionless, unable to speak or scream.

"What are you doing to her?" Blake asked, growing uneasy. "Stop, you're hurting her!" he yelled to the Pixie King, taking a step forward. Ace had to hold him back.

If Blake interrupted, all of this would have been for nothing—her pain would have been for nothing. My stomach felt sick at the awful display. Seconds turned into a tormented countless amount of time, until at last, he straightened back up, and released her.

Without looking at Ace's, or Blake's face, I knew they were as relieved as me it was over.

It may have been over for us, but what if Pixie-girl's worst nightmare just came true?

After, the Pixie King did his weird glitch thing and was gone in a blink of an eye. Blake grabbed Pixie-girl into his arms, while Ace and me stood back and watched her sob, finally able to take back her body and emotions again. Waiting patiently was not easy to do, believe me. Especially knowing Pixie-girl had all the answers about where Abaddon was.

Apparently, her father had told her Abaddon was being held deep within Ryu, also known as The Void.

"Damn!" I cursed under my breath. Ryu was a place in between Apollyon's terrain and Osiris' Underworld. It was where some of the worse traitors and Hell's rogue creatures were held prisoner. Worst of all, getting to Abaddon would prove to be more difficult than I'd originally hoped.

"Are you sure you're all right?" Blake asked, voice chockfull of concern.

"Yes, I'll be fine," she told Blake, though I had my doubts since I wasn't convinced either, and guessed she was trying not to worry Blake any more than necessary.

"I think you should lie down and get some sleep," Blake told her.

Pixie-girl gave a small, tired smile at him before agreeing, letting Blake wrap an arm around her, leaning some of her weight on him as he walked her toward his bed. I wasn't sure how I felt about Pixie-girl sleeping in Blake's bed, though I was pretty sure I knew Blake well enough to know he'd probably take the couch later.

"You guys should probably go, I'm going to stay here and make sure she's okay." Blake turned his head to look back at us.

"Yeah, probably a good idea," Ace said to Blake. Standing there beside Ace quietly, not knowing what to say—knowing there were no words to offer that would make things better. It was because of me Pixie-girl was turning an odd shade of gray again.

As Ace and I turned to leave, I doubled back needing to say one more thing, "Um, Ebony wait," I said. Blake, who held Pixie-girl stopped walking, looking impatient, wanting to get her to bed. "Thanks, for what you did. That's all." Pixie-girl looked weary and frail, as though at any second she might collapse. She gave a small smile before Blake toted her off.

Ace and I kept silent while we walked side by side out of the Hellhounds' living quarters. I could guess why Ace was quiet, probably replaying the disgusting scene we'd witnessed back there. It was partly my reason too. Mostly my concerns lay within not knowing what deal Pixie-girl had to make with her father. Whatever he had told her, an anxious feeling in my stomach made me think something particularly atrocious occurred.

CHAPTER FOUR

Jealousy

Later on in the day, the halls of the Institute were buzzing with the constant chatter of students talking excitedly about their new mentor. Girls gushed over how handsome he was while the guys tossed around exaggerated stories of Kione single-handedly putting an end to the Lamia-demon attacks against the Morning Star and all its inhabitants.

Around the corner from the cafeteria, I heard a group of girls talking, and stopped in my tracks when one of them wondered out loud if Kione would be into dating someone younger than him.

A huff of annoyance slipped out of my mouth, and when I rounded the corner unable to take anymore, I immediately faltered. The girl who spoke was a Succubus, I hated with a passion. Scarlett.

You have got to be kidding me!

The feeling was mutual. Scarlett and I have always hated each other. Even more so after Scarlett had tricked me into joining the Sisters of Selene—a sorority who praises the Moon Goddess, Selene—in attempt to humiliate me. Scarlett had brought out a young Hellhound-boy wearing a spiked dog collar for her and her evil minions to torture for fun! That and she used to date Ace—if you could call it that—before Ace grew a brain and ended it with her. His love-hate feelings for me may have had something to do with the last part.

Scarlett's eyes gleamed at me like emeralds cut into two menacing slits upon seeing me. "Well, well, well, look at what the hounds dragged in—Dessi Starr, never a pleasure," Scarlett said, looking around at the group of girls who were a part of her bitchy sorority.

Holding Scarlett's glare, appearing unaffected by her open hostility, I said in equal disdain, "And you're still you, the Succubus-bitch."

Scarlett's eyes beamed jewel-toned daggers at me, before she flung her fiery red hair back over one shoulder huffily. "Since you are here, and there's nothing we can do about you being, well you, humor me, and tell us your view on something…we were talking about Kione—you know the new mentor? What do you think of him? Personally I think he's sexy as all hell and I have half a mind to give him a big, warm welcome," Scarlett said, making my stomach lurch into my throat making me want to vomit.

Scarlett had no idea what Kione was truly capable of, even I was still trying to figure it out, but still smart enough to know he was no good. Walking away and not answering Scarlett would have been the smart thing to do, because—well because Scarlett's an evil bitch who deserved whatever karma brought her. For some reason, it didn't settle right with me until I'd officially warned all of the Sisters of Selene. "Look, Scarlett you don't have to believe me—and you probably won't —please try to hear me when I say Kione is bad news. There are things about him you don't know, and he's dangerous. You guys need to stay as far away from him as you can," I said gravely, making sure to look at the faces behind Scarlett; she, Scarlett, wasn't going to believe me, maybe one of her spawn would.

If I thought Scarlett looked menacing before it was nothing compared to now. Her arms uncrossed and her fingers stretched out into claws at her sides. "You've got to be kidding me, first with Ace and now you're after Kione?" Scarlett shouted angrily. "You were right. I'm not going to listen to anything you say. You want Kione all to yourself. Now I'm warning you—"she threatened, taking a step forward, putting herself only a few inches from my face, backing me up until I hit the wall and a large framed poster resting on an easel, advertising the end of the year dance. The whole set crashed to the floor, causing Hellions who hadn't noticed the feud going on, to stop and watch.

Me want Kione? Gods this was so not going the way I'd wanted it too. If her theory weren't so revolting it would have been comical since it couldn't have been any further from the truth.

"You better stay out of my way or else watch your back, because I *will* make your life a living hell, if you try to get in my way," Scarlett said.

"Suit yourself," I told her. Trying to warn Scarlett off Kione had been a complete and utter failure in more ways than one. I'd been trying to avoid drawing any more attention from Scarlett than necessary. If there was one thing you could count on with Scarlett, it would be making good on her threats. Scarlett turned on her heels and stormed away.

Good riddance!

* * * *

"It was her decision, so stop beating yourself up about it," Ace told me the next day while we sat in our desks impatiently waiting for class to let out.

"Humph," I said in somewhat of a daze while watching where Blake sat eating his lunch and laughing at something Pixie-girl was saying. I frowned; only one month ago—before this little rift of ours, we always sat together. Blake looked up and caught me staring, offering a small smile before shifting uncomfortably in his seat and returning his eyes back on Pixie-girl.

"Dessi, are you all right?" Ace asked.

"Huh?" I said, not paying much attention, still fixating on Blake, unable to glance away from Blake.

"Well you're not eating your lunch which is a huge red flag since you're always stuffing your face, and you've hardly said two words since sitting down," Ace said.

My eyes left Blake reluctantly, turning toward Ace's concerned face, "Yeah, fine," I said, shoving the last of Ace's bagel into my mouth, hearing him exclaim having wanted to finish it himself and stood. "See you later, I'm headed to class," I told him.

"Okay, bye, I guess," Ace said watching me run off.

* * * *

"The raven has not signaled class end, Miss Starr, please take your seat." Mentor Grubbs, who's a Sluagh meaning he's a soul hunter, said when I stood and began gathering my things. Sitting back down, and slamming my back into the seat, wishing this day could be over already, a loud screeching sound filled the hall when outside of the classroom the raven swooped down and signaled class end.

Perfect timing!

On my way out of the class, I gave my mentor a victorious smile and veered out into the halls.

Rushing out of the classroom allowed me to get into the halls first before the rest of the Hellions emptied out of the classrooms. It allowed me to book it down the hall running, only stopping to turn right where the hall split into a T toward Apollyon's office. I needed to speak with Zola. Apollyon's wing of the Manor looked more impressive than the rest of the Institute, with even more gold on the ceilings and fancier intricate designs on the walls; Apollyon's need of grandeur *things* was over the top if you asked me.

"Correct me if I'm mistaken, aren't your classes in the other direction dear child?"

"Eh." I shrugged, smiling at the old, white-haired Seer, Zola.

Zola was pretty much the only real parental figure I'd ever had, really more of a grandmother than anything—she and Abaddon *were* my only real family. "I think they can manage without me for the rest of the day," I told her while throwing my book bag into the corner of her office, receiving a disapproving glare from her.

"Harrumph," Zola gave me a half-snort, half-grunt. Zola was sifting through some papers on her desk; Seers had psychic abilities, and once discovered by higher creatures such as Apollyon, they were usually given two choices: to become enslaved and bound by dark magic to not speak of these foresights, or to be killed, in fear their knowledge might be used against them by an adversary.

Zola had been acting as Hell's secretary since before my mom, Lilith was with Apollyon. "I know where Abaddon is," I told Zola what I'd been in such a hurry to get here and tell her.

Zola stopped what she was doing, instantly, forgetting about my poor attendance record or the book bag on the floor. I'd caught her attention. Pushing her glasses down her nose all the while looking intently up at me, "Oh thank heavens child, I didn't think I'd be able to keep it from you much longer, but you know, the rules are the rules," Zola said with tears welling up in the corner of her eyes. As much as Zola had become my family, Abaddon and I had become hers as well. "That Pixie King never was any good with keeping his mouth shut, though I suppose I am glad, this time anyway."

"You already knew?" I asked. Of course Zola would already know where Abaddon was, along with who would be the one to inform me. Zola usually saw things play out before the rest of us did, unable to warn though because of Apollyon's binding her powers, preventing her from speaking her insights.

Zola's furrow deepened, troubled by another thought. "Ebony made the deal—I don't know what exactly—not me. Blake's not exactly happy with me about it, though not being happy with me has become his new bad habit lately," I vented for a second.

"Uh-huh," Zola said, watching me with amusement. The twinkle in her eye suggested she knew something I did not.

"It doesn't do any good knowing where he is if we can't reach him Zola," I said getting back to Abaddon.

"I have an inkling time will work it all out—" Zola responded, sounding very much the Seer.

"He's in Ryu, Zola."

By the fearful look on her face, the unease I felt within grew. The dread I'd been feeling inside came rising up to the surface when Zola confirmed my doubts.

"That does pose a real challenge now, doesn't it?" Zola asked sounding thoughtful, not ready to give up.

"Wait, you still think there's a way?" I gushed, trying not to let the small sliver of hope rise to the surface quite yet. It didn't work; hope was all I *or* Abaddon for that matter, had at this point.

Zola looked almost indignant I even had to ask, "There's always a way, child."

"Oh, Zola, can you help—I mean obviously you can't tell me direct information, but maybe you can tell me something anyway—a clue or tiny hint even—or maybe you could try writing it down instead—" I rambled on, excited for new possibilities. When Seers, and other fortune telling creatures are discovered, they are often captured in fear information will land in the wrong hands.

"Dear Gods child, get a hold of your tongue, and quit babbling on. We've got work to do!"

Knowing better than to argue with Zola, my mouth quickly closed. "Better. Now, I'll need you to go see what arrangements can be made with your Hellhound suitors while I'm gone."

"Where are you going?" I asked. "And what do you mean by suitors?" Exasperated with the term she used to describe Blake and Ace.

"To track down a few promising leads of my own," she said furtively, and ignoring the last half of my question.

"Pains in my sides are more like it," I said, still talking about Blake and Ace.

"I'm glad to see you knew who I was referring and how not everything inside that head of yours is full of feathers and impossible tasks."

Easy for her to say, she wasn't caught up in all this boy drama.

Shortly after Zola left her office, tracking down Ace and Blake—which was easier than I thought it was going to be since they were both in the same place—was my next task. The only problem was they were both tied up running a drill under Aeg's order and their help was out of the question until tomorrow.

* * * *

Back in my own room, I feared it would be a long night ahead of me, and almost immediately began pacing back and forth, trying to think up my own so called mastermind plan, always coming up short. "Okay think, if you were in Ryu, what would you be seeing? Probably a whole lot of nothing because you'd be locked up probably in some deep hole in the earth with no rocks or windows and nothing to climb." Images of cold, dank, and dark prisoner cells began flipping through my mind and were too much for me to take, so much so a scream of frustration burst out. A plan to break Abaddon out of jail wouldn't be figured out overnight. An idea came to me. I looked over at the grandfather clock which stood in the middle of my bedroom, and wondered if Ebony would still be awake.

Almost midnight.

Storming across my bedroom, I grabbed my black leather jacket from the chair, and then hightailed it out of my room. I may not be able to figure out Abaddon's escape tonight on my own, there was still another way to help settle my nerves—something that has been bothering me. So while Blake was preoccupied with his Hellhound training tonight, now was my chance to find out what Pixie-girl promised her father in exchange for information on Abaddon.

<u>CHAPTER FIVE</u>

Taste of Winter

Ebony

Ebony knew she was dreaming, and still, could not stop it from happening. *"Please!"* her mind begged, trapped from somewhere within, wishing her dream would stop before it could take her to the place most feared.

Caught within the spiraling web of sleep, Ebony was already lost, too deep into it now to make it stop.

It started the same as it always did.

Ebony stood motionless, frozen in terror underneath twisted vines and bare trees, making branches reach out to her in all directions. Her wool dress did little to protect against the elements of the woods that jabbed their bony fingers into her ribs and scratched the delicate skin of her arms and legs.

She'd had this nightmare a thousand times before, but something was different about it this time. The dream somehow had a tangible quality about it. Ebony wondered what would happen if she picked a flower and stuck it in her hair. Would it come back with her to the waking world? Bending down at the hips, Ebony reached out and placed a little yellow daisy in between her fingers before pulling it up and out of the ground. Standing back up, she brought the flower to her nose, inhaled deeply, closing her eyes. She imagined standing in a whole field of them, the sun beating down on her face and warming her soul. Daisies were her favorite. Opening her eyes, she was saddened to see no such field of flowers. There were only trees forming a canopy above her, concealing any chance for sun and warmth—only coldness touching her core.

There was something strange in the air around her—a foreboding feeling of being watched. She could feel the gaze of someone—or something—not belonging. "Finish this," her will told her, knowing it would do no good prolonging the inevitable, and began walking forward with her arms crossing over her chest, hands held tightly to the opposite arm, trying to warm the skin where raised gooseflesh prickled the air.

Ebony continued to look around uneasily, watching the woods, seeing nothing out of the ordinary.

Holding her arms out in front of her, she examined the short length of them, pondered in wonderment at how tiny her hands were. She knew without having to look in a mirror how she would also be wearing the face of a small nine-year-old girl's face.

During these awful slumbers she felt young and afraid again—vulnerable, again at that place in time in her life from all those years ago. Her young face, with the same peachy-skin, minus the fuller baby-faced cheeks a young child often has. Ebony looked the same except her face had more defined lines framing her feminine features: a more angled nose and fuller lips.

As Ebony continued to walk she kept looking up toward the canopy of trees, gauging the time by how the bottom layer of leaves made shadows dance across the forest during the twilight hour.

It was the exact scenario from years ago. The only reason she was lost was because her cousin, Carrick, had played a distasteful joke on her during a game of hide and seek. When it was Ebony's turn to seek, he would call out from behind trees, and when she thought he had been found, he'd call out to her again from another tree. It went on and on until they were so deep into the woods, it would be near impossible to find her way out again. After calling out to him saying, "Carrick, this isn't funny. I want to go home," he would ignore her, and she'd hear her name whispered in the wind. Even now, Ebony could hear his residual laughter grow farther and farther away, leaving her there alone and scared during sunset.

She wrapped her arms in front of her chest to ward off the cold racking her body with chills. Fall was nearly over and as she breathed in and out heavily, the taste of winter landed on her tongue. She felt it again, the menacing sensation that something not belonging in this memory-induced nightmare of hers, was watching her. An intruder of dreams perhaps.

Continuing on, thoughts about why her father hadn't come looking for her left her feeling abandoned. Ebony was too young at the time to question anything the Pixie King did, and why should she anyway? He was her father; he was supposed to keep her safe from others like Carrick—to keep safe from the dark and the cold.

Ebony was, however, old enough to understand what would happen if shelter was not found...she'd be as good as wolf food; Werewolves in particular, Pixies were their number one delicacy of choice.

While the dream-Ebony wandered aimlessly alone in the woods, she thought about a trip she and her father had made in the woods once before. When they left their home that morning, her father had told her how, "We're going on a little trip to the woods to find the rare winter rose."

Ebony remembered asking, "What's a winter rose?" in her small, trusting voice.

"A miniature spot of color, which lies hidden beneath the change of the season—a real extraordinary find. Do you know why, Ebony?" She shook her small head and her father went on, "Because the one who finds it is the first one to know of winter's arrival."

Ebony had smiled up at her dad in wonder, burying her small hand in his tighter. Even though her small legs were growing tired and her stomach hungry, Ebony did not complain in case her father should turn them around and take her home before she'd a chance to see the rose. It was a fairly cheerful memory, one of the few with her father.

Ebony walked for hours, even after the sun had long since gone down. Her steps were small and clumsy leading her to fall and scrape a knee on a rock. Sitting on the forest floor, holding her knee to her chest, a dreadful howl of a wolf echoed through the night, scaring her half to death. As quickly as possible, Ebony turned around and crawled onto her knees to stand. Frantically, she gazed around for a place, any place to hide. The wolf howled again, this time much closer, and her knees began to shake. The only place to hide was within the wild thorn-filled branches of a rose bush. Throwing herself on the ground she quickly dug at the ground with her small fingers, removing rocks and the forest floor's debris until able to fit underneath the branches. Ebony had to lie on her stomach and wiggled herself to fit just right within the hollowed out area. Several rose bush thorns caught the delicate skin of her arms, legs and even the scalp of her head. Once inside, she reached back, trying to camouflage the small hole with rocks, needles, and forest mulch.

She sunk as deeply into the shrub as possible, uncaring of the thorns clawing at her arms and legs. The thought of a wolf finding her was more frightening than a plethora of bleeding scratches. A few seconds later, the sound of a large animal sniffing around the bush had her heart jumping into her throat. She didn't dare move or breath. Everything was still and quiet. Maybe the wolf had moved on? Her mind pondered, until there was urgent scratching and pawing at the bush as the wolf tried to get in there with her. Too frozen by fear to even scream, Ebony backed up as far as possible while thorns pulled at her hair and head. She turned her face to the side and squeezed her eyes shut.

Movement beside her had her reopening them only to see a rabbit trying to make its way through the rose bush with an urgency. It ended up getting caught on a thorn before it managed to slip its way out of their hiding place. The wolf, distracted by the rabbit, forgot all about Ebony in hopes to catch the rabbit for its meal, and darted off into the woods after it.

Quite some time had passed, probably hours, fearing the wolf would come back for her.

Ebony did not see the spot of crimson-red hiding within the damp leaves of the soiled forest floor at first, too overrun by fear. For a moment, she forgot all about being lost, all about the howling and thoughts of wolves. She reached her small, scratched and bleeding arm out and ever so carefully cupped her hands around the ruby-blossom and pulled it up out of the ground, holding it gently as though it were a baby bird having fallen out of its nest. She was the first person to know of winter's arrival.

Her breath made little clouds around the rose. It had grown colder still and when something cold fell from the sky, landing on the tip of her nose, her face rose upward to see little specks of white snow falling like pieces of white confetti. Ebony didn't even remember falling asleep afterward, only remembering hearing twigs snapping close to her head and then feeling the warmth of something's breath spill down upon her face. The Ebony that was stuck inside her own head, reliving the same nightmare, braced herself for what was about to happen next...

CHAPTER SIX

Disaster Plan

When there was no answer after knocking for the fifth time on Pixie-girl's door, I thought about giving up and going back to my room; unsure if this was her room at all since I'd never had any reason to go there until now. Aiming to turn and leave, the sound of a door being unlocked made me turn around.

The door opened and there, leaning on the frame, was a peach-skinned Pixie girl wearing a slightly dazed and confused look on her face. It was obvious by her disheveled hair and dark circles under her eyes I'd awakened her—*Of course you did, it's the middle of the night.* Her being tired wasn't all surprising, what was odd, though, was the pale-grayness of her otherwise peach-colored skin. There were also beads of sweat formed on her forehead.

"Are you ill?" I asked, frowning, feeling bad for waking her.

"No, I was, um, sleeping," she said, shaking her head.

"Sorry to wake you…um, can we talk for a minute?"

"No, it's fine. I'm kind of glad you did," she said, appearing anxious. "Come on in."

"Thanks." I moved past her into her bedroom.

Before closing the door, she peeked her head outside her room and into the hall as if looking to see if anyone else came with me. When realizing it was only me, her eyebrows furrowed deeply while shutting and locking the door quickly.

I took a moment to look around her bedroom. It was much smaller than mine and even smaller than Blake's and Hunter's which was saying something—though it was tremendously cleaner than the Hellhound duo's. The room held a small bed positioned not far from the entrance. The space felt tight, and when she reached over to grab her robe from behind the door, I had to move out of the way. It was hardly a living space, allowing only bare necessities in here: minimal furniture of one nightstand next to her bed, a desk pushed up under the one window opposite the doorway, and an ornate chair to accompany the desk. Bathroom and closet were probably miniscule too.

I'd temporarily forgotten Pixie-girl stood behind me, her blonde-bobbed haircut a disheveled mess, and something was definitely off with her soul aura if the black clouding around the edges of her soul were any indication.

After slipping on her robe and tying it tightly around her waist, Pixie-girl turned her attention back to me.

"Are you feeling okay, I'll leave and come back tomorrow—or do you need anything? Tea, a hot water bottle maybe?" I rambled awkwardly.

I'd undoubtedly made her feel bad causing her to glance down at her robe, feeling insecure and embarrassed. "No-no, I'm not sick, I've been having these dreams, if you could even call them that, keeping me up most nights," she said around a yawn.

Having dreams that kept her up at night that made her look like this? Something about that unnerved me. I was going to tell her as much when Pixie-girl caught a glimpse of my face and changed the subject.

"Thanks though. You needed something?"

Getting down to business was probably a good idea. "Right," I said, looking around for a place to sit.

"Here, um you can sit there if you want—or here." Pixie-girl gestured first to the wooden chair and then to her bed.

"The chair's fine, thanks." I sat. "You should really sit too," I said, mostly wanting her to sit before she ended up passing out or something.

"Okay." Pixie-girl tucked some of her hair behind her ear nervously before settling into a cross-legged position at the bottom of her bed, looking all off key in a sweet, complex way. I'd had a brief epiphany to why Blake might be interested in her. I supposed there was something about her, some kind of natural allure from Pixie-girl just being herself, uncaring to what others thought of her.

"You wanted to ask me something?" Pixie-girl brought me back.

"Right, yes. Sorry," I said, wondering if my inability to form clear thoughts had something to do with being around a Pixie, not necessarily

Ebony here, but I'd heard being around Pixies in general could mess people's minds. Definitely something worth finding out when less pressing matters were apparent.

"It's about the Pixie King," I said, waiting her to respond angrily, or lash out or something, not appreciating me bringing him up to her after everything.

Pixie-girl shifted uncomfortably on her bed; not the freak-out I'd been expecting. Instead, her response was more anxious than anything while twirling a piece of her yellow-blonde hair around her index finger and thumb. "What about him?" she asked, warily.

"I know it must be hard for you to talk about him—I get it, believe me, it's awful having a father who doesn't care. So I'm sorry, I have to know since Abaddon is my brother and Blake, he's my—" I paused, struggling to find the right word for what Blake was to me; friend didn't seem quite enough to describe what he meant to me. Without knowing how to finish the sentence correctly, leaving the answer in question up for grabs, I continued, "Blake cares about you, which is why you should tell me what you promised the Pixie King, so I can at least try and help."

"There's nothing anyone can do, what's done is done now," Pixie-girl said, and as impossible as I thought it would be to accomplish, she looked even more tired with the mere mention of her father, and having to talk about any of this.

"Yeah, you're probably right," I said, dejected. There had to be something else to be done to help out our situation. There was one topic popping to mind not involving the Pixie King or deals made, "So Blake, you like him?"

Her eyes widened, not having expected the change in topic, or the subject choice "Yes, he's a good friend."

"Friend only?"

Pixie-girl laughed at the insinuating tone behind my words, catching my drift. "Yes, no—I'm not sure exactly. I mean I like him, *really* like him."

"But?" I asked, ploddingly following her hesitation.

"I'm not sure if he feels the same way about me."

"Oh," was all I could think to say. The idea of Blake not liking her back the same way evidently got to her, if the way Pixie-girl began biting her bottom lip was any indication.

"What makes you think so?"

"Little things here and there." She shrugged.

I nodded, not knowing what else to do. Telling her something along the lines of—Yeah you're probably right about Blake not returning your feelings—crossed my mind, I'm not going to pretend it didn't. Thoughts of my father's games of twisting the truth, and whispering lies into people's ears, corrupting them in hopes to create more hurt and chaos in the word, put a screeching halt to it before any real damage could be done. It wasn't my proudest moment, and the fact Apollyon could get into my mind at all pissed me off. Gazing over at her seeming all fragile and self-doubting, reminded me of me. I sighed and said, "You're a smart girl, you don't really think he doesn't have feelings for you."

Pixie-girl looked away. "I guess."

"Of course he does." I waved my hands through the air dismissively.

"He does?" Her head turned back to face me, the smallest sliver of hope turning her eyes into a happy-blue color.

"Yes. I mean he is a guy isn't he? And you—you're this mysterious creature, some kind of exotic treat, which is saying something around here," I huffed around a short laugh. "Guys like that."

A smile brightened her face. "Thank you."

"Sure."

"It seems kind of silly now, for the longest time I thought he was in love with you," Pixie-girl said, catching me unguarded, in turn making me choke on my own saliva.

Coughing a few times, I finally said, "Wow, hmm, sorry, is the air dry in the room to you?" I asked, feeling lame.

Pixie-girl tilted her head, curiosity on her face.

"What made you think he was in love with me?"

"Little things mostly; the way he watched you all the time, always concerned about what you're doing, if you're okay. Plus he always talks about you incessantly, more than he talks about anything."

Blake was talking about me to Pixie-girl? It felt strange to have Blake telling her things about me, and I wondered how much he was sharing with her. "What kinds of things?" Hesitantly, not sure why I cared so much, unable to hold back anyway.

"Oh nothing bad." Pixie-girl misjudged my hesitation. "Nice things—good, impossible-to-live-up-to in his eyes things."

We'd spent so much of our childhood together, it wasn't surprising he'd have lots of stories to tell her. A sense of melancholy swelled up within me, making me miss the way we used to be. I sighed. "Don't worry about trying to live up to anything. You guys will make your own stories, tales to be envied." I winked at her, burying any sadness deep down, surrounding to the possibility of Blake and Pixie-girl.

"Seeing you with Ace helped squash the idea of you and Blake together," Pixie-girl said. "I mean, don't get me wrong, you have this indestructible beauty every girl would kill for, what with your long dark hair, and ability to be sporty yet still feminine in the best way. And after getting to know you better, the idea of you and Blake together seems ludicrous."

"I guess, and Ace, yes." I sounded less confident talking about Ace over Blake.

"Not the kind of love where you feel like your heart desperately longs to be with another's," she said, followed by a sigh, getting caught up in the moment.

This is when enough friendliness-girl bonding for one day came in. It was time to get back down to business. "The Pixie King must've said something to you," I said, not so tactful.

Pixie-girl nodded her head. "A promise to return back *home* when I turn eighteen." Her eyes wandered down to looking at her hands grimly. Her home, did not sound like a place she wanted to be going.

"Is it going to be bad?"

Her eyes looked over at me sadly, and she sighed. "It's already done," putting an end to our conversation. "Please don't tell Blake, it should come from me."

"Yeah, you're probably right," I said. It should have been me to make the deal with the Pixie King.

"He did tell me one other thing, though I don't know how helpful it would be since the guards at Ryu are supposed to be impenetrable."

That was a detail I was willing to overlook until a more imminent time. "What did he tell you?" I eyed her intently, waiting for her response.

"When he told me Abaddon was being kept in Ryu, he also mentioned how the wards on his prison would be at their weakest during a new moon."

That was helpful news. Now all I needed to do was figure out how this bit of news might help us free Abe. The Pixie King wouldn't bother mentioning it if it wasn't imperative to helping us. "You said during a new full moon?" A plan began to form in my mind.

Pixie-girl gave me a strange look while watching the gears turn in my head. "Yeah, why?" she asked, voice full of caution.

A smile widened my mouth at her suspicion. "I overheard Scarlett talking to Adana, one of her other Sisters of Selene minions. Though Adana really is the lesser of evil amongst the evil bitches," I said, getting slightly off track for a second. "Anyway, they were talking about a new moon ceremony coming up." It would be the perfect guise to getting what we needed from a full moon ritual and a chance for me to get Scarlett back, but that was beside the point.

"How does this help?" Pixie-girl asked, not quite following my train of thought. In all fairness, it wasn't a fully formed plan yet, and still had holes to fill. Somehow, we should be able to use Scarlett's ritual to our benefit.

"I'm not exactly sure yet; it's a good place to start though. And besides, we have until the end of the month for the full moon giving us plenty of time to form a better plan." My mood quickly shot up to cheerful. For the first time in weeks a plan to free Abaddon, instead of sitting around and complaining, was beginning to form.

"Why does it unsettle me to hear you say this?" Pixie-girl asked, and I was unable to keep a laugh from bubbling up my throat and out of my mouth when Blake's words came out of her mouth.

"Because you're not stupid."

"Speaking of…I think there's a way to get in with Scarlett." Pixie-girl hopped off the bed to grab a notebook from within the small drawer of her nightstand.

"Uh, whatcha doing there?" I watched her in bewilderment.

"Jotting down some notes, it helps my planning process," she said as though it should have been obvious.

"Want to clue me in on it?"

"I'm trying to decide how to go about convincing Scarlett to let me join the Sisters of Selene," she said, shocking the hell out of me.

"Oh-no, no way is that a good idea," I said, already shaking my head before I began to speak.

"Why not?" Pixie-girl sounded outraged.

"First off, because Blake will kill me. Second of all, Scarlett and her evil gang of sluts will eat you alive," I said, trying to scare her, to put some sense in her.

"Blake will have to get over it. And that's why you both will be there, I don't know, hiding behind the rocks, to bale me out, if I need it." Her plan sounded seamless, if not over the top in the secret agent Pixie-girl category. I liked it!

Standing with vigor in my pose, the feel of purpose took over my senses. "I could kiss you right now!" I said fervently, and had to stop myself from reaching out and hugging her.

"I've been warned about the look you have right now," Pixie-girl said.

"And for good reason," I said, unable to stop the corners of my lips from turning up into a wicked smile.

"I really hope I don't regret joining team Dessi."

You probably will. "How do you feel about crashing a séance?" I asked ruefully.

"I don't know, I've never been to a séance, but seeing as it was pretty much my idea, I'll have to get used to it."

I didn't blame her for being wary; the last time I'd gone to one of Scarlett's séances, I'd been tricked into joining a *blood-letting*. It still gave me nightmares. After Selene's grotesque appearance, Scarlett had gone so far as to bind a young Hellhound boy by the name of Oran, so she could have some sick, personal slave for her and her sisters to drag around in chains and a collar. It had made me sick with vengeance and I'd hastily put an end to her ritual.

Oh, Pixie-girl was in for a surprise all right. Instead of telling her about the disaster I'd made the last time I'd foolishly joined in one of

Scarlet's Sisters of Selene meet-and-greets, I said, "That's okay, I have. Piece of cake," I lied.

* * * *

During the walk back to my room, finally feeling a goodnight's sleep lay in store for me, echoes of someone in pain—*or was it pleasure?*—had me coming to a stop down the hall right before the stairwell leading up to my room.

Taking a step toward a door cracked partially open, brought me closer to the disturbing sound. From a safe distance back the room appeared to be consumed in darkness, once close enough to peek inside, I could see a faint light flickering. Another loud moaning noise nearly had me jumping out of my skin. Swallowing down the scream I'd all but freed on accident, I pushed myself closer to the door. Careful not to open the door too fast, making it creak, I gave it a nudge, allowing it to open wide enough for me to see a large, looming shadow on the wall.

Recognizing it as a male's shadow, my gaze scanned around the room for him. Another shriek, leaning more on the painful side this time, had me drawing back slightly and giving me the direction to look in next. I'd found him sitting with his back to me in the corner of the room adjacent to the door. In his hand he held a knife. A bloody knife. Without him having to turn around, I recognized his sun-kissed skin and shoulder-length surfer hair, all alarms went off in my head. Kione sat on the floor, cutting himself—*and enjoying it!* I thought horrified.

Giving the room a more detailed scrutiny allowed me to take in the entire gruesome scene, and to see a circle surrounding him made up of what appeared to be dark-red sand. Also stationed before him, a bundle of dried herbs—or brush, twined together and smoldering similar to how incense is used. It smelled of sage and something displeasing making the smells clash…algae and mold.

For a brief moment I thought Kione was singing, until everything fell into place, the blood-red sand surrounding him, the burning brush, the cutting…*Kione's dealing in Dark Magic!* A sound began to pulse around Kione, forming into prickly staccato peaks while he chanted. Another deep hum matched the beat of the sand-peaks, responding to Kione in a conversation I couldn't understand. The whole scenario seemed perverse and troublesome.

I'd gone unnoticed until the moment when Kione arched his back writhing in pain as two bloody stumps protruded from his back, unfurling a set of wings made from charcoal and ash. The shock of seeing them made me jump back, grabbing onto the closest thing near me, a coat rack, and ending up throwing it on the ground, in turn breaking Kione out of concentration. His wings retracted when he spun around to see who had interrupted him. It all happened so fast, I'd already begun to doubt it had been wings I'd seen. Mostly because none of it made any sense.

Kione didn't show any emotion when seeing me, at first. He simply cocked his head to the side to gaze curiously over to the position I'd fallen down in. Kione stayed in the kneeling position breathing heavily in and out. I could see small beads of sweat on his forehead getting ready to run down his face. Other than the sweat, there were no tell-tale signs he'd been cutting himself, or ever having just been talking to some dark entity. If anything, Kione gave the impression of being tired maybe, and definitely more vulnerable, and real and exposed than I'd ever seen before.

For some reason, this reaction frightened the beejesuss out of me and acted as cold water thrown in my face. Gathering myself up off the floor, not sparing a second glance back at Kione, I booked it the heck out of there. But not before seeing Kione reach one arm out for me with a look of sadness and regret on his face.

I ran the rest of the way up to my room, needing to feel some security as if I were a child again needing to lock my door, check for monsters in the closet before burying myself in the comfort of my bedding. Tonight would no doubt be another sleepless night with visions of deep looming voices reverberating all around me, sand the same hue of blood with a life of its own, and the images of wings—especially the wings, unfurling above and raining ash over me.

CHAPTER SEVEN

Kisses and Confessions

"**O**kay, what are you up to?" Ace finally asked at the library during study hour, he'd been on the verge of asking this all day.

"Nothing," was my immediate response, again thinking about the disturbing scene in which I'd caught Kione in last night. Ace didn't know anything about it though, and was referring to the shadiness from both Pixie-girl and myself ever since we had formed a plan.

"Bullshit," he said, slamming the book he was holding closed.

"Hey wait, is that a book you're reading?" I tried veering the conversation elsewhere, genuinely surprised. Ace wasn't exactly the studious type, unless it involved studying girls. Ace took his Guardian exams seriously though. *Could he actually be worried about passing them?* Well there's a first for everything, I thought, making a mental note to ask him about it later.

Crossing his arms over his chest, managing to keep a hold of the book, he said, "I can smell trouble on you a mile away."

"Being a geek looks good on you." My body's proximity to Ace's was close enough for me to rub my shoulder against his playfully.

"Of course it does," he said, smiling briefly before getting back to me. "Now stop trying to distract me and answer my question."

I sighed, knowing any attempt at keeping secrets from Ace was a predetermined failure. His probing mossy-green eyes stared at me with an intensity that may have well been truth serum, because everything I'd been holding back all day spilled out. "So last night while talking with Pixie-girl I made her leak what the Pixie King told her, you know, when he did that creepy-thing that sorry, but kind of looked like her father was kissing her, right before she turned that awful color and scared Blake half to death?"

Ace sighed heavily in exasperation. "Yes, I remember all of that, and we already know Abaddon is being kept in Ryu."

I place my hands on my hips in exasperation. "Pixie-girl didn't tell us everything. Now, do you want to find out what? Or would you rather forget all about it."

"Go on."

Pausing momentarily to look around and make sure no one was listening in on our conversation, I continued in a low voice, "What if I told you that we know *how* we can free Abaddon from Ryu?"

Ace's eyebrows rose in question. "All right I'm listening. How?"

I almost took a second to gloat and dragging the suspense out a little longer, but the look on his face suggested I do otherwise. "First, Pixie-girl and I are going to have to get our hands a little dirty." Meaning convincing Scarlett to let Pixie-girl attend one of her rituals.

"Please don't tell me you're going to use that damn fountain again?" he asked. His face went rigid with the memory of the last time I'd dragged him to the fountain and hundreds of bone demons came crawling out of it when I'd mistakenly messed the spell up while opening it. Luckily for Ace and I, the two angels, Lain and Ethan, had come to the rescue and closed the portal to the Underworld before any real damage could occur. There are many layers of Hell. The deepest parts are known as the Underworld, and are ruled by Osiris, an Egyptian god and sort of an ally to Apollyon. When I say sort of what I mean is that they have a business-like arrangement to keep from waging war on each other. Apollyon was arrogant enough to assume his precious Hell being tightly managed, and could never be at fault, further casting blame on Abaddon and Lain.

I shivered with the memory, knowing how easily things had gone wrong. I cleared my throat uncomfortably, "No, definitely not. Are you opposed to crashing a midnight ritual?"

"You're not talking about one of Scarlett's rituals by any chance are you? I mean we all know you're a masochist, but you're not stupid— please tell me you're not going crazy, Dess." *Okay, so it hadn't exactly been a brilliant, top secret plan—Pixie-girl and I had made it out to be.* "How did you know, and here Pixie-girl and I thought we'd outdone ourselves this time," I joked, though I really was disappointed I'd been easy to read.

Agitated I huffed away, walking behind a long bookshelf knowing Ace would follow. I'd gone halfway down the aisle before turning back around, making Ace almost run into me. "Look, I'm not stupid, or a masochist. Her full moon ritual happens to be when the wards surrounding Ryu are at their weakest," I replied, crossing my arms over my chest. I didn't know why I was getting so upset, not realizing until then how much I'd needed his approval, especially because no one else had come up with a plan of their own yet.

His face softened when he saw the way I nervously bit my bottom lip. "I know it's not what you want to hear…you do remember how the last one of her rituals you attended turned out, right?" he said softly, reaching out and placing one hand on each of my arms, tender yet firm.

"No you really don't need to remind me."

He nodded, until something I must have said caught up to him. "Wait, you said during the full moon?"

"Yes."

"The full moon is almost an entire month!" he said, not missing a beat, though I wasn't sure where he was going with this veracity. "You actually think this whole scheme of yours is going to work?"

"Pixie-girl—err, Ebony," I needed to quit calling her that, especially if I was going to work with her to free Abaddon, "has confidence we'll be able to pull it off." The bitterness from before, cut through my tone.

"That's because Ebony doesn't know any better, yet." He gave me a disapproving look suggesting Pixie-girl was being taken advantage of.

Cringing and thinking about it, finding Ace wasn't entirely wrong. "Hey what's up with all the Q-and-A anyway? At least Pixie-girl's got my back." Deflecting was one of my many talents.

Ace hunched his shoulders. "I'm sorry. You know I'll always have your back, Dess." Something Ace had proven time and time again over the past few months together, making me grasp that maybe I wasn't the one being reasonable here.

"I know you have, sometimes it would be nice to see you have a little more faith in me, is all," I told him.

Having his hands around my arms still, gave him the leverage he needed to pull me to him, so he could place a kiss to my forehead. "I have more faith in you than you know," he whispered next to my ear. And just like that, all the tension surrendered, like the sea's tide after sunset. I found I could breathe again as a result.

"One more question, and then I'm done, I promise," Ace quickly said after watching me roll my eyes at him. "How do you plan to convince Scarlett to take Pixie-girl into the Sisters of Selene?"

Damn, that was a good question.

"How do you mean?" I asked to buy me more time to come up with an ingenious answer. It irritated me Ace kept asking about Scarlett in the first place, let alone think of her as someone who could stop me from getting what I wanted, in this case, to use her to get to my brother.

Ace's past relationship was the one thing I disliked about him, not because she was pretty, or voluptuous, or every boy's dream-girl; petty jealousy stuff, mainly because Scarlett was the biggest bitch I knew. The saying how "judging someone based off the company they keep" came to mind. In so many ways they made more sense than me and Ace did together: both voted to be the best looking the last three years in our upper-class, both zealously over-confident in everything they did, and both in leadership roles.

All the tiny hairs on my arms stood when the diminutive black serpent, which spent its days coiled tightly around my spine, awakened its ugly, snarling head. The way it did every time my anger started to spiral out of control.

No! Determined not to allow Scarlett any power over me, I willed the thorny creature back in its state of sleep. If I wasn't careful one of these days this demon inside was going to get the better of me.

"I know her enough to know she'll never fall for it," he said. When I didn't dignify his answer with a response, he continued by asking, "Does Blake know this so-called plan of yours and Ebony's?"

"No, Ebony doesn't tell him everything, and besides, even if he did know he would have a lot more faith in us than you do!" I don't know why I felt the need to throw Blake's loyalty in the mix, especially when we both knew it probably wasn't true, and Blake would want us to try and find another solution first.

There wasn't any, and this was going to work, it had to! I stormed back over to the table we'd been studying at and began gathering the books I'd been using to help me write a paper on Banshees, due in the morning.

"Ha!" Ace exclaimed, following me over to the aisle where I'd retrieved the book, to put it away. "Asking a Hellion to have faith is like asking me not to be an acid slobbering Hellhound, or Blake not to be annoying, or asking you to not be a pain in the—"

"Yeah, yeah, I get it—" *Sheesh! Someone put their collar on too tight today.*

Once my books were all put away, Ace grabbed me by the wrist and spun me around to face him. "It's not that I don't think you won't be able to find a way to find your brother—if anyone can do it, it's you. I'm just worried you're going about it for all the wrong reasons."

"What reasons?" I asked tiredly. I was so tired of fighting; we've been doing so much of it lately, not only with Ace, but with my father, with Kione. There was even my unresolved issues with Blake. It was all starting to catch up with me.

"I can only think of two actually, both involving Kione showing up and lighting this fire of revenge in you that might be clouding your judgment. I'm worried about you is all," he said, his tone changing into something softer. His voice filled with a warmth I wanted to wrap around me like a blanket.

After a few moments of letting his warmth drown me, my arms relaxed in his hold. I was short enough my head fit snug against Ace's chest and I had to tip it way back in order to look up into his eyes. "Maybe you're right," I said.

"What did you say, I didn't quite catch it?"

"This thing with Kione is definitely getting to me. If it makes you feel better, I'll try to keep it in consideration while scheming," I said, echoing his earlier words.

He pulled me away from him far enough so he could look down at my face while giving me a half smile. "That's all I'm asking for," he said and then surprised me by drawing me in and crushing his lips against mine.

The kiss was sweet and spicy and ended way too soon, like a fireworks show that ended halfway through the grand finale. I should have been upset by his yo-yoing with whatever this was between us. The kiss shocked me momentarily, and all I could do was relish in the way he'd tasted.

Our heads whipped so fast in the direction of another voice, I felt my neck crack a little. "A stolen kiss will create a lifetime of heartache and bliss." Kione was standing at the other end of the book aisle. Kione's face filled with delight over having interrupted a private moment.

I didn't have to look at my face to know it would be wearing a similar expression like Ace's, one of detest and hatred. "What are you doing here?" I growled. Seeing Kione brought back all the anger I'd been trying to suppress since his arrival at the Morning Star. I remembered the promise I'd made to Ace and thought about how this might be the fastest I'd ever broken a promise.

Ace stood behind me and had thought to clasp his hands tightly around my shoulders as if knowing the internal struggle within me, rightfully so since I was considering lunging out at Kione. Smart of him, though a part of me wished he'd let me punch him, even once.

"Reading," Kione answered my question tranquilly, contrary to the unwelcoming tone I'd used. "Though now I'm pondering if I shouldn't report when students begin to sneak off to the library for a little romantic interlude?"

I snorted loudly. "Go ahead," I said, uncaring.

"Yes, well then, I suppose this could be our little secret." He winked at me. "I'll be on my way and leave you two. Please carry on, and do try and remember not to be a stranger, little Starr," he said, calling me by the nickname Ace had first given me, before turning around and leaving.

"I hate that driftwood bum," Ace said, eyeing the direction Kione had gone with furrowed eyebrows, appearing puzzled over some inner turmoil. I tried to shake off the gross feeling Kione somehow managed to leave in his wake. Reluctantly his gaze shifted back to me, "I should be going too," he said.

"Go figure, you're going to leave now. Weren't we in the middle of something here?" I asked, hopeful, staring at his lips.

"Look, Dessi, about that kiss…" he started, guessing where my thoughts were leading me. "I still don't know if our dating right now is a good idea. I've got finals and passing the Hellhound's placement assessment is pressuring me." His low voice sounded strangled like he was forcing the words out.

"Wait, you're worried you won't have a place here?" Being worried about passing his classes was unexpected since Ace, of all creatures, wasn't known for worrying about his academics, but it wasn't nearly as bizarre as Ace being worried about securing a place as one of Apollyon's Hellhound Guardians.

Ace looked anxious to be saying as much. "It's not set in stone, Dess —I'm not like you. When I mess up that's it for me. I can't just make a few mistakes, get slapped on the hands and then sent on my way. There are real consequences for everything I do. Someone like me doesn't get a second chance." He stepped back and then ran a hand through his hair; it's what he did when he was anxious.

I recoiled as though I'd been slapped. His insinuation hurt. For him to think I had a *free pass*, and not be held accountable for my actions. He might as well have put a wedge between us because being daughter of Apollyon was one thing I'd never be able to change. Only, I never thought he'd actually use it against me as a reason to not be with me.

My voice felt hollow and lost somewhere inside. When I finally found it again, I had to choke out my next words, "I see, I'm sorry, I won't be a distraction anymore."

I wasn't sure how my face looked right then. Whatever it was, it crushed him. He sighed before reaching out and taking my hands in his. "No, Dessi, it's not like that, it's a good distraction, which is sort of the problem."

My shoulders stayed slumped forward. Thoughts going a million miles an hour in my mind. *What if he became one of my father's Hellhound guardians, what then? Would he be worried about how my inability to not screw up might affect his future?* It would be obvious for me to point out how we couldn't possibly have any kind of future together if he didn't see us as equals, and we certainly wouldn't work if he felt he had to hide our relationship.

Unaware of the thoughts churning inside my head, Ace reached his hand toward my face and softly traced my jaw with his finger. "You drive me crazy. You know that right?"

All I could do was sigh, feeling too dejected to do much else. "Seeing you before in the healing chambers, you are the most sinfully-beautiful creature I've ever known."

So, my plan had worked. I forced a smile, even though his earlier words still haunted me. Tormenting him *had* been my earlier objective, and it worked. "You're also the most obnoxious, and maddening creature I know. Only the *gods* know why I had to fall in love with someone as complex as you."

"I'm not obnoxious!" I exclaimed. He laughed, negating what I'd said. "Sure, maybe I can be a bit maddening at times, but so can you," I went on to say, gently hitting Ace's chest in exasperation. It wasn't until then something he'd said finally caught up to me. "Wait, what did you say?" I asked, voice rising too loud and the Hellions nearby had to "shush" me.

"I'm in love with you," he said, amused, watching me as though I'd done something cute.

"Oh," I said, eyes widening in surprise. *That's all you're going to say? Tell him you love him back!*

He reached out and pulled me to him, "I think I always have."

A moment later, I let my breath out and pulled away from him. "I love you too," I said, unable to mask the sadness in my tone. "Let me guess, you loving me doesn't change your mind, and you still don't think it's a good idea to be together right now?"

His eyes looked at my face sadly—knowing the answer I desperately wanted to hear but he couldn't give me. I had the urge to open my soul-reading gift up to him to get a better sense on how he was feeling, but somehow it seemed like an invasion of his privacy, and I refrained. "I think it's best right now."

Folding my arms over my chest and hugging myself tightly in order to try and stop my heart from aching inside my chest, I watched him turn and leave, regret filling his face.

His parting words had acted as fingers of cruelty pricking at my heart, leaving me wounded and exposed. I turned on my heels and stormed off in the opposite direction, feeling dejected and more confused than ever.

A loud screeching sound from the big black raven signaled the end of class. I gazed upward in time to watch as the ominous bird's wings in their full expanse as it glided overhead.

For a moment in time I wondered what it would feel to fly; to simply lift my wings and soar away to escape my sorrows.

<u>CHAPTER EIGHT</u>

Ghosts and Lullabies

A couple of days had passed since Ace dropped the L-bomb on me. During our next group training with the other Hellhounds, you could cut the tension between us with a knife it was so tangible.

Originally, these trainings were Apollyon's way to try and induce me into blossoming into my "gifts" as he called them. Needless to say it worked. He still believed he could push more out of me and now required us to have additional trainings after our lessons a few days a week. I had a feeling the twelve Hellhounds would start to resent me for it sooner rather than later.

On that note, I decided to stay and run at the back of the group during today's training on the black and red sands of the beach.

Ace had been drilling me pretty hard the past few weeks, so I didn't mind taking things at my own speed today, enjoying the way my strong legs carried me across the sand at a steady pace. Ace was at the front of the group leading the other eleven boys, which resolved my worries about having to talk to him. I'd been avoiding him all week, always finding excuses to avoid him by starting up conversations the moment he came over to me at my desk before and after classes, and again during meals.

I often wondered if I was just being cruel. The way I saw it, if Ace could tell me he loved me and how we couldn't be together all in the same sentence we had nothing more to say until he figured things out. I wasn't going to sit around and wait like some love sickened fool. *Desdemona Starr does not wait for anything!*

"Don't think too hard you might burst a blood vessel or something," Blake said teasingly, appearing next to me. Distracted, I wasn't sure when he'd fallen back behind the others to run beside me, or for how long.

My eyes wandered over to him and found his soul aura a comforting array of clear red-tones showing me he was feeling energetic, powerful, and maybe even a little competitive. I smiled. His ability to lift spirits came naturally. "Noted," I said.

"I usually am," he teased, wiggling his bushy eyebrows at me.

Blake received a half-hearted smile in response, my heart not in it today. Blake noticed and asked, "So, you want to talk about what's troubling you today, and making you wear one of those?" He pointed to my mouth set into a frown.

Definitely not! "Nah, I'm all right, but thanks." It would feel too weird talking to Blake about issues with Ace, especially our particular romantic issues.

"If you say so. I'm here if you need to talk, about anything," Blake declared, sounding sincere. I could tell he wanted to press for answers, and refrained; thank the Gods.

"Ebony and I talked the other night. She's nice, Blake," I admitted, changing the topic.

"Yeah I heard about that. Ebony is…great," he said, trying to find the right word for her, blushing with the thought. "Could you promise me one thing," he asked.

"Sure, anything?"

For a moment I thought maybe he'd ask me not to tell her about how he told me he loved me less than two months ago, and felt foolish when he said, "Whatever plan this is of yours involving Ebony be careful okay, make sure Ebony doesn't get hurt."

Well this was new. My head was nodding in compliance, even though his worry for her left me puzzled. "Sure, Hellhound promise," I said, holding my hand up into a salute, trying to deflect some of the weirdness stirring between us.

"You do know you're not a Hellhound? And besides, we don't exactly have a salute," he stated, giving me a good-old lopsided Blake grin.

"I know," I smiled sheepishly over at him.

"Thank you." He reached out and squeezing my shoulder, and then ran off ahead to catch up with the others. Once again, I ran by myself, alone to battle my thoughts. His gratitude felt weighted; he wasn't only telling me thanks for the promise there was more behind his gratitude. He was probably relieved I hadn't mentioned the whole telling-me-he-loves-me thing to Pixie-girl, I thought dryly. It bugged me he hadn't told her for some reason. *Was he ashamed for having feelings for me at all?*

My stomach felt twisted up inside. I hated how selfish I was being where Blake was concerned. *He's your best friend and you love him, it's not his fault you can't love him the way he wishes you did, and you should be happy he's found someone else—someone who might love him back,* the rational part of my brain won the inner battles.

Slowing my jog to a walk, before stopping altogether, and feeling breathless, I bent over at the waist, grabbing a hold of my knees in a deep stretch. Turning my head to look up at the sky, I watched as pastel colors of pinks and oranges streamed across signaling sunset. Training would be almost over, and since my absence probably wouldn't be missed, I had no problem taking it slow to get back to the Institute.

Carrying my shoes tied together in one hand, I walked along the edges of the water. Icy-blasts of the cold water felt good after the strain I'd put my feet through. Aromas of the Aegean Sea settled around me smelling of crisp salt, and minerals from the nearby cliffs breaking loose into the air. It smelled of the only home I'd ever know. If ever I left, it would be missed.

Enjoyments of the solitude I'd found was cut short when whispers carried by the wind had me pausing in my tracks. Startled, I looked up only to see nothing out of the ordinary. Still, the sound surrounded me.

Every bone in my body was on high alert; there had been too many surprises of late to *not* be wary. Gazing silently around, a movement caught my eye.

There, twenty feet away, was a woman standing in the sea. The wind had caught the fabric of her long sleeves of the white dress she wore. It's what tipped me off she was there at all, or else I wouldn't have seen her since the sun had almost completely set now. With tourist season approaching, it wasn't uncommon for people to leave the mainland and venture over this way; we never had to worry about tourists spotting the Institute since it was protected by a glamour, even so, the woman in white was an odd sight to see and didn't settle right in my stomach.

She could have been accompanied by someone, I thought, and began looking around for clues of another person. I didn't see any.

Once sure there was no one else around, I hesitantly approached. The freezing water was up to the woman's knees and still she continued to move deeper into the icy water. By the time I was close enough to get a better look at the woman it covered her waist.

The woman heard me behind her and whipped her head around in my direction. Her tear-streaked face caught me by surprise, and I sucked in a sharp gasp of surprise. There was something terrifyingly familiar about the heart-shape of her face, and those large almond-shaped eyes.

And then, like waking from a bad dream and gasping for air as though the wind had been knocked out of me, I knew why; it was the face that had haunted my sleep every night since I was a child.

Lilith. My mother.

Had I seen a ghost? It's impossible, it can't be! The logical part of my brain screamed at me while the other part, the part that made wishes when blowing out birthday candles, or when I saw a shooting star—the part of me that still believed good things could happen if you believed enough— desperately wanted to reach out at even the slim possibility it could be her.

Before I knew it, I was wading out toward her—calling out to her. The woman who looked like my mother smiled at me in approval, wanting me to follow her.

Only the slightest hint of twilight lingering at sea level gave light. When I was only a few feet away, the woman stopped walking, and turned toward me.

"Desdemona," the woman called in a voice no louder than a gentle whisper, the same whisper I'd heard in the breeze earlier.

Extending my arm out toward her, merely fingertips away from reaching her, I opened my mouth to ask if it was truly her, when a scream burst from my lungs when the woman was pulled under the water before disappearing into dark waters.

"No!" I spun around frantically searching for her, waiting to see if she'd come back up. When she didn't I began to move deeper in, near the spot she'd gone under, struggling to touch the sand on the bottom with pointed toes. Desperate beyond a measure, I took in a quick breath and submerged myself beneath the water. It was too dark to see anything and I had to come back up, gasping for air. It didn't stop me from trying again, and again, until I grew dizzy. "Help," I tried to yell, but my voice shook too badly from being in the cold water too long, and it didn't carry.

If no one can hear me, I'll go get help! I began to make my way back to shore, but didn't make it far when something in the water caught hold of my ankle and pulled me under.

I didn't have the chance to hold my breath, and already felt as though my lungs were empty and seizing in panic while whatever had a hold of my ankle, continued to keep me beneath the water's surface.

It wasn't long before I was too tired to struggle anymore, my limbs weren't responding to my brain telling them to keep moving, to keep swimming. Without my thrashing around and struggling, I could see clearly for once.

At first, all I could see was her dark, auburn-colored hair floating upward, until the woman let go of her hold on my ankle, probably knowing I did not have enough strength to swim to escape her anyway. She glided up closer, putting us face to face. And then did something strange. She smiled.

The resemblance this woman had to my mother was shocking. Maybe it was because I was drowning and near death, I'm not sure, but at that precise moment, I didn't think I'd ever seen anything more beautiful.

I fought to keep my eyes open when all they wanted to do was to shut. All I wanted to do was sleep. It took all of my might to keep them open to see *her*.

"No, my sweet, beautiful Angel, you mustn't die, not now," the woman's voice filled my mind. My eyes widened. That voice, so familiar, like a lullaby once forgotten and only heard again recently. Her hand floated up to my face where she ran one finger down the length of my cheek. *"You have so much to do still—go, go back now."* Her voice trailed off into the crashing waves overhead. The woman was telling me to go, but I was too tired to do anything. The sea pressed down on me and my mind closed off. My body felt light, like I no longer weighed anything at all. Reaching a hand out trying to touch her, just once, that's all I wanted before my imminent doom took me. A doom which never came. Something strong reached down into the water, grabbed a hold of the back of my T-shirt, and pulled me free from the sea's cold, unremitting fingers.

From then on, my vision went in and out, not allowing me to connect all the pieces of what was happening. All I could hear was the sound of a man's muffled voice trying to break through to me.

Finally managing to get a few salty coughs out from having swallowed too much water, the strong hands that had pulled me free from the sea's prison, rolled me over and began patting me on the back, making certain I'd gotten it all out.

Elevated to a sitting position, still trying to catch my breath, my lungs heaved in and out, rejoicing in finally getting air to fill them back up again. The sounds of someone nearby breathing heavily reminded me I was not alone. Hair and sand needed to be removed from my face first in order to see who had rescued me.

Kione, of all people, was the last person I'd expected to see sitting across from me, worry he'd almost lost me evident on his face. *I had to be dead for this to be happening.*

On instinct, I began putting as much distance between me and Kione as fast as I could by digging my heels into the sand, crawling backward. He remained where he was kneeling in the sand, watching me, and making no effort to come closer or calm me.

My throat felt scratchy and raw when trying to speak, and at first no sound came out. After clearing my throat a few times, I finally managed to get a few words in. "You pulled me out of the water?"

He gave me a curious expression, "Yes." "Why?" This was Kione we were talking about here, and as far as I was concerned saving my life one time—okay so he saved me twice now, not to be keeping score—it didn't make me trust him anymore. Abaddon had trusted him once, and look where his trust got him.

"Why did I save your life?" he repeated, humored by my blatant hostility.

In answer, I found my feet and stood over him, wobbling from the light-headedness of almost drowning. Kione reached out to steady me, "No, don't," I told him.

He huffed once before following suit to stand, dusting off his knees and saying, "It's my duty here as a mentor of the Morning Star to ensure the Dark Princess's safety," he said simply.

I snorted at hearing this. "Don't think this will change anything between us, I still don't trust you."

"Of course." He glanced in the direction of the water which was now under the glow of the moon.

The worry I had spotted on his face earlier had returned. He seemed just as unsettled as I was by what had happened. I shivered with the memory of almost drowning.

Kione mistook my shiver and said, "You must be chilly, and it's going to get cooler. I need to take you back to the Dark Manor now. With your permission of course," he added smoothly.

With the mention of the Manor, visions of crawling into my bed and pulling the covers over me and putting this awful night in the past took precedence, and I let Kione lead me back toward the Manor. All the while an unsettling thought crept its way into my mind, knowing that if Kione tried to pull something, I was too weak to do anything and my voice too raw to scream.

Sleep rolled over me the instant my head touched the pillow. That night, I dreamed about auburn hair caught in the black waves of the sea and whispers beckoning me to come back and find her.

* * * *

Apollyon

"Kione was seen escorting Desdemona to her bedroom late this night." Apollyon looked over at his guest impatiently wanting him to get to the point. "Do you think it wise to entrust the man who goes by Kione when we have not learned his origins?" Aeglaeca, the old demon and trusted advisor asked Apollyon.

"Kione has proven as to which side he is on when he laid out evidence against the Destroyer. If I thought him a threat, he would have been smote in front of the council. War would have eagerly done my bidding for me if I had asked," Apollyon said, not pausing while his brush strokes created an array of red paint suspiciously like the color of blood, across the canvas positioned on an easel before him.

Aeglaeca took an insistent step forward, "Yes, my lord, forgive my ignorance. It is with the way he easily dismissed the friendship he had with your son which worries me. Could he not do the same with your trust?"

Aeglaeca cringed away, hunching his tall, bony frame in on itself as he backed toward the exit. He looked like an old, molting crow. Apollyon sat in silence, only giving conscious thought to his brushstrokes. Time seemed to lag on longer than reality, when finally Apollyon sat back and laced his hands behind his head, admiring his work. "You need not worry about my use of trust. It would be negligent of me to trust even my closest advisors, precisely why I have a handful of spies lurking around every corner of my domicile." Namely, there were a few watching his daughter Desdemona closely.

"Treat me as you would one of your young Hellhounds, Aeglaeca, and I shall have your tongue removed from your mouth with a hot iron," Apollyon said. He liked to remind his faction who was the superior one every now and then. He had been wondering what game Osiris, Lord of the Underworld, was playing at exactly. It was impeccable timing, he should make himself known before the attacks on the Dark Manor began; also around the same time Abaddon had returned and betrayed him, as he'd always known he would. He didn't feel he should mention this to the old demon however, and let him grovel on his knees, where he put himself immediately after being threatened.

"Yes, my lord, it will not happen again."

"Find your feet, old friend, your knowledge is not needed for the time being. We have more important things to pass our time."

"Yes, my Dark Lord. Is there anything an old friend can help you with?"

Apollyon raised his eyebrows at his word choice but chose not to mention it. "As a matter of fact, I would like you to find out whether or not my son had any contact with the Lord of the Underworld before his timely arrival at my Institute."

If Aeglaeca was surprised by the request, he didn't show it. Instead, a cruel smile lit his ashen face, making him look far beyond the old age he was. "Make necessary arrangements with one of the hounds out front if need be, and be gone with yourself. My dinner should be arriving momentarily and the sight of you lessens my appetite." Apollyon waved his hands in a dismissive manner.

Once Aeglaeca had gone, Apollyon looked upon his latest artwork in silence. He grinned recalling the way the traitor, whose blood he'd used to paint this piece with, had pleaded for his life to no avail. Apollyon only reserved such punishments for those he had mistakenly trusted. This one had been one of his most trusted Hellhound guardians, Thann. It was a shame it had come to this, but the Hound had been spotted conversing with Abaddon the night Abaddon had betrayed his own kind. Apollyon had no other choice, the Hound had been bled by the Imps, his title removed before he was tossed away to live with puny mortals. Apollyon could not think of a worse fate.

CHAPTER NINE

Banshee Unleashed

I was rudely awakened sometime early the next morning by someone barging into my room unannounced. I sat straight up in my bed, trying to focus on the figure standing next to my bed with sleepy eyes.

"What did he do to you?" this irate person demanded to know.

"Ace?"

Of course it's Ace—who else would storm in here as if he owned the place?

"You're damn right it's me! Now, are you going to tell me what he was doing out there alone on the beach with you? I swear I'll tear him to pieces if he so much as laid one finger on you."

"Who?" My mind was still in sleep sluggish mode.

"Kione! Who do you think, Dess? It's all anyone is talking about—news about you and Kione," he practically growled.

Ah, right. The memory of last night came crashing back in waves.

This was not good. Gods only knew what kind of things Hellions were saying about us. I groaned, rolling over and opening my eyes. "What kind of news?" I asked, reluctant to hear the answer.

"About how you two were caught out after hours, and how you guys came in together last night soaking wet."

Well that sounds about right.

"Please tell me it's true so I can kill him."

Throwing the covers off me in one annoyed motion, sitting up, I said, "Okay it's true—but it's not what you think. He didn't do anything to me." Ace wasn't listening to me, already livid. "Ace, he saved my life."

"You expect me to believe that? After everything he's done to you—to Abaddon?" he exclaimed, pacing in front of my bed.

"It's true, Ace. You don't have to believe him. Believe me."

"Okay fine, I'm listening."

"I saw something in the water and went after it, got caught under water somehow, and couldn't find the surface. Kione must have seen me struggling. He pulled me out of the water." I left out the part about having seen my mother. I didn't know how to explain what happened, not entirely understanding it myself. Besides, I didn't want to chance Ace thinking I was in danger after explaining to him how something tried drowning me last night. It would be like when the Lamia was after me all over again, only this time instead of getting assigned to guard me every second of the day, Ace would volunteer to do it.

"I still don't buy it. No way did Kione just happen to be at the right place at the right time. How do we know Kione hadn't planned the whole thing, right down to your almost drowning?" Ignoring him was getting harder to do when he insisted on barging into my room making demands.

Ace wasn't saying anything I hadn't already considered. By the wild look in his eyes, I could tell he wanted me to agree with him and wouldn't settle for anything less. All it would take was one simple lie on my part and Ace would shift into Hellhound form and probably be able to take Kione out himself. The prospect of having Kione out of the picture was enticing, yet, I couldn't do it. Kione deserved much worse for betraying my brother. I wanted to prove to Apollyon—to the whole council Kione's true snake-like intentions. I shook my head and those tempting thoughts away with it.

Ace stood poised and ready, watching me intently for my response. "He saved my life, Ace," I repeated.

Ace looked at my face for the space of several more breaths until finally letting it go. I could tell by the rigid set of his mouth he wasn't happy or convinced, and was probably going against every instinct he had by not leaving now and confronting Kione.

Ace left, grim expression still in tow. I'm glad he woke me up, even though he could have been a bit more tactful about it. If he hadn't, I'd have slept through the day and missed my classes.

The rest of the day proceeded as I'd expected after hearing Ace say the whole Institute was talking about me. Everywhere I turned, blatant stares as hushed whispers trailed me down halls and surrounded me during classes.

Though our meal times were somewhat formal in the way that we had servers in the form of Hantu-demons, there was also a side table with extras for us to help ourselves to fruits and desserts. While waiting in line at the salad bar during lunch, I finally caught wind of what people were talking about. "Desdemona Starr is sleeping with Kione. I don't know if I should be appalled or jealous." The first girl who I recognized as Donella said to her friend, whose back was to me.

"Tell me about it, it's so not fair. Who knew our little Dark Princess was such a little Succubus?" the other girl said in reply, and when they started laughing, the one girl whose face I couldn't quite see before, turned enough for me to see...Brigitte. Anger shot through me and I had to clench and unclench my fists, my tray of food shaking in my hands. They confirmed the worst.

I cleared my throat, letting them know they'd been heard. Instead of ignoring them and walking away; I reached over them and grabbed an apple off the top of a basket of fruit. "I know right? Who would have thought? Maybe I unconsciously picked up a few tricks from Scarlett over the years—if anyone knows how to be a slut best, it would be her. But seriously guys, there's no need to be jealous, really, there's nothing even there worth mentioning," I said, in my best superficial voice, and then turned and left, rolling my eyes as I went. I looked back to see Donella and Brigitte standing there aghast with their jaws hanging open.

It was probably uncalled for and only aided in drawing attention to this bullshit story; seeing their dumbfounded faces made it totally worth it though.

On my way to go find somewhere to eat, I spotted Kione eating his lunch at a table nearest the exit out into the courtyard. I'd been planning on taking my meal outside in order to avoid hearing anything else, but didn't want to walk past him. Instead, I turned around and went in the opposite direction, choosing a small table in the far corner of the room.

While I picked at my bagel and a dozen other bread-type foods and about three pieces of fruit having not paid attention when filling my tray, I kept glancing up to cast accusing eyes over in Kione's direction.

He was a source for attention, like a circus freak, I thought bitingly. I sat there quietly observing Kione's social niceties, his presence creating excitement and curiosity amongst everyone. Students gathered around his table, asking questions loudly and with enthusiasm, wanting to know all about where he's been and what he's seen. When a couple of kids moved out of the way, it opened up a small window for me to see a certain redheaded Succubus I hadn't been able to see before. It didn't surprise me to see Scarlett sitting right next to Kione, putting herself the closest to him. Evidently, whatever rumor was going around about Kione and I didn't put a damper on her efforts to chase him. If anything, it only seemed to make her more desperate.

Good riddance, Scarlett can have him, I thought, reaching up and grabbing my throat. It still felt sore and scratched up on the inside as though it had been rubbed with sandpaper.

"Please tell me none of it is true?" a familiar voice asked and stole my attention from Kione's table. I looked up to see Blake set his tray of food down on the table in front of me before he sat down.

"Two days in a row, huh?" I asked, surprised but otherwise happy he was talking to me again.

"What?" he asked, not understanding my demented sense of humor.

"Nothing." I waved what I'd said away. "And it depends on who you ask." Stealing one more glance over at Kione, and instantly regretting it. This time he saw me looking. His smile faltered, though he never quite lost the humor in his eyes as he returned a meaningful gaze at me. He probably took some kind of perverse satisfaction in what people were saying about us. Scarlett noticed our exchange and went rigid beside him. Her feline-shaped eyes narrowed in fury, and I was pretty sure the temperature dropped a few degrees with the icy glare she was giving me.

"Why do I not feel comforted?" Blake asked sarcastically.

I shrugged, "Because you have killer instincts. Go with your gut on that one, trust me, you don't want to know."

"Sounds fine to me. My gut instincts are telling me to eat," he said, leaning back and rubbing his stomach. We both laughed, and soon the rest of the dining hall's presence dimmed to a meaningless backdrop of shadows and voices as we fell into old habits, laughing and making fun of each other.

Things stayed like that for a while until he brought up going to the dance at the end of the month. "Are you thinking about going?" he asked, after taking a long pull of soda from his straw.

"No," I answered a little too fast, receiving a famous one-eyebrow raise only Blake could pull off and somehow still look regal.

"Why? Are you?" I asked.

"Eh, I'm not sure, I haven't really thought much about it." Blake shifted uncomfortably in his seat.

"Yeah, I can tell. Are you worried Ebony will say no?" I asked, finding his nervousness trivial. I didn't see any reason to tiptoe around what was obviously a sensitive subject. Hey, he brought it up!

"Nah, it's not that. I mean it's part of it, sure. There's more. We're just getting to know each other. I'm not sure Ebony even likes to dance."

"Blake, she's still a girl. She wants to dance with you, believe me. Besides, you could always dance to the slow stuff, no one will notice if either one of you can dance or not."

"Yeah?"

"Yes. So will you please ask her so you can shut up about it already?" I said teasingly before play shoving him. Any other time it might have seemed weird for me to be pushing Blake and Ebony to go to a dance together, but doing this for them somehow seemed right. Plus, I *owed* Pixie-girl one for helping me find out my brother's whereabouts. This made us even.

"Um, yeah I guess…sure," he said, starting to sound a bit more confident.

"There you go champ," I said, taking his soda out of his hands and drinking it. Blake left his now empty hand up in the air for a second while giving me a disbelieving look. Shaking his head at me, he finally dropped his hand back down, cutting his losses with the soda.

"What about you? Are there any certain hounds calling to escort the Dark Princess to the ball?" he teased.

Thank the Gods I never had a chance to answer that ridiculous question when the deafening Threat-sirens blared out over the Institute.

Blake and I both jumped up out of our seats, our meals long forgotten. Panic was scattered all around the dining hall as Hellions ran around to seek shelter, some covering their ears against the deafening tone.

Whipping my head over to look at Blake and seeing the crease of alarm on his face told me this was not a drill. "Come on, let's go find Ace," he told me, motioning for me to follow him.

Usually Blake and Ace told me to wait behind when the possibility of threats arose, for whatever reason, not this time. This time Blake was asking for my help. He didn't need to tell me twice.

I followed him out into the courtyard before we stopped since it was as far as we needed to go. We'd walked right into the danger and the cause for the sirens. Our Banshee mentor, Malinda, had apparently fallen off her rocker or forgotten to take her crazy pills because she was flying overhead distraught and frantic.

"What's gotten into her?" I asked, leaning in close to Blake's ear.

"What do we do?" Blake looked uncertain. This was our mentor, what *could* we do?

"There," Blake said, pointing over to where Ace stood with Ignacio, Sheldon, and Braedon. Those Hellhounds looked clueless to what should be done about the situation too. We took one step forward and immediately had to duck when the Banshee let loose an ear-piercing wail right before Malinda swooped down on us. Lucky for us, she missed. Not so luckily for the Hellion who was standing next to Blake when her outstretched claws grabbed him by the shoulders and flew upward with him.

He didn't stay up for long when the Banshee began tearing at him, clawing him up before releasing him to fall to his death. I had to look away from the gory scene, feeling rancid bile forming in my stomach and threatening its way up my throat. Mentor Malinda killed someone. What the hell was going on around here?

I looked back up in the nick of time to see Blake shift into his Hellhound form; killing Hellions was the green light for Blake, Ace, and the other Hellhound-guardians-in-training to take matters into their own hands. I noticed a few of my father's guards had also shown up to handle things.

Hellfire formed in the palm of my hand when Malinda continued to swoop down at Hellions who were stupid enough to be outside in the courtyard wanting a front row seat. The blue-tinted flames of hellfire burned eagerly in my hands, I was ready to use it, but couldn't find an opening without accidently hitting a Hellhound. There was too much movement and chaos for me to get a clear shot. "You can't make me leave!" Malinda shrieked. "I won't go!"

So, that's what this is about? Apollyon must have fired her—or banished her, whatever you want to call it; sometimes he made mentors leave once he felt they were no longer a value to the Morning Star, and Malinda wasn't going without a fight. One of the hounds let out a loud yelp when the Banshee's talons caught him. Instantly my mind begged it to not have been Ace—or Blake. If anything happened to either of them.

A few more casualties fell from the sky.

I felt helpless unable to take action. Her blood curdling screeches felt like glass was slicing the meat inside my head. I cringed, and thought desperately of something, anything, I could do. Desperation and fear for the people, or in my case the Hellhounds I loved, led me to discover a new ability I hadn't been aware of. Desperation formed into black vines coming from within me, acting as extensions from me, slithering out from under me like shadows with their own will to move. The vines shot up and into the air finding their victim and snagging her by the throat. The shriek she'd been wailing was choked off as I dragged her before me. Everything else had gone silent, and I was vaguely aware of how everyone was watching me. All that could be heard now was the gargling sound of Malinda being choked to death.

Realizing what I was doing, I immediately released her. My first mistake. Malinda lunged at me with her claws stretched out toward my face.

Her razor-sharp nails barely managed to leave a scratch when I heard the vicious growl of a large animal, probably one of the hounds fearing for me, at the same time her body was jerked backward in one swift violent motion. Looking over, I saw my father standing in the middle of the courtyard, lifting Malinda into the air with the same tendrils of darkness coming from him as it had from me, only he became part of the shadows wholly, lifting up into the air with Malinda. He looked like some ominous black cloud wrapping completely around our former mentor. Her screams were cut off when he continued twisting around her until at last, there was nothing left of her.

When he floated back to the ground, becoming his person form again, little black grains of sand misted down all around us. I was going to be sick if I thought about the sandy stuff as what used to be Malinda.

"Well done, daughter, though you still seem to lack a bit of conviction. It is something we can work on though." Apollyon rubbed his hands together shaking off any residual Malinda on them. He strode over and stopped directly in front of me with a look of what only could be described as satisfaction.

After the crowd dispersed, I was still in shock from not only the whole ordeal, but also from what I'd been capable of. Apollyon who remained in the courtyard, showed his disappointment at my lack of gratitude toward what he considered to be a compliment, his fiery glare in turn making me cringe. When Apollyon used his power through his eyes, it felt as though a hole were being drilled right through your soul until you felt miniscule in size, having beaten down all your will. He turned and barked out orders for his Hellhound guards to clean up the mess, and then he left the courtyard.

He'd done what he came there for by putting an end to the mess he was responsible for making in the first place. He made no mention of the Hellions, his precious Morning Star Pupils he'd lost today. They did not truly matter to him.

I needed to sit down.

I turned and banged open the doors to the dining hall and then threw myself down onto the first chair available. I wasn't sure how long I'd been sitting there trying to get a handle on my heart beating rapidly inside my chest, when I saw Ace, back in normal form, come and sit down next to me. His presence comforted me.

"I don't know what's happening to me," I said, burying my face into my hands.

Without saying anything, Ace reached out and drew me into his arms, holding me close. Our heartbeats synced together, and I knew as long as Ace held me this way, nothing else mattered.

CHAPTER TEN

A Stir in the Darkness

The bad thing about having so many sinister creatures living, and schooling, under one roof—things were destined to go bad at some point.

Getting caught in the crossfire bites, big time. I wasn't the only one paying for it. We were all paying for it even days later. The Institute was a wreck after the fiasco with Mentor Malinda ended; Hellions were still grieving for the ones we lost. And you would think that after the disaster with the Banshee, the rumors about Kione and me would stop. Nope, no such luck. Kione's popularity was unyielding.

Everywhere I went students were talking about him. If Apollyon had caught wind of these rumors he either didn't care, or found the whole thing meaningless and a waste of his time.

It wouldn't surprise me if a monumental bronzed statue of Kione in all his false glory, showed up in the middle of the courtyard tomorrow!

Wouldn't that be something for Abaddon to come home to? With Abaddon in mind, I couldn't sit around and do nothing while waiting for Scarlett's full moon ritual to roll around.

Walking across the Institute to get to the Hellhounds' living quarters nearly killed me. I was tempted to cover my ears and run past any student talking.

Finally, I'd made it to the secret door on the stone wall hidden by overgrown vines making their way inside the Manor. Reaching one arm into the mass of vines, I began searching for the door handle. A moment later my fingertips closed around an oval shaped handle. One quick turn of the handle and I was surrounded by mild winds carrying fragrances of the sea and flowers from the mainland as they blossomed into spring.

A cliff threatened my immediate fall to a certain death, mere inches away the moment I stepped outside and onto the narrow pathway. I wasn't scared of heights, but I wasn't fond of them either. Carefully I placed one foot after the other, keeping one hand stretched out along the side of the Manor at all times, slowly creeping forward. There had to be another way to get to our mother's secret courtyard, I thought. Right on cue, my foot caught on a root from an overgrown vine in the path. My foot slipped off and over the edge of the narrow path. The rest of me would have fallen off if my hand hadn't caught hold of the root on which I'd originally tripped.

Oh for shit's sake, why can't anything be easy? I pulled myself back up over the side with trembling hands. Once standing back, I allowed myself a few moments to get my breathing back under control while second-guessing my fear of heights.

* * * *

When finally arriving at the courtyard, I took in how it appeared exactly the way it had when last I'd come here with Ace. It seemed impossible since we had done a real number on the place during our battle with Bone Demons when I'd accidently opened the portal to the Underworld and dammed creatures began climbing out of it left and right. The only evidence left from then was the black singe mark on the bench near the fountain. That's where the Angels, Ethan and Lain, had used *white-lightning,* a heavenly weapon of mass destruction, to save the day.

Since it was the peak of May, roses bloomed vibrantly in different shades throughout the fenced-in courtyard garden. Reds, pinks, yellows, white, and peach blossoms looked striking up against the gray of the lion-head statues and fountain; the smell was intoxicating. It was easy to imagine my mother tending to the foliage. I could understand why Lilith loved coming here so much; it was a quiet escape from the dark chains of the Manor; an escape from Apollyon too, my mind added.

Pausing to take a deep breath first, I walked over to the fountain; I'd promised both Blake and Ace I wouldn't open the portal again anytime soon, and knew they'd both be mad if they ever found out. This time I'd get it right though. Bending down to retrieve the small blade Lain had given me after the last fountain incident, my fingers gently ran over the hilt of the knife where jewels of black and citrine set it apart from any other knife. Its name was The Star. Like people, an object such as a knife could be given a name making it belong to a certain person indefinitely, and sometimes if misused by another, any trace of magic left over in it could be disastrous. Lain had hinted how this particular knife had belonged to my mother at one point, though its rightful place was with me. Remembering the proper way to access the magic within the fountain, I recited the written words. "Only truth can illuminate the darkness." Repeating it three more times in a few of the different languages, and ran the blade smoothly over my forearm, thinking first to make the cut high enough it could easily be concealed from sight later.

Blood streamed down my forearm in droplets of crimson rain, and straight into the murky waters of the fountain. All traces of nervousness vanished when the water began to slowly circle clockwise; counter clockwise had been the first telltale sign I'd done something wrong the last time.

Thoughts of Abaddon filled my mind. I wasn't sure if focusing on what I wanted to see would help or not since there was no way of knowing Abaddon's exact location. Abaddon once told me the fountain had a life of its own, and only showed what we truly needed to see the most.

Darkness rippled like dark folds of fabric, and a moment later a silent picture-show swirled to life.

I saw a woman wearing a black dress. A second longer into the show, realized I was looking at an image of myself, and I wasn't alone. Kione was standing behind me with both of his hands on my shoulders. He held me close. His breath moving stray pieces of my hair against my cheek. Once identifying who I was watching, the pictures changed, they began scrolling more slowly. The dress I wore in the fountain's image was the same one I'd been wearing during the disturbing dream I'd had about being in the old underground tomb with Kione. It put me back there again, and all the same feelings of confusion and hatred also flooded back. The expression on my image's face was all screwed up though; I was actually smiling, taking pleasure in Kione's presence. The way we gazed at each other made me think we were together—as in a couple together. My stomach flip-flopped in disgust at the thought of being attracted to him, even knowing it was only the image trying to fool me.

A second look made me notice how there was also something odd about my eyes; the color was red and frightening. There was something feral inside the fountain me that scared me to even witness; I did not recognize myself in the image. Still, I could not tear my eyes away from the motion picture. Kione's mouth was moving but I could not hear what he was saying. When he was done, Kione stepped back, and a pair of wings unfurled behind me in a cascade of feathers. My wings had been black in the dream, here in the fountain's image, only one was black and the other was swan-white. Kione stepped away, leaving me standing with my wings still spread, and holding a knife in one hand. The image me jerked her head up and looked directly up at where I stood outside of the fountain in my mother's garden. I jumped back startled, continuing to watch as a slow spreading smile transformed her face, and all in one motion the image me reached out with the knife and made a swift slashing motion toward me. Out of reflex, my eyes closed shut, and my hands came up to protect myself. When I reopened them again, the whole picture-show display was gone, and I was left to stand there, my heart feeling as though it had leaped into my throat.

Hands shaking, I reclaimed my breath and resumed my position over the fountain. The distorted version of me was gone as was Kione, and in their place was another familiar face.

"Abaddon," I breathed out a long sigh of relief.

It was dark wherever he was being kept at Ryu. The only way to identify the person as Abaddon was by his heart-shaped face and perfectly angled nose he'd inherited from our mother. My face was similar to hers too, except I'd inherited our father's more peaked nose, and strong squared jaw.

The space seemed cramped, I thought, as I watched Abaddon turn toward a wall and began to do what looked like scratching or drawing something onto the wall. I couldn't quite make out what it was he drew, and the fountain didn't deem it necessary for me to see; it's not like there was a zoom button for me to push, so I bit my lip, and continued to watch, hating every second Abaddon had to spend in that horrible place.

I was about to call it a night, finding the fountain to be of no help when all of a sudden, Abaddon fell to the ground, arching his back in pain, his mouth stuck open in a silent scream. "No!" *I cried, a feeling of sickness swarming in the pit of my stomach.*

What was happening, why was Abe screaming? What caused him to be in pain?

Seeing Abe lying on the floor crippled in pain, reminded me of when War had had me in her merciless clutches during the council meeting, when I'd stupidly provoked her.

As though thinking of War had persuaded the fountain to show the image, War, and her pet Vampire, stood on the other side of Abaddon's imprisonment, staring down at Abaddon with a look so cold, a set of chills ran over my entire body. War's mouth was moving with no way for me to know what she was saying, the same way if had been with Kione. What's worse was feeling helpless while watching Abaddon's body continue to jerk on the hard ground for what felt like an unbearable amount of time. At last, all movement stopped, and his face showed instant relief. War had released her hold on him, I realized, watching the fountain's waters still, putting an end to everything it wished to show me.

What is War doing there?

All I knew was nothing good could come from War and her pet being there. Her intentions were always to cause more discord and chaos, which was exactly what I needed in my life…more chaos.

CHAPTER ELEVEN

Moonstone

When evil lurks in unexpected forms, the chances of destroying it become an impossible feat—and this is coming from someone who knows her evil.

If War was somehow involved in dealing with Abe, my plan would prove more difficult than originally expected.

It was barely sundown when I made my way to Zola's office, in hopes she hadn't already gone to dinner. Disturbing images of Abaddon with his mouth stuck open in a silent scream, played repeatedly in my mind.

Once I'd made it down the long hallway, I noticed my father's guards were missing. He was probably away on one of his visits to the mortal world, I thought, since his guards escorted him when he left the Manor.

I'd let curiosity steal my attention momentarily, but I had more pressing concerns and needed to focus. If War was in league with Kione, then we were in bigger trouble than we thought. Not to mention, clearing Abaddon's name would be damn near impossible.

I entered Zola's office just as she was gathering her coffee cup and shawl, getting ready to leave. "Zola, are you busy?" I asked, peeking my head in.

Zola looked up at my approach, and all it took was one look at my face for hers to lose its color and turn gray. She frowned. "You've learned the truth of Abaddon's whereabouts," Zola said, using her Seer powers of perception. "I've been expecting this day to come. I have something I've been holding onto for a while now in case a troubling day like this should come."

Unable to speak, afraid my voice would crack, or I'd start crying, I strode over to her and threw myself in for a hug. Zola's Seer powers proved proficient yet again.

Zola reclaimed her composure, snapping back like a buoyant rubber band. "Well, child, I don't see any point in dragging it out any longer. Gather your wit, and come with me." Zola grabbed me by the shoulders, forcing me to see her stern face. "Good. Now let's get something to eat, I'm starving." She led us out of her office, keeping one arm wrapped around my waist, steering us to the dining hall.

Instead of ordering her food and sitting down at a table to eat the way everyone else did, Zola headed us back into the kitchen where the chef prepared our meals.

"Why don't you have them bring you your meals the way the rest of the mentors do?" I asked, more curious than anything. Zola always did things unconventionally.

"I wouldn't dream of it. It seems foolish having someone else wait on me when I'm a capable being," Zola said, sternly. "I do fine on my own two feet," she went on to say while ladling soup into two large bowls for each of us. I didn't have the heart to tell her I wasn't hungry, mostly not wanting to listen to her scold me for not eating enough or something.

"What was it you wanted to show me?" I asked, leaning over the counter to sip my soup off the spoon. I wasn't sure eating this way was sanitary. Even so, the soup warmed up my stomach, and helped settle my nerves a bit; as Zola probably knew it would.

"Okay, it's time," Zola said, gesturing to one of the cooks who slowly stirred a large stockpot. He was a Hantu-demon. They literally fed off the pain caused to others. His grotesque appearance was made up of rotting flesh, exposed bones, and tiny larva crawling over his skull eating away at all his death and decay. *Despite his unsightly exterior, man he could cook!*

The Hantu-demon reached his rotting hand into the boiling pot, pulling it back out with something clutched in his bony hand. Zola's face lit up with a smile, "Ah, there it is." She took the stone from him and held it up to examine as though it were some rare jewel. It was a white, almost translucent stone on the outside while on the inside I could swear every color that existed was captured there.

"Is that a—"

"A Moonstone," Zola finished for me.

"Where did you find this?" I asked, unable to keep the surprise from my voice. Moonstones were hard to come by because of their absorbent trait, making them an impressive carrier for all sorts of magic, dark or natural, it doesn't matter.

"Never mind any of that, it is no concern of yours," Zola said, voice grave. "You be sure to keep it well hidden. I won't have it landing in the wrong hands—heaven knows what'll happen if something gets a hold of it —besides sendin' me to an early grave," she said, forcing it into my hands.

Holding it in my hands tightly cupped together, frankly, this much power frightened me. "I will keep it safe." It wasn't lost on me of the dangers Zola and whoever had helped her must have gone through to get the Moonstone, and my nerves were uneasy all over again.

Carefully hiding the Moonstone in the side of my boot, opposite the one which held my knife, I patted it with my hand once, after making sure it was safe and snug.

On my way back across the Institute, the weight of the stone was a constant reminder of what I had to do in order to free Abaddon. It was also a reminder for what would happen if I got caught. They probably wouldn't even bother taking me in for questioning. An act of sedition was grounds for death in the most gruesome ways imaginable.

It would be disastrous to be found with the stone on me. There were several days until Scarlett preformed the Moon Ritual, and so I needed a safe place to store the stone. But where? I thought of only one solution, hating how I was going to have to tell someone and risk their safety as well as mine.

There were only a few other Hellions I could trust with this information —only one certain shaggy-haired hound coming to the forefront of my mind since I was not keen on going to Ace for help, mainly to avoid any discomfort.

It would have to be Blake.

* * * *

Blake was swimming laps in the pool located near the healing chambers when I found him. He was so focused on his form, he didn't hear my entrance. His strokes were powerful, his body a perfect, muscular swimming vessel. Stepping up to the side of the pool where he was making his way back, I crouched down onto the balls of my toes and grasped the side of the cement pool, waiting for the right moment to make my company known. Just as Blake's hand touched the wall, and before he had the chance to spin around for another lap, I shouted, "Whoa, what did the pool ever do to you?"

He startled, coming to an ungraceful stop. Spinning around, obviously disoriented from wearing goggles, he held the side of the pool, his hand next to mine. "Who's there?" Blake asked.

"I'll give you one guess?"

"What? Dess, is that you?" he asked.

I laughed and then reached out to take his goggles off him. "Who else would barge in here and interrupt you while you were unleashing your inner dolphin?"

Blake smiled and then rubbed the chlorine from his eyes, "Of course, my mistake, now scoot back," he ordered, and then smiled. Doing as I was told, Blake used the side of the pool to grab onto before jumping up and out, shaking the water off. It was the perfect set-up for some dog joke, one I refrained from with effort.

"Now, do you want to hand me one of those towels over there?" he asked, pointing behind me where a stack of white towels lay rolled up on the bench by the door.

"Can do." I spun around to retrieve the towel. Returning with the towel in hand, Blake stood so close, my outstretched hands bumped into his smooth, still dripping with water, stomach. It forced my eyes to look down at where my hand pressed up against his diaphragm, and notice how the recent exertion he'd put his body through left his muscles defined and hard to the touch.

"Oh, sorry," I sputtered, quickly taking my hand back, and raking my eyes back up to his face. *Had Blake always been so defined?* I'd never really given him much notice even though there were plenty of times I'd seen him without his shirt on during our trainings.

"Thanks," he said, taking the towel. He didn't hide the look of amusement at my embarrassment very well; it wasn't often I got embarrassed. "So what do I owe for the pleasure of this visit?" he asked, running the towel over his hair quickly, before throwing it into the laundry bin.

"Right," I said. "To ask a favor." I bit my bottom lip. He didn't say anything, instead, crossed his arms over his chest, waiting for me to go into more detail. "I know I've been asking for way too much lately and I'll probably never be able to pay you back for everything. I had no one else to go to. I'll owe you big time!" A look of unease overcame him while he took in my pleading face before eventually sighing.

"How big are we talking?"

"Monumental," I said with a smile, and then bent down and retrieved the stone from where it hid snugly in my boot.

Blake, being the bookworm he was, gawked at the stone with wide, astonished eyes, before reaching out and snatching it from my hands. "Is this real?" he asked in a loud whisper, defeating the need to whisper in the first place.

"Whoa, slow down turbo, we need to be careful with the merchandise," I exclaimed. "And I'm assuming so, it isn't like Zola to deal in counterfeit belongings."

Blake missed the note of cynicism in my tone, too busy obsessing over the stone. "You're the only one who can know I have this," I told him gravely.

"You haven't told anyone else?" Blake asked, his head immediately snapping to attention. I could guess his reason for being surprised—he probably assumed I'd already told Ace about the stone.

"Just you, and I want to keep it that way," I said, guiltily, hating to be keeping secrets from Ace, or asking Blake to keep them from Pixie-girl.

He seemed slightly uncomfortable, nevertheless didn't press for an explanation. "What do you need my help with exactly?" he asked, handing the stone back over.

"I need somewhere safe to keep it."

Blake's stance went rigid with the enormity of the favor requested of him. He'd be breaking a lot of rules by keeping it hidden. "Look, I know it's a lot to ask, and I'd keep it myself but the risk of someone finding it is greater with me." I had too many enemies right now, Kione and Scarlett, to name a couple, who were both fixated on tarnishing me in their own messed up ways. I couldn't chance keeping it.

"Okay, I'll do it," he said, holding his hand out to take the stone back. It was starting to feel like we were playing a game of *hot-potato*. It was a game we learned during our first year at the Institute as an ice-breaker for Hellions to meet each other, only instead of using potatoes, we had to use the old skull of a Lepus Europaeus, otherwise known as a brown hare, found in Greece.

"You're sure you can keep it safe?" I couldn't help asking.

"Not at all, but like you said, you don't have another choice. Besides, I could never say no to you," he said, smiling sadly at me.

"Thank you." I handed the stone over, already feeling less anxious to have it out of my possession.

* * * *

"It will be safe with Blake," I told myself when I was alone again. What couldn't have been foreseen though was the dark loom of shadows, which seemed to be everywhere, yet invisible at the same time; some dark force seeing everything I did, hearing every word spoken, and always watching.

The price I would have to pay for the choices made this time would be unbearable, and even worse, unforgiveable.

CHAPTER TWELVE

Warnings from an Angel

Carrying a secret is like playing with fire, eventually someone is going to get burned.

I just didn't like being the one holding the match, and hoped Blake was smart enough not to get caught, for both our sakes.

When the morning came back around, the temptation to pull the blankets back over my head and sleep for the rest of the day lured me. There were three days left until the full moon, meaning Scarlett's full moon ritual as well when the wards at Ryu were at their weakest. It was enough pressure to make anyone curl back up in their hole and stay until the inferno passed over.

My duty to rescue Abe trumped wallowing in self-pity, and the only reason I launched myself out of bed, throwing the blankets off with more force than necessary, practically rolling out of bed. After brushing my hair and teeth, I went to my closet and mindlessly picked out the first thing my fingers touched. While leaving the closet, fully clothed, I looked up to see a certain baby-faced, blond Angel leaning up against one of the posts of my bed. Jumping back a step out of surprise, I said, "What on earth are you doing here?" and thought to lower my voice, not wanting to be caught talking with Lain, the infamous Angel on the wrong side of Apollyon's naughty and nice list.

"Hello Lilith's daughter. You're looking...hmm, I'm not exactly sure." He began studying me. "There's something about you undeniably different though."

"Um, thanks, I guess." It wasn't the strangest thing he's ever said to me.

What was strange was the way he carried food around with him everywhere he went, I thought, looking down at his hand, noticing how Lain was holding a small piece of fruit. "Wait, is that a kiwi?" I asked, pointing at the object in his hand.

"It is indeed. A kiwi is a delightful piece of fruit, don't you agree? Tarter than an orange, and the color is far more appealing," he said, cutting off a small piece of the green fruit before biting it right off the knife I'd just noticed he was holding. *Sheesh, some guardian I would be*! The way I so easily overlooked details reminded me of what Blake said, about how I was not a Hellhound-guardian-in-training even though I trained alongside them, it was not my forte.

"Sure, I guess." I shook my head, "But, Lain, seriously, what are you doing here?"

"To warn you against your upcoming venture involving a certain Angel of Hell," he said.

"How do you know about that?"

"I am a warrior of Heaven, it is my duty to know what Eve's Beloved is up to," he said, the fruit and knife vanishing into thin air from his hands. The disappearing act was such a cliché.

Of course Lain would already know my plans to seek out Abe. He probably knew where Abe was being kept this entire time.

I was about to mention how in all actuality, he wasn't a warrior to the heavens anymore, a retribution for helping me, deciding against it since the fact wouldn't help either of us.

"I don't know why I'm surprised by anything you do or say anymore," I said, stepping closer to him.

Lain didn't cringe with my closeness, he never did. Most Angels probably would have. Ethan, his other more disapproving half, certainly did the few times we'd met. "*I* surprise *you*?" he asked, astonished by this revelation.

"Well it's not every day that I get the chance to talk with, you know, the *other side*."

"Oh, right," he said, not picking up on my mockery.

Shaking my head, I said, "As much as your concern touches me, you need to understand one thing: I don't care about the risks. I'm going to do this anyway—I need to do this."

"I know," he said, sadly, looking at me as though he suspected as much. I was tempted to ask what he knew, if he could give me specifics, but quickly decided I didn't want to know.

"Hey, cheer up, fly-boy, I'm tougher than you think."

"No, you are as tough as I always knew you would be," he said, in all seriousness.

It was a relief to hear him say. "I appreciate you risking yourself to come here. However, you don't need to worry about me." Why an Angel worried about me in the first place was the real question? One I'd be sure to ask at some point during these unannounced visits of Lain's.

"You are not a risk, you are a possibility—the only possibility. I made a promise to someone to keep you safe," he said simply. *Maybe there would be an answer sooner rather than later.*

"Why exactly, and who?"

He seemed startled by this question, and took a second thinking it over. I'd rendered him speechless for once.

Faintly aware of holding my breath, I watched Lain turn his head sideways while watching me curiously, I thought about how he reminded me of an oversized bird—*which he sort of is, he has wings anyway.*

When he spoke again, his answer seemed to surprise us both, "Because you're worth saving. As for the second part of your question, now is not the right time."

Right time for what? Riddles were all Lain wanted to give.

"I'm limited in my callings, unable to interfere with fate. My callings won't always allow me to help. Promise me you'll endure, that you'll always find a way?" he pleaded.

It was a strange thing to promise, but when I stared into Lain's crystalline blue eyes, I saw only concern for me there, and resolved to promise him anything he wanted. "All right, I promise."

Once he was *sure* I'd meant it, his face softened and then transformed into his usual happy-go-lucky self again. "Excellent. I can leave knowing you'll be sufficient on your own until my return." Lain's need to tell me he was leaving must have meant he would be gone quite a while, Angel business, or whatever, to deal with. "Thanks for the load of confidence," I told him.

"Here," he said, throwing a small object at me that had magically appeared in his hand. Lucky for me I had fast reflexes and caught it in hand. It was a whole kiwi.

"Um, thanks." I stared at the fruit before my head whipped back up, searching for Lain. All I was met with was a blinding light to shield myself from. When the light was gone, so was Lain.

A sense of loss followed his absence. It was a feeling like no other… like being stuck in the dark for too long, and finally coming out for sunshine; amazingly warm. I stood there for a few more seconds, holding a kiwi in my hands and thinking about all Lain had said to me.

If Lain was worried about my going after Abe enough to risk coming out of hiding, it could only mean one thing: things would go horrible wrong.

* * * *

After leaving my room, I headed to class, needing to run the last half of the way since the raven had screeched for class to start right after Lain had vanished.

I'd made it to class in time for the mentor to smack his gold cane against the front board beginning our lecture. He was a Rakshasa that used to be a human. You see in order for a human to be turned into a Rakshasa when they died, they had to have been a very bad person in the human world, monstrous even to get the job, so to speak. A trait specific to Rakshasas were how they could create illusions in order to capture their victims. Here at the Morning Star, we used Rakshasas as mentors since they could teach how to live among humans without getting caught.

Quietly, I tiptoed across the room and sat down in the only seat left available, right next to Ace. "Hi," he mouthed silently at me.

I sighed in exasperation, and gave him a small, sad smile, mouthing "Hi," back before turning all my attention to the lesson being taught in the front of the classroom.

"Today we are going over how to feign normalcy in a mortal dominated world," our mentor began saying. For once, the lecture held my attention, fascinated by idea of being among ordinary people. An absurd idea really, since I doubted Apollyon would ever let me out of his sight for too long a time, even though we Hellions had our advantages. For instance, we're stronger, faster, and we usually live longer, plus we have plenty of other magical and physical abilities humans do not.

And still, I envied them.

They could be whoever they wanted to be, live and go wherever they wished, and love whoever they wanted to love without having to worry about any new magical ability popping up and ruining their day. Everything about being a human sounded great.

The raven signaled the end of class, winding up our lecture. Ace turned to me in his seat and was about to say something, my queue to leave, not allowing him to get a word in edgewise, by rushing out of the classroom. He didn't get to choose when it was convenient for him to act all friendly with me again; not after making it clear he wanted to focus on his big test and think about us, right now.

An idea had formed in my mind last night when lying wide awake in bed, one I needed to run by Pixie-girl; an idea to ensure our safety in case things went awry at any point during our rescue mission. I decided to blow off the next class since the mentor running the *Element Fundamental* course couldn't care less if his students came or not. Knowing Ebony would be serving her elective as the Library Assistant during this study hour, I headed toward the library.

Pixie-girl was sorting a pile of books from the return box to a cart on wheels, getting them ready to be shelved. "Hi, Ebony. Are you busy?" I asked after stepping up to her desk.

Pixie-girl's head whipped up after hearing her name, looking caught off guard. "Hi," she said, glancing over at her full cart of books with a weary expression, and then back at me. "Definitely busy, but why not?"

"Good," I said.

"I'm all ears, what's going on?"

"It's about this Saturday—during the full moon," I said, leaning over her desk so no one else would overhear.

Pixie-girl dropped the book she'd been holding, nervous with the reminder. "Okay, you have my full attention. What about this Saturday?" she asked, sounding tense.

Before any more could be said, a familiar voice dropped in on our conversation, "I might be able to help some." We both looked to our left to see Blake walking over to us, stopping on the other side of the desk next to Pixie-girl.

"Hi, I wasn't expecting to see you here," Pixie-girl told him genuinely surprised.

His butter-rum colored brown eyes glinted with humor and fondness toward Ebony. "Yeah sorry, my last mentor gave our class a free period to study, so I thought I'd come say hello. It's okay that I did right, I mean you're not too busy or anything, are you?"

"Yes, of course it is." Pixie-girl returned his affectionate smile.

"Good because I have been wanting to do this all day," Blake said, leaning over the desk to give Pixie-girl a small kiss on the lips. When he leaned back away from her, she blushed a bright shade of orangey-red.

I cleared my throat from beside Blake, not wanting to intrude on their gag worthy moment but also needing to hear what Blake meant when he said he could help. "Um, you said you had an idea or something, Blake?"

He took his eyes off Pixie-girl reluctantly, turning them on me and said, "Right. I was thinking that if I go to Scarlett first, instead of having you two crash her ritual, I can maybe convince Scarlett to invite Ebony to one of her secret Sisters of Selene charades. Of course I'll have to make it seem like it was her brilliant idea, but I think it could work," Blake said. Out of the corner of my eye, I saw Pixie-girl shift uncomfortably from the idea of getting recruited by the Sisters of Selene. I did not blame her one bit for feeling uncomfortable with the idea; Pixie-girl should be terrified out of her wits.

I didn't think it crucial to inform Blake how Pixie-girl and I had already considered something similar, and rolled with his newfound knowledge. "No, it could work. Are you sure you want Ebony recruited into the bitch-witches though? Not that Ebony would be categorized as such if she did manage to get in," I clarified smoothly. "And what makes you think Scarlett will agree to invite Ebony?" I crossed my arms over my chest. In theory it was a good idea, but I knew Scarlett enough to know she was pretty hard to win over.

"Ah-ha! I knew you'd say something along those lines, which is why it's all already covered…I figured I'd mention something about how Ebony is practically royalty, having a Pixie King for a dad and all—a detail Scarlett will not be able to stop obsessing over once I plant the idea. She'll invite Ebony in for a chance to add a new influential friend to make her look better."

Pixie-girl let out a sigh next to Blake, showing her unease for being used as the subject matter. "He's right, as much as I dislike it, it could work,' Pixie-girl said to her own dismay.

I stood there, biting the bottom corner of my lip, rummaging the idea over in my mind, trying and failing to find any reason why Blake's plan might not pan out. I was aware that they were both watching me anxiously, waiting for an answer. It was a brilliant plan, much better than my idea to wear all black since it would be dark out and then sneak up on Scarlett and her group when they least expected it. The fact was, we were running out of time to come up with anything else since the full moon was approaching fast, with only three days left.

Before saying anything, I tapped into my soul-reading gauge, and sized up Blake's aura as a last measure to making a decision. A smile tugged at the corners of my mouth when the familiarity of his soul-name which meant "Gleam" or "Shine" shone true to his potential; I could feel his confidence dripping off him like rays of sunshine. My mind was made up.

"Fine. But if Scarlett tries anything I can't promise there won't be an incident where her hair accidently gets set on fire or something," I told them both, receiving a small laugh from Blake and an absolutely horrified expression from Pixie-girl; eventually she'd get used to my demented sense of humor. Until then, I'd be lying if I said I didn't take some pleasure in freaking her out.

Now that the plan was in place, all we had to do was make sure nothing went wrong in the meantime. I could think of only one person who might stand in our way. Kione.

It wasn't lost on me how we should probably be paying closer attention to his movements, especially since his involvement in meddling with my plans had been pretty quiet so far. But you know what they say about the silence before the storm…

I had a feeling this storm was not going to blow over anytime soon.

Since I'd already blown off one class today, I had to make the rest of them, and left Blake and Pixie-girl in the library when they got the *look* like they were going to start kissing again, and headed for class. While walking to my next class, a strange sinking feeling hit like a ton of bricks again, of someone watching me, giving me all-over goosebumps. It was the exact same feeling of dread I'd had in the pool room after bringing Blake the Moonstone. There wasn't anybody I didn't recognize in the hallway; nothing out of the normal, only a heavy eeriness that seemed defining over the loud buzz of Hellions coming and going, making me pick up the speed in my step, and hurry to class. I was too blind yet to see.

<u>CHAPTER THIRTEEN</u>

Charms and Spells

"In order to bind an evil spirit to you, one would have to endure a certain degree of dark magic that is not only a challenging task to do,; but also a perilous feat." I listened intently as our mentor answered a question from a fellow curious Hellion, still trying to ignore how shaken up I'd gotten while walking through the halls before class.

I was in my *Art of Malicious Intents* class, and we were going over how Shakespeare was a stickler for adding a degree of wickedness to his plays, when someone made some smartass comment about how it was because evil spirits must have been controlling Shakespeare's fragile, mortal mind.

"Exploiting evil spirits is a danger to your own soul, if you should fail to control the spirit, it will control you. It would be peril to your existence to be left unguarded and vulnerable to one of those," he said drastically. "It would be just as effortless for the spirit to seize *your* soul and trap itself inside of you, before forcing you to endure endless torture," our mentor, said, using dramatic antics to get his point across, what else would be expected from a theater teacher? There was an unmistakable look of excitement behind the prospect of his words, that wasn't lost on me.

Once an evil being of Hell, always an evil being of Hell.

Dealing with evil spirits sounded scary enough, but I couldn't help thinking how controlling one of those might come in handy.

"Don't even think about it," a voice spoke next to me in a firm tone.

Ace's breath was warm against my ears, sending shivers down my body. I'd been so occupied listening to the mentor's lesson, I hadn't heard Ace sneak up on me. "I don't know what you're talking about," I said, indignantly, even though Ace had been spot on when guessing where my thoughts had taken me.

"It would be the most reckless, idiotic thing you could possibly do and that's saying something because I've seen you do some pretty reckless stuff."

"Hey!" I exclaimed to his accusations, unable to avoid giving him exactly what he wanted: for me to talk to him again, it wasn't fair, Ace knew exactly how to get under my skin.

"I'm worried you're going to go off on some crazy mission and I won't be around to fish you out this time," he told me.

His caring about me was infuriating, especially since he was constantly giving me whiplash and a headache. "Look, you don't have to worry, I'm not going to mess with an evil spirit, all right?" I said, mostly to get him off my case.

We held each other's gaze in a kind of standoff to see who would back down first. Ace was the one to finally take a breath and concede. He never relaxed during the rest of our lecture, and out of the corner of my eye, I kept seeing him look at me with worry.

"By the pricking of my thumbs, something wicked this way comes. Open, locks, whoever knocks!" our mentor said, quoting Shakespeare's *Macbeth*, Act IV: Scene I.

Chills ran up my spine with how spooky the verse touched the audience of Hellions in the classroom. The words behind this particular scene, struck a nerve, making me think about the intuition of wickedness following me in the hallways. As the mentor continued, I understood he was talking about the three hags who came to deliver a prophecy to Macbeth, which would inevitably set off a whole chain of bloody events.

It must have made me more anxious than I realized, because Ace had to reach over and grab my hand to stop the pencil from tapping spastically on the desk. "You okay?" he asked, in a low, rushed whisper. In doing so, he practically made me jump out of my skin, and I had to swallow down a small yelp.

Looking at his face before turning my gaze down at his hand still on mine, feeling its warmth and comfort, thinking how it was exactly what I needed right now to help calm my nerves and take some of the edge off. I hated how much I needed his comfort, and how he wasn't able to be there for me this way all the time; how he had to turn all noble and perfect when it mattered most, and then become a jerk and selfish the rest of the time. *He just needed to get through his Hellhound trials, and then everything could go back to normal between us again.* Even with this knowledge, something inside me wanted to be mad at him, and so I shook my hand out from under his along with Ace's attempt to comfort.

"No, I'm not okay, Ace, not with any of this." my voice caught on a small sob, glad to be sitting at the back of the classroom.

Ace frowned. "I'm still here for you, Dess, maybe not here in the way you need me to be as a boyfriend, all the same, you don't have to be alone, to do any of this."

Somewhere in the back of my mind I knew he meant it, and he was right, about everything. Maybe it was me who wasn't being sensitive enough or the one who was there for him when he needed me to be, I thought.

"I know. It's frustrating, wanting something that's right there in front of you, and unable to attain it, you know?" I asked, voice sounding small and pleading.

"I know," he said simply before reaching out and tucking some loose strands of hair behind one ear. This time I didn't remove his hand from touching me.

"I wish we were both free from this God-forsaken—free from all influences holding us back from each other," I said, reaching up and grabbing his hand still placed on my ear, holding it to my head in a gentle, hopeful embrace.

We looked at each other for a long pausing moment, before he sighed because there was nothing else to do, and say, *"We know what we are, but not what we may be..."* Ace surprised me when he quoted Shakespeare. "Desdemona Starr, there is nothing you can't attain. You already have my heart, isn't that proof enough that anything is possible?"

* * * *

Though schooling for the day was over, the look Ace had given me was burned into the back of my brain. While walking aimlessly around the Institute, unsure of where to go or what to do, too anxious about something the mentor from last class mentioned, I finally made a decision—I was going to invoke a spirit.

Probably not one of my soundest plans, I admit. If it worked though, we would have an advantage in freeing Abe we didn't before. The tricky part now would be dealing in dark magic, and only one certain hound known for finagling with dark magic and not getting caught came to mind; Ignacio. He was one of Ace's fellow Hellhounds known for his mad science skills, I remembered he enjoyed creating all kinds of concoctions to enhance supernatural performances, and spells, and stuff like that. The only problem I might have would be if Ignacio decided he needed to blab to his Hellhound leader (and comrade), Ace.

* * * *

When the initial shock of seeing me, of all people at his door, Ignacio finally said in a booming voice, "Well look what the hound dragged in." That was Ig for you; everything he did was loud if his soaring green Mohawk was any indication. "What do I owe for this special occurrence?"

"There's a favor I wanted to ask. Can I come in?" I felt anxious on my feet, making it hard to stand still for too long.

Ignacio looked baffled but appreciated my energy. He held the door open for me with a wide smile spread across his face. *"Mi casa es su casa,"* he said.

"Thanks," I said, stepping past.

His room was the same size as Ace's, only instead of having posters with different city scenes on them plastered throughout, Ignacio had seductive half-woman half-creatures posters on the walls. To each his own, I thought, before turning my gaze back to Ignacio when he spoke.

"Not to be rude and certainly not trying to rush a lady out of my room, but what can I do for you, little Starr?"

I gave him half a smirk; it looked like Ace's nickname for me was catching on. "Rushing works for me. I need you to make a potion to allow me to access distressed spirits," I said, seeing no point in lying.

Ignacio was good at concealing his surprise (if he had any), about my demands, instead he seemed curious. When he spoke again, he was all business. "The only one I know of is a near-death remedy, but it's risky."

Near-death would be risky, I thought but didn't say. *It would be a small price to pay in return for the help I'll receive.* "Doesn't matter."

This awarded me a one-eyebrow raise from Ignacio. "Right on! Give me a few days and I'll have it to you."

"A few days, you've got to be kidding me! No, I don't have a few days." *Did I not make the urgency of this clear?* "I need it tonight," I said firmly.

"This kind of mixture takes ingredients that are, um, off the market. It'll take me days to get all the supplies." he shook his head in similar frustration.

At this point, I was ready to scream. Ignacio must have seen it by my facial expression, and quickly said, "But maybe for the right price I can have it done, I'll have to ask my suppliers what it'll take, shouldn't be too difficult though." *Now we're talking.* "Anything; name it!"

After Ignacio named off a few key items he deemed worthy of trading for the ingredients he needed, most of which could be found in Apollyon's stash of precious jewels and gold in which he had an abundance of, and probably wouldn't be missed, we parted ways.

* * * *

While evening settled in around the Institute, I found myself pacing back and forth outside on my bedroom's balcony. Ignacio's package was finally delivered, five hours after my initial request. Impeccable timing since most Hellions would be going to bed now, no one would come looking for me and interrupt. I'm not sure how Ignacio pulled it off, or who his supplier was—and probably didn't want to know—I was just glad it was here.

"If you're going to do this, do it and get it over with already!" I scolded myself after questioning my sanity for the thousandth time. After sitting down and folding my legs up, clutching the small teal vial of liquid Ignacio created for me I said, "Bottoms up!" popping the lid off and tipping my head back. I drank the concoction, and had to hold back the bile which rose in my throat. After managing to gulp it completely, the world began to spin around me, and cries of despair from the dead threatened to swallow me whole. Everything became a jumbled mess, and then the scenery changed; one second I was sitting on the floor in my room, and in the next, a narrow path and a whirlwind of spirits.

This must have been the near death part Ignacio had been talking about. I focused on walking the path of the lost souls again, like before in order to sit in on the council meeting where my brother Abaddon had been betrayed by Kione, and fed to the wolves by our father. It had been the first time I'd ever been down there, and hoped it would be the last; it was too easy to lose yourself to the sorrow-filled souls. Unfortunately, tapping into those dreadful feelings was the only way to access one of them. Having never done this before, I didn't realize the similarities between tapping into a distressed spirit, and my own innate abilities to read souls; except instead of seeing the colors of a living creatures aura, all I saw was an endless sea of dull, lifeless gray. My room filled with smells of death, coldness, and anger.

Residual emotions of their past, when they were still living, poured into me. I was filled with a thousand transferred feelings, a few of those feelings taking precedence over the others: regret, fear, and sorrow, and worst of all anger, probably because many of the souls had died too soon or horrifically. There was one soul in particular that stood out among all when it threatened to overwhelm me with its callousness.

That's the one! I'd found the right soul to aid me in freeing Abe. I was going to need a spirit that felt it had a chance to turn some of the unfinished business into action.

The darkness that had followed me around my whole life came in spades right away when opening myself up to it, not something I'd ever tried on purpose before. You wouldn't think I'd be susceptible to the darkness since I was born with it already in me, when in all actuality it only made me more vulnerable. Once my mind and soul latched onto the distressed spirit, my body shifted back to the position I'd been sitting in my own room, eyes remaining tightly closed until sure the binding was complete.

The dark matter, which made up the spiteful soul, hungrily seeped into me, awakening the thorny creature on my spine so it could feed off this new form of malice. It eagerly snaked up my spine, sitting in its favorite spot at the nape of my neck, feeding off emotions spilling into me. This binding ritual had to be done in front of the mirror, which is why I had my floor length mirror before me now. Opening my eyes, gazing at the reflection of myself sitting crossed-legged was a girl who looked exactly like me, all except for the beady eyes glowing ruby red, and her (my) lips, which were curved up into a malevolent smile. Right away I knew it was the spirit I was seeing within my reflection.

Reaching my hand out toward the mirror and placing my hand on my reflection's hand, I grasped onto the soul and began pulling it right out of the mirror.

My reflection wavered as the possessed soul fought to stay within my emotions. Two occupants fought each other in the mirror reminding me of two opposing magnets swaying away from one another. I continued to pull the soul out of my image while trying to keep it in the mirror since it needed some place tangible to go until fully bound. My arm muscles began to shake with the exertion, and for a terrifying moment a thought about how the soul would win by choosing my body to be its welcoming host, occurred.

"I don't think so, you old soul, you do not get to stay!" I said, not allowing this distressed intruder to win. Giving the spirit one final hard yank finally freed it from me, sling-shooting it forward where it was trapped inside the mirror. *I'd done it, I effectively bound a distressed spirit ready to use at my disposal!*

I jumped back in the sitting position when the soul sprung itself at me, stunned for a moment when it hit the glass inside the mirror, unable to reach me.

Finding my feet, and some humility, I stood and dusted off my hands. Carefully stalking forward, I leaned down and said, unsure if it could hear me or not, "None of that will do any good, you're mine to control now."

Its beady red eyes shone with hatred, surprising me when it first spat at me, its saliva sticking to the mirror in a disgusting array, and then it spoke, "When I possess your body, and exist again, it is *I* who will control all you do, wreaking havoc wherever desired, in your name."

So, it can speak. "That's where you're wrong soul. When you're done helping me, you're going right back to circling the Underworld where you'll stay for all eternity." In response, acid-like foam bubbled out of the soul's mouth as it growled in rage.

Looks like you picked a real winner there, Dess. Sure to keep the fear from showing on my face, not wanting to show any sign of weakness in the face of an evil, distressed spirit, positive it would make good on its promise to inhabit my body the first chance it got. I smiled through my teeth and said, "You're unneeded for the time being, so go away," I said, dismissing the soul.

"Oh dear Gods," I said, feeling overwhelmed while plopping down in the Green Beast otherwise known as my super comfy, oversized green chair. A quick glance toward the clock on my nightstand told me it was early into the next day, halfway through the Manor's sleeping hours. I thought about getting some rest before school started in only a few hours from now, but the thoughts of sleeping in the same room where I'd conjured a spiteful spirit, didn't bode well in my stomach.

As if on cue, my stomach let off a huge, annoying growl; summoning the soul had required a lot of energy and I was feeling the repercussion of going all night without sustenance. Food became the next main focal point.

I left my room quickly raiding the pantry of the dining hall, shoving anything with a large amount of carbs and sugar into my body, leaving me with mouthful of yawns and a stomach full of food. Still unable to shake the unease of having the soul linked to me, I needed to catch a few hours of shut-eye without doing it in my room, and the chaise lounge in Zola's office sounded like a good place to find it. Hopefully, the decision to bind the distressed spirit wasn't a bad judgment call on my end.

I could guess what Ace would say when, and I mean when not if he found out because let's face it, keeping secrets from Ace was useless. They would all begin and end in blaspheme of words about how irresponsible and idiotic I'd been; and he was probably right.

You're already too deep in to turn back now, was the last thing I thought before sleep pulled me under, wrapping me up in her forgiving embrace.

CHAPTER FOURTEEN

Midnight Blue

Dabbling with the dark arts weighed on my shoulders even long after waking. Venturing to the little coffee stand, which sat in the courtyard outside the dining hall, ranked highest on the plans for the morning. Our coffee addiction was one of the greatest positive traits we Hellions picked up from mortals; one I commended them for.

After ordering my favorite, an orange latte, I stood waiting, unable to shake the heavy feeling having the spirit bound to me. It felt as though there was this invisible chain linking the distressed spirit all the way from the Underworld to me.

"Dess, there you are!" I heard my name being called, and nearly jumped out of my skin. I spun around to find Pixie-girl walking toward me, hand-in-hand with Blake.

"Gods! You scared me," I said, already feeling jittery even though I hadn't had my coffee yet.

"Sorry," Pixie-girl said, the impish smile negating her apology, while Blake openly laughed at me.

"What's up?" I asked, turning to the barista and thanking her for the coffee before turning back to them.

"I was just telling Blake how I think that since we're one day from crashing Scarlett's ritual, maybe we could use a little trip to the mainland to take our minds off things for a while. Plus, I could really use it as a chance to find a dress for this dance since there's no way I'll be able to order something in time. We decided to go last minute," Pixie-girl said, rambling in an annoying yet endearing superfluous way she did sometimes. All I could do was to shake my head in confusion while trying to keep up.

"So…what do you think?"

"Say it again…sorry, I didn't get much sleep last night, or fulfill my coffee quota for the day," I said.

"Do you want to come with us or not?" Pixie-girl repeated.

"Sure, I'll go. Sounds fun." Pixie-girl let out a little squeal of excitement before jumping forward and grabbing me into a tight hug, catching me off guard. "Thank you, this is so exciting!"

I froze with my arms raised out in surrender as Pixie-girl hugged me. It was such a normal teenage-girl mundane thing to do, I thought. "Is Ebony always like this?" I looked to Blake helplessly who settled for an uncomfortable shrug and a lopsided grin.

A small laugh escaped from me while watching Pixie-girl continue to happily jump around. "When do we leave?" I asked Blake, since Pixie-girl was still on the euphoric high of cloud nine, and dancing around.

Blake shook his arm out in front of him so his watch slid back down to his wrist where he could read it. "There's a boat that departs from here with a whole group in about forty minutes," he said.

After the three of us had agreed to go back to our rooms to pack our day bags, we would meet at the boat's landing. I almost didn't make it after running into Ace, who demanded to know what Ignacio and I were up to. Apparently keeping a secret around here was a futile endeavor. Eventually, and with great effort, I managed to blow Ace off and escaped his scrutiny by reminding him as nicely as possible, that he wasn't my boyfriend, and it wasn't his job to keep tabs on me anymore, immediately regretting it once it came out.

When I finally got to the top of the boat launch dock, Blake and Ebony both waved their hands for me to hurry, hearing them arguing with the captain from the Institute half a mile away, asking him to wait another five minutes.

"Look. There's Dess coming right now," Blake told the captain in relief while gesturing at me.

"Finally," I heard a girl's voice snarl at my approach. It looked like Scarlett and a few of her evil minions had also decided to do some last minute shopping.

Just great.

"Sorry, had to dodge a bullet," I said inwardly, climbing into the boat referring to Ace ambushing me. This only landed me another curious gaze from Blake, one I directly shrugged off. "It's nothing," I had to tell Blake.

"Are you sure, because you don't have to come if you don't want to," Pixie-girl said, frowning.

"Nah, I'm sure," I said, relaxing into one of the seats on the boat, stretching my arms behind me. The captain departed and I breathed a sigh of relief. Watching the Institute get smaller the farther we went made me feel calmer. All of my problems were back there. A sense of freedom had me thinking more and more how Pixie-girl had been right; I needed this.

* * * *

We made it to the mainland of Santorini all too soon. I could have basked in the sun and wind all day given the chance. Blake offered a hand when we landed to help me off the boat, using it as an opportunity to say, "Hey, I wanted to say thank you for doing this for her." He nodded toward Ebony who was a little ways up ahead of us. "I appreciate your effort to play nice."

"Who says I'm playing?"

"Either way, thanks," Blake replied.

"So, what do we do first?" I asked, after we caught up to Pixie-girl, while I looped my arm together with Pixie-girl's, wondering if this was what it was like to have a girlfriend.

"I've always wanted to buy fruit from one of those stands, even though it's probably the same stuff we get at the Morning Star," Pixie-girl said.

"Sounds good to me." I turned my head in time to catch Blake watching us with a reserved expression. I wondered if it was weird for him to see Pixie-girl and I looking like friends. I winked over at him and then turned back to Ebony who was going on about pesticides. *Was I just being nice to Pixie-girl because I honestly saw friendship in her? Or to do it to get Blake back in my life?*

Maybe a little of both, I decided, knowing that if Blake suspected anything besides honest intentions, it could be the end to our friendship— for good this time!

Per Ebony's request, we walked up the cobblestone streets where merchants lined up their goods for tourists to search for treasures. There was everything you could think of, from good quality fruit—which Pixie-girl bought a bushel of as though she'd been deprived for years, to name brand shoes. There were soccer jerseys of local teams and heroes, Greek police shirts as well as military shirts for tourists to take as souvenirs. Some of the jerseys were of American sports teams that were obviously made by someone who did not know anything about the sport and barely spoke English, but otherwise anything you wanted could be found.

This time of year, the streets of Greece were treated like a never-ending fair with musicians. My two favorite things about living here in Greece were watching families enjoying time together, or couples sneaking off for a romantic interlude.

Nothing really caught my attention until I spotted a blue-bannered merchant stand selling bangles and necklaces, as well as some other trinkets and accessories. I rummaged around mindlessly, not looking for anything in particular.

"Normally I like to choose the outfit before picking out the accessories to go with it," Pixie-girl said, giving me a disapproving look at my lack of knowledge of dress shopping.

"I wasn't planning on buying a dress," I said, not realizing what I'd said until it was too late.

"What do you mean you're not buying a dress, aren't you going to the dance?" Pixie-girl asked not disguising her concern.

"I, uh, I'm not sure. Ace hasn't exactly asked yet,"

"But he's going to, right?" she asked. I sneaked an uncomfortable peek at Blake before turning back to her and reluctantly said, "Things are kind of complicated right now." I hadn't wanted Blake to know about mine and Ace's issues, but when Ebony cornered me I didn't think I could keep it a secret anymore. Not if I wanted her to drop this whole dress-buying-thing anyway.

Blake who had otherwise been pretty quiet until then cleared his throat, uncomfortable by that amount of girly-ness. "I think this is my cue to leave. You two girls have fun. We can meet later for lunch, okay?"

"Okay," Ebony told him, while I could barely make eye contact. I felt like an idiot for mentioning my relationship with Ace or actually lack thereof.

Pixie-girl and I were left to explore the whitewashed town alone. Even though hanging out with another girl was still little lost on me, I enjoyed every opportunity to be free from the Morning Star Institute, and could relish the time surrounded by Cycladic architecture.

"He's not really into all this," Pixie-girl said, apologizing for Blake.

It sort of irritated me that Pixie-girl felt the need to make excuses for Blake when he and I had been friends first, and for a lot longer.

"Can you blame him?" I asked, grabbing a tiara bedazzled in gaudy fake jewels from a nearby merchant and placing it on my head. When the merchant gave me a fear-provoking look, I quickly returned it back onto the table. "Not really his scene, come on, let's go." I grabbed her arm so we could make a quick getaway, both of us laughing.

"He was frightening," Pixie-girl said, once we were a safe distance away.

We ran inside a shop showcasing wedding dresses, where Ebony found the perfect bridesmaid style-dress. It was a dazzling blue-topaz color, which looked gorgeous in contrast to her peachy skin tone, and after trying it on, confirmed it was a perfect fit. After buying the dress, we went and sat down at a quaint bistro table waiting for Blake to meet us for lunch, Pixie-girl turned to me, "Sorry about earlier. It's easy to forget you know Blake better than anyone."

"It's no biggie, really. I'm glad he has you. It means he has someone else's ears to talk off," I joked.

"Thanks. I'm sorry you didn't find anything you liked."

"Its fine, I'm not much of a shopper." I didn't feel the need to mention how online shopping was a different story; with all the training I had to do, dressing up seemed pointless.

"Yeah, I could tell," she laughed, right as Blake showed up.

Unfortunately, I'd only been able to eat a few bites of my Tzatziki—a Greek sauce made from goat's milk, cucumber, dill and mint over meat—when something caught my eye. Mid-bite I noticed a beautiful dress in the window of one of the white-washed structures, romantically lit with rose-colored lighting. I didn't know what came over me right then, only that I needed to go check it out in person. I skillfully excused myself from lunch after first checking the time on the clock tower; there was twenty minutes left before our little venture was over.

A bell chimed when I opened the front door to the dress shop, and immediately greeted by the smell of rose-incense. Carefully stepping down the three steps into the shop, I called a quick "Hello," to see if anyone was there, and was only met with silence. I debated leaving, but didn't want to until I found *it*: the dress in the window.

Dresses of every shape, size, and color hung from wardrobe racks throughout the dress shop. With all the glitter and shiny materials along with the incense, it was almost a sensory overload.

On my way to the back window where I was sure my dress hung, a pretty plum colored dress modeled by a mannequin caught my eye. I ventured over for a closer look. Folds of fabric were cinched in at the waist where delicate appliqué covered most of the bodice. It was a sleeveless dress with a light dusting of sparkles throughout. It was perfect. I wasn't sure I even needed to look at the one I saw hanging in the window.

"That one is not right for you," a raspy voice startled me.

I let out a small yelp of surprise while spinning around. I expected to see someone standing behind me, and it unsettled me when there wasn't. "Hello?" I called out again, apprehensively.

"I said, the dress is not for you," the person said again.

"Yeah, I got that," I said scathingly, slowly stepping around the rack of dresses in search for the woman. The woman ducked out from under the rack right next to where I was standing, and faced me.

"Eeesh!" I said. "You scared me." Someone needed to get this woman a bell to wear around her neck to avoid scaring off customers. The shop owner was an older lady with wild frizzy hair that was gray with wide black streaks all over. She didn't say anything in return, instead continued staring, seemingly unimpressed by me.

"Um, I'm looking for a dress."

"Yes, I know," the shop owner said in a monotone.

"Okay, I'd like to try on the purple one," I began to say when she immediately started to shake her head fervently at me.

"No, that one is no good. Come," she said, turning and motioning for me to follow her.

"And people think I'm the freak," I said under my breath. "Could I at least try it on?" I asked as the old woman led us to the window at the end of her store.

"No," her answer came hasty.

"Okay, maybe I don't need to find a dress after all," I said, giving this whole absurd situation a second thought.

"You pay me for this one," she said, after stopping and pointing toward a big bay window.

Going against my better judgment, I let curiosity guide me forward, watching the owner as she reached up into the window and unhooked the hanger, pulling her hand back down holding a beautiful midnight-blue dress.

That's the dress I'd spotted from the boardwalk!

Seeing the plum dress had made me forget how spectacular this one was. The dress, unlike the other sleeveless one, had one sash-like sleeve going across the front from one shoulder to the other. It also had a corset bodice tying up the back in a crisscross pattern, true to vintage corset fashion, and instead of using tulle most of the other dresses had, this one appeared to have real lace embellishing the skirt and bodice of the dress.

"It's Victorian satin," the old woman said, making me have an odd feeling of déjà-vu, sensing I've heard that phrase said in a distant dream perhaps. Dreams aside, I could picture myself in this dress. From the smile on the old woman's face, I could tell the owner was pleased by my reaction to the dress.

It was perfect in every way.

I reached one hand out, wanting to touch, but ended up pulling my hand back instead. From out of the corner of my eyes, I could see the disappointment in the old woman's face.

"Take it, it is yours," she told me, shoving the dress at me.

I stepped back out of her reach. "No I can't."

"You do not like it?" Her voice corresponded to the confused look she wore.

"No, I mean yes, I do like it, but I—"

"Then take it," the owner said, and this time when she reached out to me, I was not fast enough to escape her. The old woman grabbed my wrist and shoved the dress in my hands. That's when something really strange happened. The old woman's mouth went slack, hanging open in an unnatural O-shape while her eyes rolled in the back of her head, so all that was left for me to see were the white parts. The woman started babbling words I did not understand, "Darkness and death...Angels weep in fear. The darkness will come, I can smell it everywhere, it is in the air," the crazed old woman said, letting go of my wrists and jumping back away from me. "You must leave! Go now," she said, jumping back away, scared of me, her eyes going back to normal again.

"Wait, I don't under—" I began to say but was cut off by her shrieking.

"What have you brought into my store, you must go. Leave!" she screamed while pacing forward, herding me back toward the door.

Turning around, I ran up the steps, fumbled and nearly fell trying to open the door before finally managing to open it and step outside. The door slammed shut as soon as I found the outside world again.

What the heck just happened? One minute the old woman was trying to throw the dress at me, and the next she was literally throwing me out of her store. And what was all the babbling about? Crazy old lady, I thought. *Could the old shop owner sense the evil spirit I'd bound to me?*

It wasn't uncommon for the natives to be educated in what was otherwise known as mythical or folklore. Chimes of the clock tower gave warning of the hour; and for my ride back to the Institute. I turned and ran back down the cobblestone hill, my legs carrying me with ease from all the training I'd put my muscles through of late. When I got to the dock, the captain piloting the boat had already left; I'd missed my ride back home.

"Wait, there's Dess, stop the boat!" I heard Blake yell over to the captain.

"Don't you dare!" Scarlett, who I noticed was sporting a new pair of sunglasses and a scarf, hissed in warning at the captain. That was the last clear thing heard before they'd gone too far, leaving me standing there watching the boat go farther away. Great! I thought, trying to think how to get back to the Institute on my own, when the boat was no longer getting smaller, instead it was getting larger. *The boat was coming back!*

As the boat pulled back up to the dock, I knew it had been Bake who was responsible for its return if the large goofy grin he wore was any indication. I could only imagine what he must have told the captain to make him change his mind.

"How did you do it?" I asked Blake once aboard.

"Nothing much, mainly how Apollyon would probably have him fed to the Devoraks when he learned how the captain chose to leave the Dark Princess behind," Blake said.

"You did not!" I exclaimed, smiling at the thought of sweet rational Blake threatening anyone.

"Proof is in the water?" he said, enjoying his moment of rebellion.

"I'm impressed." I folded my arms over my chest while leaning back into the cushions of the boat.

The whole ride back I received menacing glares from a Succubus whom I was fairly certain was already planning horrible ways to get back at me. All I could think about was the midnight blue dress, and the old woman wrinkling her nose up at me in abhorrence. Alarms started going off in my head. *If the old shop owner could sense the distressed spirit bound to me, I wonder who else might be able to sense it?* It was a loose end needing to be tied up.

Spider-like sensations crawled up my back, pricking at the hairs on my arms and making them stand up, before the emotions began pouring into me—emotions full of dread and spite.

No, it couldn't be!

Immediately, I began looking around for it; my thinking about the spirit had summoned it. There it was, sitting on the bow of the boat directly in front of the captain. It was watching me with disdain-filled eyes reminding me of rubies. My gaze flitted over to Blake and Pixie-girl who were too busy talking to have noticed my alarm. And by the fact that the captain had not shrieked in surprise, told me I was the only one who could see it, because how would I even begin to explain something like an evil spirit following me around? I wouldn't even know where to start.

CHAPTER FIFTEEN

Sleepwalking

"**G**o away Spirit," I said, flinging my arms out in front of me to no use. We arrived back from our shopping trip several hours ago, and I immediately ran back to the privacy of my room's closed doors. I couldn't remember how I'd managed to banish the thing before back to —well wherever it went.

"I am Riker, the Great Havoc!" it shouted at me as though I'd insulted it.

"Great, I probably found the only distressed spirit with an idol complex. Look, technically you're not anything anymore," I said brazenly, knowing it wasn't scoring me any points with the thing.

"I *am* Riker, the Great Havoc, and when I inhabit your body, I shall be great once more."

"So I've heard."

The spirit took a step forward, rage making its dull gray skin turn crimson, matching its fiery eyes. "Riker the Great Havoc will make you suffer, better still Riker will make everyone you have ever cared about suffer, and you will watch unable to save them when Riker—" it started to say, tone dripping with abhorrence.

"Be gone already!" I shouted, having had enough, and then something strange happened: it actually went away when those final words seemed to do the trick. One second it was threatening me, and in the next it vanished. "Finally."

Exhaustion set in, and it wasn't long before the lack of slumber from the previous night finally caught up to me. Before I realized what was happening, I was drowning.

Again.

My dream state had taken me back to a few weeks ago when I almost drowned (and would have), if Kione hadn't pulled me out of the water first. Angry, ominous black waves pulled me under, water began filling my lungs, and even though I was aware I was dreaming, it felt as though I was being smothered by a pillow, and unable to catch my breath.

And then everything went still.

There she was, exactly how I remembered the woman who resembled my mother. The woman wore the same elegant white gown, her long russet-brown hair fanning out around her head while pulling me deeper into the merciless sea. Even now, I believed the woman was a ghost and had been trying to tell me something, whether dead or alive.

Dead.

Definitely dead, I thought. Nevertheless, the doppelganger of my mother was as beautiful as my fading memories imagined her to be.

Her mouth was moving from under the canopy of the sea, it didn't take long for me to realize the woman was trying to speak to me. My brain feeling tired and slow, as though my mind was drudging through mud could not make out her words. Not until miraculously her voice somehow came through, "Open your eyes, Desdemona." It sounded all echo-y, and far away. Not only did the woman resemble my mother, her voice sounded exactly the same as if coming back to me from a dream the way a mother's voice could never truly be lost in their child's memory.

"Mom?" I asked, blinking in opposition of the water in my eyes, which felt like blinking away a thousand specs of sand.

"Open. Your. Eyes," the woman said again.

It took all my concentration to break free from the dream, and when my eyes opened, I was seeing my bedroom in the present world.

My mind was no longer moving slowly, instead, it had kicked into overdrive in order to protect itself from any more intruders and my thoughts were going a million miles-an-hour. Sitting upright in bed, I began to take in the disorienting scene before me, shivered from being cold and noticed for the first time the sheets blanketing me were soaking wet as was the extra-long T-shirt of Ace's I'd worn to bed. *If it was only a dream, how could the bed be sopping with water?*

To further complicate the vexing situation, I wondered how it could have only been a dream and still be able to see *her*? The little voice in the back of my mind stated as I stared at the woman standing at the foot of my bed. The woman looked exactly the same from both: the night in the water, and in the dream I'd had moments ago.

Unless...

"I must still be dreaming," I said out loud, receiving an immediate head-jerking response from the woman, shaking her head side-to-side as if to say I was wrong.

"This isn't a dream?" I asked, feeling my eyes widen in shock when the woman shook her head that is wasn't.

"Perfect, I'm having a psychotic breakdown," I said, throwing back the wet covers off the bed and standing up, shivering once more.

My teeth chattered as I turned to face her, crossing my arms over my chest to try and keep what little heat there was left. Walking closer to the woman, I examined the ivory nightgown, remembering having studied the lace hem before; I could remember rolling the pads of my fingers over the scratchy surface of the lace with tiny hands long ago. It looked familiar, and I immediately recalled my mother having a similar nightgown. The last memory I'd had of Lilith, she'd been wearing it the night she left after having tucked me in and kissed me for the last time. Putting these pieces together only made me more confident I really was delusional.

"Okay I'm up, so what did you want to show me?" I asked, figuring if I ever wanted these visions to go away I needed to humor her.

"Wake me, Desdemona," the woman said, her voice sounding like it was being translated through an old radio or intercom or something because it came through to me in static bits-and-pieces. Her image was just as elusive, and began flickering in and out of view. The woman continued wavering in and out as she turned and walked all the way around my bed, heading toward my door to leave, stopping once to reach a hand out and grab the doorknob, and then turned her head to look back at me.

"You want me to follow you?" I asked. It was sort of weird to be giving into the dream version of the woman who tried killing me, but presumed she'd continue to harass me if I didn't; the only reason for playing her game.

Out in the halls the cold managed to seep into my bones, and I realized I probably should have put on dry clothes before we left, and I would have if not for being afraid she'd disappear the moment my back turned.

Even in my dream state, the halls looked the same from my waking hours, dull-gray, cold and over the top in gothic decor. As I walked, my breath bellowed out of my mouth in puffy iridescent clouds.

We walked across the entire Dark Manor, eventually making it to a pitch-black stairwell. I paused at the top, apprehensive when she started making her way down into the lowest bowels of the Manor; these very steps led us down into the same dark chambers Scarlett had led.

My mother, or the dream-figure who looked like my mother, stopped to turn back and beckoned me to continue following. The fabric of her white nightgown floated through the air gracefully with the movement.

Well, whatever is down there, it could not be as bad as Scarlett's devious plan for me, I decided, and continued downward, swallowing my fear.

I kept one hand on the left side of the wall in order to help guide me down the stairs, because unlike the last time, the candelabras on the walls were not lit. There was only darkness. The lower we went, the colder it got and the harder it was to keep my bones from rattling and my teeth from chattering.

We finally reached the bottom. I knew it was because of the perfect, circular shaped reflection sitting in the middle of the floor made by the roofless structure above. My mother walked across the length of the room, stopping in the middle of the moon's soft glowing reflection to tilt her head and gaze upward.

"What, so you brought me here to look at the moon?" I asked, I was pretty sure I'd have a similar view from outside on my room's balcony.

Her head turned to me where she gave me a sharp look, before pointedly looking back up at the moon. I sighed, walked across the length of the cold, stone room, and stopped once positioned next to her, feeling exasperated when nothing happened, no surprise there.

"Okay yeah, the moon looks spectacular tonight—as it does every night, now what?" I asked, stepping into the white, circular reflection to turn and look at my mother. What I wasn't expecting was for the woman to have shifted directly in front of my face, and before I had a chance to let out a yelp of surprise, her hands were squeezing tightly on my shoulders trying her hardest to pull me down. Taken by surprise, I tripped and fell while taking a step back away from her hold. The back of my head hit the cold stone floor, my head throbbing in pain right away.

While on the ground, the woman hovered over the top of me. No, not hovering, I couldn't breathe because her hands were wound tightly around my neck. "Wake up," the woman called while shaking me. I tried screaming for help, but no sound came from my mouth since she was cutting off my airway. Why was she doing this to me? My mind screamed. I was sure I could smell the tanginess of blood, probably from the wound on my head. It took all my concentration not to pass out from a lack of oxygen.

Wake up! My mind exclaimed, since there was no possible way illusions can physically hurt you. It felt like an anvil was sitting on my chest, pressing on my lungs and heart.

"Help me, Desdemona, you need to wake me up!" was the last thing I heard the woman say before I slipped out from under the woman's callous hands.

Astonishingly I felt the weight lifted off my chest, allowing me to breathe again, and began gasping, trying to reclaim the air I'd lost. My mind was too fuzzy to make anything out at first, but my hearing worked perfectly fine; someone was speaking over the top of me. "Open your eyes, Dess," the all too familiar voice said.

My catatonic body remained unmoving on the floor where I took in shallow breaths. "Ace?" I asked, my eyes trying to flitter open.

He didn't answer my question, too concerned with other matters. "You have some bleeding on your head…are you hurt anywhere else?" Ace asked, voice breaking slightly; I must have given him a real scare right then.

It took me a second to find my bearings. I was in the lowest part of the Manor, a room once used for prisoners before Apollyon decided on having them kept deeper within Hell, my mother tried to drown me—no not this time, this time the woman tried strangling me my mind corrected, and now Ace was here.

Ace was here! What if he hadn't showed up in time?

"I thought I was dreaming, and this is where she led me," I said trying to sit up, but the pulsing in my head reminded me I'd hit it pretty hard, and ended up swaying before leaning back into Ace's arms. "Ow."

"Don't move too fast," Ace told me. "Who is she?" He glanced around the room checking for a possible threat still in there with us.

"No one, probably just my alter ego in bitch form," I said, wincing when trying to sit up again, not getting much further this time.

"That's one hell of a dream, Dess," he said, before I felt strong arms scoop me off the floor to position me on my feet, not letting go of me entirely yet. "Let me help since it's obvious you need some. Can you walk?" he asked. I nodded, not wanting to speak in fear my voice would crack on the sob I felt buried deep wanting to come out. The woman was relentless on killing me, and it was too much for my fragile and tired mind to handle tonight.

"Yes, I think I'm okay. Dizzy, I must have hit my head on the floor," I said, reaching up and touching the tender spot throbbing on my head. When my fingers smoothed over wet, sticky stuff, I brought my hand in front of my face to exam bright red blood coloring the tips of my fingers.

"Careful, it's gashed pretty deep, we should get you to the medic," Ace suggested, and once he was sure I wasn't going to topple over, he released one of his hands, keeping the other around one shoulder in case.

"Ace," I said, voice trembling.

"Yeah, Dess, I'm here, you're safe now," he said, hearing the desperation in my tone. It had all become too much for me to take. I just wanted to bury myself in his safe embrace.

"It was horrible. I-I was running, but couldn't get away!" I said, turning my body into his hold, so his chest shielded my face, and began telling Ace about the horrible, nightmarish world I'd been trapped in, starting with the real reason for wading out in to sea and nearly drowning.

"I'm not understanding, Dess, who is this crazy woman…why was she here, and why is she after you?"

"My mother. Oh Gods, Ace, the woman looked like my mother. It was her. I'm so certain it was her. She wanted me to follow her, and led me here before she…" I said, unable to finish the rest.

"Shhh, you're safe now, everything's going to be all right," he crooned to me the way someone might a child. I wasn't sure everything *would* be all right, but did feel much safer now Ace was here.

There was no more talk about ghosts or my mother while Ace led me back to my room.

We stopped outside my room, and I could tell by the worried look on his face he didn't think I should be alone tonight, and honestly, I didn't want to be alone. Things may have been complicated between us, but after all the strange things that had happened recently we both needed each other.

"What are you thinking about?" Ace asked, his hand in front of my face where he began smoothing out the worried creases between my brows with his thumb. His touch felt good, it somehow calmed me and made me feel safe. Reaching up, I grabbed his hand with both of my hands when he went to move away. I placed his hand near my ear so I could lean my head into it.

"You…"

He echoed my hungry look filled with need and want. He moved his gaze from my eyes down to my lips, where he concentrated for a long time. "I'm thinking about you too," he said.

My breathing came out staggered. I needed Ace for more reasons than I dared to mention to him.

Ace moved with precise control as he bent his head down to mine and slowly kissed me, taking his time, relishing every second. I hadn't been aware that while he kissed me, he was slowly leading me closer to my room, until my back hit my door with a loud thud. His hands traveled up my neck and into my hair where he grabbed on tightly as though he couldn't get our heads close enough together to really deepen the kiss.

Kissing Ace allowed me to escape from this wretched place. Right then, I could be anywhere I wanted to be, as long as I was with him.

One of his hands released my head so he could grasp the doorknob behind my back. I was only slightly aware he was leading me into my bedroom and then toward my bed. Before I could say anything to question his motives, he was kissing me again. I had half a mind to stop him, and remind him how it was his idea to take a break—except other prominent thoughts took over.

This is what you've been wanting isn't it? For Ace to be fearless, maybe even reckless again?

He leaned over me on the bed until I was lying down on my back, continuing to kiss me. It wasn't long before all thoughts other than the way Ace was kissing me, were gone.

When Ace came up for air again, it allowed me to see the all-consuming look in his eyes, like I was the only thought on his mind right then too. Watching him look at me hungrily made him irresistible, and before I knew what I was doing, I pulled Ace down to me and rolled over on top of him, crushing his lips with another kiss. We continued to fight over control like that for some time, reminding me of when we first got together, always challenging one another.

It's how Ace and I worked best together.

* * * *

Golden light filtering in through my cracked-open curtain awakened me the next morning. Ace must have woken some time earlier since he was already dressed, by dressed I meant shirtless while wearing jeans, and standing by the balcony doors looking out at the terrace. Leaving his shirt off allowed me to appreciate the way the dawn light shone down on all the right spots, highlighting his muscular physique.

Sitting straight up in bed stretching, I thought about joining Ace over by the window, and wrapping my arms around his waist as way of saying good morning. He heard me shuffling around and turned his head back toward me. The happy smile I wore began to wane when I caught sight of Ace's small, sad smile which completely negated the happiness I felt inside after the night we shared together, and decided against joining him; he obviously wasn't having the same take on last night as I was. Instead, I wrapped the sheet around me, worry taking front stage, fearing he regretted last night and was about to tell me how it was a mistake or something.

"How long have you been up?" I asked, trying to keep the concern from my tone. He continued to condemn my happiness with his look of regret.

"Not sure. I couldn't really sleep last night," he said.

"Wait, you mean like at all?"

He shrugged before turning his gaze back to whatever held his attention outside before speaking tiredly, "No, it's hard to sleep with these crazy dreams I've been having. They feel so real. You know the kind I'm talking about, that just make you feel even more tired?" He turned back to face me.

"Oh yeah, I know those kind," I said, and got the chills with the memory of the dream I'd had last night, well technically it wasn't a dream I guessed, since dreams don't usually reach out and try to choke the life out of you.

How long has Ace been having trouble sleeping, and having peculiar dreams? It was kind of strange we were both having vivid, nerve-wracking dreams. Instead of saying anything to him, I asked, "So what did you do all night?"

Reluctantly he turned away from the terrace and walked back over to the bed, sitting down on the edge in front of me. He had an impish smile on his face, "Most of the time I watched you sleep…you snore."

"I do not!" I exclaimed. Ace laughed probably at the horror-stricken expression on my face. It was good to hear him laugh, even if it was at my expense. And then I realized I couldn't ignore the regret-filled look he'd shown before.

"Last night was…" I wanted to say perfect, or amazing or something to that effect, but I took too long and Ace finished my sentence for me.

"I shouldn't have led you on, not after everything," Ace said, confirming my worst fear.

Well it was nice while it lasted. "Because you still don't think it's a good idea to be together? Because last night meant more to me than anything, being away from you kills me. It's killing me Ace, so please don't ask me to stay away from you because I don't think I can."

He looked over at me, despondent but not denying what I said. He closed the few steps over to me and kneeling down onto the floor so his face lined up with mine, he reached out and hastily grabbed my hands, "No, Dess, it's not because I don't want to be with you. You're crazy if you think that. I mean, who wouldn't? You're beautiful, sexy, smart, strong, and you're stubborn as heck," he retorted with an inward laugh as though he was referring to a specific memory and keeping it all to himself.

"But?" I said in a small voice, unable to let his torturing me continue to drag out any longer.

"Until I know where I stand, I need to focus on my final test tomorrow," Ace spoke softly, still holding onto my hands.

"What then, last night meant nothing? Just a way to pass the time?" I could hear how unfair I was being, and trying my best to understand what it is Ace wanted from me.

"Gods, Dess, no! Last night meant everything to me. You don't think this kills me too, seeing you looking so god-dammed perfect every day and not able to have you? You're right though, maybe I'm selfish and I needed to be with you before everything changes for me tomorrow. Either way, it wasn't fair of me, and I'm sorry."

"You have a lot going on, I get that, but don't you dare say last night was a mistake, not when everything else going on in our life is so messy and jumbled up. The one clear thing for both of us *is* us," I said, aware my voice was starting to shake. I was afraid traitor tears would find their way to the surface pretty soon, if my emotions weren't handled, and quickly.

In truth, I'd been so busy thinking about Scarlett's ritual tomorrow I'd nearly forgotten about Ace's big training evaluation happening on the same day. Tomorrow would decide whether or not Ace would make it as one of Hell's guardians, and securing him a valued position among Hell's finest.

"You're amazing, little Starr, you know?" Ace professed, "You are the one thing that is clear to me, no matter what is decided of my future tomorrow." He trailed little kisses up my arm. "I'm sorry this is torturing you," he added.

You have no idea.

I sighed because there was nothing else I could do. "Don't be. We just need to try and take it one day at a time. Promise me as soon as this nightmare is over, you'll take me away." I said, thinking about how Blake had offered to run away from the Morning Star, telling me how all I had to do was say the words, and he'd take me away. Running away from everything right now sounded tempting, it couldn't happen until I knew my brother Abe was safe.

"That's why I love you." He reached out toward my face to run the back of his hand down the side of my cheek.

"Why?"

"You're the bravest person I know." He surprised me by saying that, mostly because Ace was the bravest person *I* knew.

"Are you going to come and watch?" he asked, shifting our conversation.

"Do you want me to come and watch?" I hadn't planned on it, figuring my being there would lend as a distraction for him.

"Sure, why not, you might learn a thing or two," he said teasingly.

"Ha!" I exclaimed with a small snort. "I'm pretty sure you've already taught me all your moves."

"Is that so?" he asked, eyes shining with humor.

"Yes, that's so. But if you could always use another critique, then I'll be there," I promised him.

"Sounds good," Ace sounded satisfied, before looking at the clock and sobering up, "I better get going." He stared over at the door for an extended amount of time with a misplaced expression, as though he could see or hear something on the other side troubling him. Shaking his head, and whatever troubled him away, he stood and kissed me on the top of my head before leaving.

That distressed look he'd had on his face before he left continued to worry me, and I began to have second thoughts about what had kept him up all night; it could have been regret from being with me last night, or it could have been something else altogether. My gut feeling on this one wouldn't subside.

If only I'd asked him about it at the time, maybe things would have turned out differently; maybe it wouldn't have been too late to save him. Because of not following my every instinct, I would lose more than I bargained for.

CHAPTER SIXTEEN

Midnight Ritual

Once the match is lit, there is nothing else to do, except for maybe to sit back and watch as everything starts to burn, and crumble in on itself.

My day started out pretty good, right up until the moment Kione decided to grace me with his presence. It happened while sitting in the courtyard across from the barista station and eating my bagel, picking at it and making a crummy mess all over my lap to be precise, Kione showed up and ruined a perfectly hellish morning.

"Lovely day to feed the birds," Kione said, noticing the mess I was making.

"You're blocking the sun," I said, blatantly annoyed. Kione's response to my malice was to sit down next to me. *There's an entire expanse of the bench circling all the way around the fountain, why does he have to sit right next to me?*

He was so close his hip touched mine from where he pressed up against me on the bench. I gave him a sneer of disgust before pointedly scooting about two feet away from him. This only seemed to humor him further, making his smile larger.

"You know, I was thinking to myself how you and I have not properly reacquainted ourselves as friends should do. There is still so much I'd like to learn about you, and I'm sure you're dying to know more about me as well," he said.

Someone might be dying, and it's not me, I thought cynically. "Thanks but I think I'll pass. Feeding the birds should really be done in silence," I retorted.

Kione ignored my subtle hint to shut him up and continued annoying me, "Really though, I'm curious to know what secrets are locked away inside that pretty head of yours. Do tell."

He has some nerve! "I'm not the one keeping secrets," I said, knowing that wasn't entirely true. But in my defense, at least my secrets would be used for good and not evil like Kione's would undoubtedly be.

"I have no secrets. Ask and you shall find I am an open book. You may also find you and I are not so different from each other."

"I highly doubt that." I gritted my teeth, growing angry he would dare compare us. We were nothing alike!

He shrugged as though he were the most easy going, carefree person in the world. "Still no? Okay, then no need to ask. I'll simply tell you how we are the same."

"Please don't," I said, voice coming out in a plea.

Kione, of course, continued again as though I'd said nothing, "Like you, I merely wish to secure my rightful place in the world all while helping those I care about."

Yeah right, like Kione actually cares about anybody besides himself. "Could have fooled me, I didn't know you cared about anyone else besides yourself." Sometimes the only thing you can do is speak your mind, especially when you're blindsided by such a human response.

His even-tempered gaze never lingered when he replied, "Admit it. My desire to belong is not so hard to understand, is it?"

Luckily I didn't have to answer when Pixie-girl walked up to the barista bar, spotted us, and detoured over to where we sat, albeit wearing a nervous expression on her face while doing so. "Um, Dess, can I talk to you for a minute?" Pixie-girl asked, voice sounding uncertain.

I raised my eyebrow up at her, not having to fake my wonderment. Was she really helping me get out of this awkward conversation with

Kione? Thinking how Pixie-girl must have been really good at reading body language or else she really needed to talk to me about something. Either way I was grateful for the excuse to end this conversation. I stood and said, "Yes please, I'll be right there."

"Before you go, it was nice talking with you, little Starr. There's one more thing before you go play," he said, making me stop in my track to look back at him curiously. "I hope you slept *well* last night."

"Wait. What?"I took one involuntary step toward him, completely thrown off guard.

"Of course she did, probably better than you since she has a conscience." Thank the Gods for Pixie-girl who threaded her arm in mine, and jerked me back away from Kione, who managed to derail me once more. He was certainly an expert at taunting me.

"Sorry, looked like you needed me to bail you out," Pixie-girl said, leading me over to the barista stand. So my first conclusion had been correct—she was good at reading people, and didn't need to be able to read someone's soul to do it.

"You have no idea," I told her. "I owe you one."

"I'll keep it in mind. It looks like you need something now though. Do you want some coffee or something," Pixie-girl asked, after telling the barista what she wanted for herself.

"Um sure, I'll have an orange latte, extra shot of espresso please, wait, better make it two," I quickly added, knowing I'd be grateful for the extra caffeine later on in the night during our *great escape*.

"Where's Blake?" I then turned to Ebony and asked.

"Preparing a few details for tonight,' she said, looking away and making me think Pixie-girl and Blake were hiding something from me.

"Is there anything I can do to help?"

"No we have it covered," she answered a little too quickly, confirming my suspicion.

I stared at her unblinking for several seconds trying to break her with my suspecting gaze. It didn't work; Pixie-girl must have had some power to withstand the menacing-Starr-glare...or I still needed to perfect it, either way. Lucky for her, our hot beverages were up, and I soon forgot about my suspicions. Besides, whatever the two of them were up to, I trusted them.

"I'm in. It wasn't easy but after talking, Blake talked with Adana as you suggested, we convinced her to formally invite me as a participant," Pixie-girl said, I think as a way to distract me from what she and Blake were really up to.

It had been my idea for Pixie-girl to get someone else in the Sisters of Selene besides Scarlett. So while Blake was busy talking up Ebony to Scarlett, convincing her it was a great idea to have Ebony join, Ebony was making friends with Adana.

"Good news for once," I said.

* * * *

When the night finally rolled around, anxiousness made it hard to sit around and watch time go by. "You're not going to be like this while we are stalking Ebony tonight, are you?" Blake asked, while giving me a nervous sideways look from where he sat on the Green Beast in my room. The three of us decided to meet here an hour before the ritual to go over the plan one more time, even though we'd already gone over it a million times.

"I'm ready," I said feeling full of energy and adrenaline, ready to take on the night. "Pixie-err, Ebony is the one you should be asking since she's playing the leading role here, not me."

"Who me?" Ebony said, looking doe-eyed and surprised when Blake and I both stared over at her.

"She'll do great," Blake spoke for her, sounding overly confident in someone who wasn't even trained in battling unrelenting sinister creatures as we were, I thought. Pixie-girl gave Blake a grateful look in return from where she sat in the window seat.

"She hasn't had any combat training, or sparring lessons, of any kind. What if things go bad, and she's, I don't know, trapped in Scarlett's nasty web of nasty-girl cat-claws, and hatred or worse?" I said, feeling the need to point those minor details out.

"Ebony doesn't need combat training, she has me and you, hence the stalking part I mentioned." Blake sounded irritated with me when he spoke. It was evident we were all on edge waiting for the details of the night to play out.

"She's right you know," Pixie-girl said quietly, pulling her legs up to her chest before wrapping her arms tightly around them. "I'm not trained, not the way you two are. What if I mess this up tonight?"

Blake walked over to her in front of the window, and bent down, putting his face in front of hers. "Hey," he said, in the gentle, reassuring way Blake used that somehow magically made you believe anything he said. I don't know how many times over the years he had used that same voice on me when I was scared or nervous, or sad. Hearing it now made something in my chest squeeze tightly, and I had to cross my arms over my torso to ease it. "I'm not going to let anything happen to you, I promise. Dessi and I will be right there the entire time, you aren't going to mess anything up."

Pixie-girl didn't respond at first, not until Blake reassured her some more, and she finally smiled over at him, "Okay, I'll do it, I'm ready."

* * * *

We walked over to where Scarlett planned on having the ritual in silence, a silence filled with tension so tangible you could have scooped it out with a spoon.

Blake and Pixie-girl had thought out every detail of tonight's Moonlight Madness, what I was officially calling tonight's mission. They staked out a cave around the corner from where Scarlett and her group were setting up. They'd even supplied it with candles so we could see when it got dark, water to drink, a few weapons hidden in the sand, in case things really took a wrong turn. And last but not least (though perhaps the most important detail), all the tools we needed to properly infuse the Moonstone with, since our plan was to come back to the cave once Pixie-girl was done hijacking the Moon's power from the ritual.

We still had twenty minutes until midnight, in that time, Pixie-girl changed into the outfit Scarlett had given her for tonight's special occasion. Blake and I turned our backs to give her some privacy. I had a feeling Scarlett was trying to recreate the night I was tricked into coming and Selene had graced us with her presence; I'd heard rumors of how it was supposedly the first time in hundreds of years Selene appeared in her true form for anyone. So why me? I wondered for the thousandth time.

When Pixie-girl was done, she walked over to where Blake and I stood and asked, "Hey Dess, can we have a moment to talk, alone?" Pixie-girl shot Blake an apologetic glance in consideration.

"I'll be right back," Blake told the two of us before walking away.

"Um, sure," I said, walking with her down the cave a little way so we could have some privacy.

"About what you said earlier, you know about how I'm not trained and don't know how to combat or use magic?" Pixie girl reminded me.

"Yes, but I didn't mean to offend you or anything," I quickly said, feeling lousy.

"No, you were right. With how clumsy I am I'd probably do horrible in combat of any kind," she admitted. "I'm not completely helpless though. I'm smart, and a fast learner, plus Blake's been teaching me how to spar a little. I'm not nearly as good as you are, yet anyway, but I'm not useless either."

"Sorry, I wasn't trying to say you were useless. Up against someone like Scarlett you, um, kind of standout is all I'd meant." I felt embarrassed for being such a bitch earlier. As an excuse, the stakes were kind of high right now, and if there was any one else to take her place, I'd probably use them. Not a fact needing to be pointed out right then. Pixie-girl was smart, but being book-smart or having decent common sense was not going to save her life if the ritual went south or demons decided to grace us with their presence, though the last one was probably unlikely to happen. Brute force, and a little pixie-dust could go a long way in her case. The point was you could never be sure when a life threatening situation might occur, and I didn't feel comfortable throwing Pixie-girl to the wolves with a handful of books to use as weapons.

Blake giving Pixie-girl secret combat training sessions didn't surprise me, being the cover-all-basis kind of guy he was. Still, I wondered how long it had been going on.

"I know you didn't say it, not exactly. You need to know I am capable though, and to have some faith in me," Pixie-girl said, her chin held high in defiance.

Good for her, I thought, seeing some of myself in her right then; it occurred to me we both weren't always given the benefit of the doubt, and always had others looking down on us and what we were capable of. It took a while for me to see this, and decided to change the way I'd been treating her. "Sorry, Ebony, really I am. Blake's a good teacher, keep working with him and you *will* be better than me."

"Thank you for giving me a chance, it's all I've ever wanted."

"You're going to do fine," I said, trying to make myself believe it.

When we got back over to where Blake was shuffling around a medium-size brown backpack, he heard our approach and glanced up at us with one eyebrow raised.

"I'm going to give the cave a quick lookout," Pixie-girl said to Blake. When Ebony was out of ear shot Blake straightened and turned toward me. "I, uh, should have told you about teaching Ebony how to spar."

"I thought you were eavesdropping. It's fine." I shrugged off his apology, Blake teaching Pixie-girl how to fight was one of those things I had no right to be upset over.

"I can't help it if my hearing is exceptionally better than yours—it's in my genes," Blake teased back, lightening the mood.

"Yeah, and you know what else is in your genes?" I asked around a taunting smile.

"What's that?" he asked curious.

"Fleas."

Blake jumped back and grabbed a hand to his chest in mock hurt, "Innocent until proven guilty. I don't and never have had fleas," he said, reaching his hand around and scratching the back of his head in show before turning the power of his full lopsided grin on me. Blake's silly-stupid smile always had the same effect on me every time he used it. With it came the power to melt away all the tension in an entire room full of Hellions, or in our case cave bats and possible flea infestation.

"All clear, and I think we have everything ready," said Pixie-girl, with a clapping of her hands to clean the dirt off from where she'd been rummaging through a bag on the ground near the cave entrance.

Her tone implied a lack of confidence, which wasn't making me feel too good about sending her, the novice, out there to be fed to the wolves, so to speak, though it wasn't unreasonable to compare Scarlett and her minions to hungry predators.

"It's time,' Blake agreed after glancing down at his watch wrapped around his wrist. He walked over to Ebony and reaching out to squeeze her hand once before letting go, showing the confidence he had for her.

When the moment came, Blake and I waited until Pixie-girl had at least a ten minute lead on us before we made our move. Knowing Scarlett, she would be ready to go well before the clock struck twelve; before she and her fellow Sisters of Selene, turned back into mice. I suppressed a giggle.

* * * *

We hid behind a large boulder adjacent to the bottom of the cliff, since it gave us extra coverage to hide behind, and it wasn't too far from the cave. I couldn't quite see the entire group of Sisters, only a clear shot of Scarlett and Pixie-girl, who lucky for us, had the position directly next to Scarlett. She always kept her victims close to her, better to humiliate them this way.

"Are you sure this was a good idea?" I asked Blake, still uneasy about putting Pixie-girl in her direct path.

"Give her a chance, and shhh, be quiet." He nodded his head in the direction of the assembled group ready to go.

I had to bite my tongue to cut off any further retorts I felt itching to come out. Familiar faces joined Scarlett in her circle: Ebony to her right, followed by Donella, Bridgette, Lana, Adana, and the new twin sisters Scarlett carefully spun into her vicious, unknowing web named Winter and Aspen. They were a part of a witch clan located out of Switzerland; apparently their mother was responsible for both the stories behind the Bundalp phantoms, and the witches' cauldron in the Kiental Valley.

Everything looked exactly as it should have, until a few seconds later when a certain someone we hadn't been expecting showed up. "What's Kione doing here?" I whispered hastily to Blake.

Blake nodded his head and looked as surprised as me to see him there. This was not good.

"As the head Sister to Selene, I would like to welcome you, Kione, we are greatly honored to have such a strong, and fearless Mentor of the Morning Star with us tonight. May the Morning Star favor you!"

"Welcome!" Scarlett's fellow Sisters chanted.

"Puke," I said, sticking a finger down my throat in mock gagging.

"Shh!" Blake repeated to me.

"Thank you, Sisters of Selene, it is an honor to be here tonight as witness to the grand powers our Morning Star, Apollyon, has sanctified you all with by giving you this link to your Moon Goddess. Please carry on, and don't pay any attention to me. I'll be observing as quiet as a mouse and you won't even know I'm here. Praise the Moon," Kione replied graciously.

"Praise the Moon!" many of the Sisters echoed Kione.

Scarlett, always the Succubus, gave an excessive flirty laugh that in my opinion, sounded completely ridiculous. "It was my profound pleasure to invite Mentor Kione to join us for our finest hour tonight, an ingenious idea of mine if I do say so myself."

Kione looked pleased with Scarlett's introduction. "You can call me Kione." He locked his gaze with a contented Scarlett.

It wasn't hard for me to guess who planted the invite tonight, I thought disdainfully.

Taking one look at all the girls' awed faces as they melted over Kione, was enough to make me want blow our cover so I could punch that smug look off his face.

Donella was sealing the circle by pouring red candle wax into the shape of a star in the sand. After Donella was done, she took her place within the circle amongst her Sisters.

It was time. I braced myself for anything, especially seeing how Kione was a part of the equation. *What is he up to now?*

"It's time," Scarlett said, echoing my thoughts.

All thoughts of Kione were put on hold temporarily to focus on Pixie-girl. When Scarlett handed her the knife I could see the horror fill Pixie-girl's eyes. It reminded me of my own reaction to seeing the blood offering for the first time. Pixie-girl took the knife, and copying what the other girls had done, she made a thin cut on the length of her forearm. Crimson blood ran in a vein-sized stream down her arm before dripping down into the circle.

Her blood was the last they needed.

All faces were looking up toward the moon expectantly waiting for Selene to answer their call. At first nothing happened. Scarlett's face transformed to anger assuming Selene wasn't going to answer her, again; the rumor going around the Institute was that Scarlett has been trying to re-enact the ritual when Selene showed her true, shockingly disturbing, yet glorious form. No such luck tonight, I realized when Scarlett reached into a satin satchel at her feet, and pulled out another knife, different than the one passed around the circle moments ago.

"Scarlett is planning something, isn't she," Blake said, thinking along the same line I was.

"Undoubtedly," I agree.

What's Scarlett planning on doing with the other knife? And what was with the dramatic presentation? None of this settled right in my stomach.

Taking a moment longer to study the knife, allowed me to see something oddly familiar about it; it wasn't just any knife, it was *my* knife! The black and citrine stones on the hilt proved it to be mine. "That little…" I said angrily, remembering to keep my voice down.

Well, technically it was my mother's, Lilith's, before it became mine. The Angel Lain had given it to me after explaining how it had once belonged to my mother, and how it was even named after me, The Star, since my soul name is The Starred One. Lain also warned me that in the wrong hands, it could be dangerous. Objects, not unlike people, can be manipulated and branded to belong to certain owners; a key molded to fit a certain lock, and if used by someone else, may open up catastrophe.

I watched as Scarlett twirled it around in the palm of her hand marveling at its beauty. I could see three familiar oblong citrine gems embedded into the hard surface of the grip, and Scarlett running her greedy hands all over them. Scarlett really put the suck in Succubus, I thought. "Where did Scarlett get my knife?" I asked Blake, who nodded at me, uncertain. Scarlett and Kione exchanged a look, Kione giving Scarlett a little nod.

Whatever they planned, it was coming now.

Scarlett turned back to her group with an all new kind of exhilaration fueling her as she pierced the night air above her head with the knife. My level of discomfort went from a five to a ten on the scale of slightly nervous to full blown panic. It might be a good time to call on my evil spirit, I thought. *What was his name again? Riker the Great something…* I couldn't exactly remember, but apparently I didn't have to because thinking of the spirit had been enough for it to have been summoned.

"Riker the Great Havoc!" it said, from somewhere behind me, sounding irritated with me for not remembering his name.

"Oh dear Gods!" I hissed in a low, harsh whisper, almost forgetting to not raise my voice since we were supposed to be incognito here.

Alarm flashed across Blake's features from where he sat beside me. *Oh no, Blake is not supposed to know about Riker!* Riker's appearance made me forget all about Blake beside me. My head whipped back and forth between Riker and Blake, and I was pretty sure a dumbfounded look appeared on my face, mouth hanging ajar.

"What's gotten into you?" Blake asked, his eyebrows were pushed down into a deep furrowed arch, either concerned or annoyed; could have been both.

Okay so maybe Blake couldn't see Riker. Now wasn't the best time to have figured that out, regardless I was glad. Shoving away the panicked look on my face, I said, "Oh, um, I think an ant bit me," I lied.

Blake continued to look at me as though I'd gone completely insane. Out of the corner of my eye I could see Riker had made himself a spot in the sand to sit, crossing his legs and appearing bored. I flashed him a glare when he started to pick up the sand and toss it around in his hands. He would scoop it up and hold it until he could no longer keep the connection to this world's matter. *So, he could make a connection to sand and probably other things for a little while at least before the connection got lost. Good to know.*

Blake might not have been able to see the evil spirit, the sand getting tossed around, however, he could see.

Riker stopped, but not without first giving me a glimpse of those beady-red eyes conveying the promise he made me when he said he would take pleasure in possessing my body someday, to use as some strange vendetta against the world. I believed Riker would try. Today was not going to be that day however, after reminding him who was boss. I glared right back at him, trying my hardest to copy the look I'd seen in Apollyon's eyes so many times. Riker's menacing gaze faltered, and he actually looked away. I wondered if Riker had seen the glossy-eyed inferno dancing around in my eyes the way I'd seen it happen in Apollyon's.

It wasn't until we heard Scarlett start to speak again Riker and I both turned back to the ritual.

"Selene, Goddess of the Moon and Watcher of the Night, watch over us now and guide us by taking our hand this night. Show us why you're named Keeper of thy Night!"

A crack of lightning resonated across the sky, and a few of the Sisters of Selene let out small screams. It was almost as if Selene had answered. By the look on Kione's face, this had been the moment he'd been anticipating. Kione was using Scarlett to get to Selene, I comprehended with a gut-wrenching start.

Colossal thunderheads rolled in and stole my attention from Kione. Within seconds the sky was completely covered in shades of Byzantium-purples and dark-grays. A lone silvery-gray cloud started shaping itself into a long, twisted shape, not exactly comparable to a funnel, but definitely not a normal cloud either. It continued to grow in size while spiraling down in front of the group of Sisters. Things got even stranger when the cloud-funnel-thing grew a giant hand attached to an even larger arm that reached out toward Scarlett; no, not Scarlett, my mind corrected, it was reaching for the knife, *my* knife.

Seeing the cloud transform reminded me of the night Selene showed herself before me: a silver silhouette of a mouthless woman saying my name over and over again. It had the same silvery-hue, and mimicked all the angles of her face, never quite reaching a full shaped body.

All of the girls' faces showed different degrees of panic. Pixie-girl also being one of them, until seeing an opening and responded ingeniously when everyone else remained frozen in terror, using this moment of distraction to pull the Moonstone out of her pocket, and chanted the incantation Zola taught her. Smart girl! I thought elatedly.

The hand stopped reaching for the knife midair, and instead turned back into something resembling more of a thin, iridescent cloud swooping down past Scarlett and circling Ebony. While swirling around, the shapeless cloud of Selene grazed over the top of the stone, somehow making all the little light prisms in the stone shine brightly and cast dancing rainbows over everyone, and everything within ten feet of the circle.

Ebony jumped back in surprise. I kept a vigilant eye on the stone the entire time, not about to let it out of my sight. Pixie-girl kept a tight hold onto the Moonstone, closing her hands around it. Once Kione realized what was happening, he took a step forward and reached an arm out toward Ebony. "No!" he yelled over in her direction.

Scarlett whipped her head over to Pixie-girl, glaring heatedly once she grasped what Pixie-girl was up to.

The wind picked up and blew the clouds away to reveal a full, silvery moon. Everyone and everything was motionless for several breaths. The silence after the storm never gets much credit, I thought oddly, thinking how it was more intimidating than the calm before the storm. At least before the storm you felt its warning charges in the air, while this kind of calm now after the fact had endless possibilities.

"Okay, I think we need to get her out of there," I said, referring to Pixie-girl, looking at Blake for the first time since Scarlett pulled out my knife. He was no longer sitting next to me, having already stood and was now headed toward Ebony.

"Shit," I mumbled, before following behind Blake. *So much for getting out of here unnoticed!*

Scarlett looked to be in shock, standing motionless with her mouth hanging partially open, and her head shaking from side to side.

Wow, she really didn't handle things not going her way well.

Ebony saw the two of us coming and glanced back and forth between Scarlett, us, and Scarlett again. That's when Ebony, once again proving her resourcefulness, broke the circle by kicking the sand over the red wax in front of her and ran toward Blake and me.

It only took Scarlett a moment longer to recover, and now she was livid. Scarlett screamed in frustration, throwing her hands up in the air. I half expected her to chase after Ebony, but instead turned toward Kione and said something I couldn't quite make out. My back was turned to Scarlett and her Sisters of Selene, past ready to put this night behind us, and proceed to step two of our plan in freeing Abaddon.

When the three of us met, we didn't waste any time before turning and running off in the direction of our cave. *We did it, we actually pulled this thing off!* I couldn't believe it.

As we were leaving, an overwhelming urge compelled me to look back, and saw Kione looking right at me even though Scarlett was standing in front of him, probably giving him an earful of complaints and name calling directed at us. And the funny thing was, he didn't look furious or annoyed at having us ruin his plans. The look he shared was much worse, he actually looked impressed.

CHAPTER SEVENTEEN

Ryu

Abaddon

There's a thin line between being a saint and being a villain. It wasn't a secret which Abaddon strived for most days, this particular day, he was neither, forced to wake the monster lying dormant inside him.

Abaddon felt as though he was stuck in an old boxing movie set on repeat, avoiding yet again another blow to his face. He'd been subjected to these fights for the past five days with little to eat and little time to sleep in-between.

Which explained why when Abaddon watched his arm swing out into a wide arc, it appeared in slow motion to him. He believed it was due to his tired brain unable to gauge time properly. His arm finished swinging fully around and squared his opponent in the jaw. The beast did not budge an inch in any direction.

Instead, the weight of his hit knocked himself backward until he lost his footing and stumbled onto his back. The beast seized its opportunity to take Abaddon out and missed. Abaddon was too quick and scarcely dodged the behemoth-sized foot before it had a chance to stomp his face in. Luckily, he had rolled over and out of its way in the nick of time.

The acidulous creature Abaddon had been forced to brawl with was called a Gigantes; only the biggest, meanest beast he could have been paired with. Gigantes' were said to be offspring to the Gods, *it* was what almost all folklore categorized as a Giant.

Abaddon knew how hard it was to take down a Gigantes; he'd already done so once in his life and had never wanted to have to do it again. The first time he was forced to take down a Gigantes was two years ago. The Gigantes had showed up at a college football game; apparently it had been living deep underground directly where the field had been built, a bad move of the city's since everyone knows Gigantes' hate noise. Some point during the game, the Gigantes awoke, erupting through the ground in the middle of the field before wreaking havoc on the entire stadium and all whom inhabited it. Abaddon remembered thinking about the gruesome comparison of watching a piranha getting dropped in a bowl full of goldfish. Lucky for the city, Abaddon had been traveling through and heard the disturbance. Eventually he took the beast down, but it was not an easy feat. This one he struggled with now seemed even more skilled than the former one he'd brawled with.

The Gigantes roared out in anger when he realized Abaddon avoided him, before letting out a string of what he imagined to be profanity. Its motives to kill Abaddon were quite clear, however.

The Angel of Hell, and Mighty Destroyer, would not be so easily eradicated though. If it was a fight *they* wanted, he would give them one.

It was ironic, he thought, how he'd spent the majority of his life masquerading amongst mortals slaying creatures from the Underworld and Hell only to have to do it again. The good news about killing them here in the Underworld though, was once they were dead here they were gone for good, and not simply vanished from this world only to be sent to the next.

All the while during his thoughts, Abaddon continued to duck and roll each time the Gigantes swung at him with arms or legs, he was trying to tire the thing out at the same time give himself a break. He was exhausting easily. Each time he did this, the giant would roar in outrage. While Abaddon played ring-around-the-rosy with the thing, he looked around his audience and noticed familiar creatures he'd already banished once before. Based on the way some of them were leering in his direction and gnashing their teeth angrily, he could tell they were eager to take their shot at beating him.

Now's my chance to finish them off once and for all. Placing his feet precisely on the ground, he kicked up the dirt behind him the way a bull would in Spanish style bullfighting, before elongating his arm out in front of him and waving the beast forward, a taunting smile lifting up the corners of his mouth. He knew provoking it was probably going to come back in the form of pain later. Abaddon, true to his nature, did not yield to anyone, or anything. He did not even submit to his father, Apollyon, the Devil himself. The Angel of Hell made decisions based off his own gathering of intellect and experience.

The beast roared its ugly head back in a massive snarl, and when it lowered it back in place, it was foaming at the mouth in anger. It growled, swinging its massive spiked club in the air around its head.

Abaddon believed it. Only, it would have to get a lot closer to do it.

Not this time big boy! Abaddon's obstinate smile never wavered as he began to back up to the farthest corner of the fighting arena, careful to avoid bumping into any beast, demon or any other malevolent creature standing amongst the eager spectators. The ground shook violently as the Gigantes ran at him in full speed.

"*Corrida de toros*," he shouted as a battle cry, meaning, *running with the bulls*. He'd been to Spain before and rather enjoyed the spectacular, though sometimes grisly, celebrations. Abaddon clutched the only weapon he'd been given firmly in his hand; a branding iron used for permanently branding the Underworld's populace.

When the Gigantes got close enough, it swung its spiked club at Abaddon. Luckily, this was a move he had been anticipating, and thereby knew to avoid it by first jumping, then rolling out of the way in perfect unison. He rolled in-between the Gigantes' feet, jabbing him once in the foot, the ankle, and again up the calf as he rolled back to his feet. Knowing this would only make the Gigantes react violently, he was sure to keep moving, light on his toes, and vigilant from all angles of any expectant blows. He'd shown his sister Desdemona this maneuver numerous times throughout their intense training sessions. He suspected he must look like a wondrous creature to anyone who laid eyes on him during a battle. What they didn't know was how dangerous Abaddon truly was.

The Gigantes roared loudly, swinging its club in all directions without having precise control. The crowd formed into the makeshift circle, scattered to evade the spiked club. Abaddon knew there would be no slowing down from this point further, and continued stabbing the Gigantes with the branding iron wherever he could get close enough. He slipped up once, and didn't get out of the way fast enough after stabbing it in the side, and received a backhanded blow to the side and shoulder, sending him across the arena made of dirt and fire, losing his weapon as a result.

Spots danced before his eyes, and he could not make out his surroundings. His hearing was also impaired, being taken over by a high-pitched sound. Rumbling of the ground was his only warning to get up and move blindly, or be trampled to death. He chose the former. With his hands splayed out in the dirt around him, he felt around in order to stabilize himself and stand. His fingers came across something hard buried in the dirt there. It was his branding iron. He clutched it carefully in his hands, and stumbled to his feet, the world swaying around him. His shoulder dangled, dislocated.

Blast! he thought, blinking rapidly in hopes his vision would clear. Finally it did, and in the nick of time to avoid decapitation by the spiked club. Doing so, he jump-rolled out of the way again, and then screamed out in agony as he bumped his shoulder on the hard ground.

The Gigantes began to laugh at Abaddon.

That one small pause was all Abaddon needed to claim the upper hand. He ran forward with all of his might and speed, and using the Gigantes' club as leverage to push himself up even higher, he jumped into the air towering over the Gigantes' head, before coming down and sticking his weapon straight into its eye.

Abaddon stood back, breathing jaggedly in pain and clutching his shoulder tightly, and watched as the creature roared in pain, and tumbled around. Abaddon, along with the rest of the Underworld's crowd, continued to watch as the Gigantes tripped and landed on its face where the branding iron still protruded, putting an end to said Beast of the Gods.

Abaddon stood back and marveled at his handy work. He was exhausted, but could still exert a bit of energy to claim his victory, even when sweat ran down his brow and into his eyes, burning them. The one thing he could make out, however, was the angry snarls growing louder as they began to close in on him—apparently he was the only one who thought it was a victory worth celebrating.

His arms went out to his sides in a protective stance, as he slowly turned around in a clockwise rotation. Was this *his* plan the whole time? *An impossible game I was never intended to win*? Even he knew there were too many for him to take on, he would be damned if he didn't try, after all, Abaddon never backed down from a challenge, test or anything else flung at him. Threats not unlike the Gigantes', (though some were quite creative and disturbingly descriptive), of how they were going to tear his limbs off, skin, or devour him, filled in the suffocating space around him. It wasn't the way he, the great Destroyer, wanted to go out. He braced himself for it anyway. A loud whistling noise filled in the space around him, making all the monsters of the Underworld clutch at their ears in agony and beckon for the giver of the noise to stop. It did not hurt Abaddon's ears. He was the only one still standing as *He*, the man, or rather creature, strutted forward. *He* looked surprisingly pleased with himself, a strange thought, given how Abaddon extinguished what was probably considered to be his most valuable beast in his collection. And, up until now, Abaddon had only imagined who it was behind this entire masquerade; he'd been right suspecting Osiris was too regal to lower himself to underground fighting, and that it had to be his brother, Seth, who was responsible for such excessive forms of entertainment.

"You and you there," Seth said, pointing at a few of his men, "Take these beasts back to their holdings, all except this one," he said, motioning toward Abaddon.

Seth didn't seem surprised the whistle didn't work on Abaddon as it did the others. In fact, he didn't seem concerned about much at all, Abaddon thought, as Seth continued forward, having to step over one of the Gigantes' limbs to get closer to him.

"The brother of Osiris does not fear coming so close to the Destroyer?" Abaddon asked, brazenly testing his theory about Osiris' lesser half.

Seth simply looked amused by such notions. His eyes were the same feline-shape and honey-brown color as Osiris'. They had a certain gleam in them not found in the old God of the Underworld—a dangerous gleam of a heart gone completely black from the rot of cruelty.

"I've been watching you for some time now. I know everything about you: how you move, how you fight, how you think. I do not fear the things I know," Seth said blatantly.

Bold, Abaddon thought, maybe a little self-assured, and definitely a horrible mistake on his part, bold nonetheless. Seth had slowly moved closer until he was a mere few feet away from Abaddon.

Abaddon thought about reaching out and grabbing the smug fool by the throat, merely to prove a point about how it would be too easy for Abaddon to kill him if he really wanted to. And he did want to. The only thing stopping him was knowing deep down it would only add to the guilt haunting him each night. It would be an easy kill considering Seth's obvious lack of skills, noticing the absence of definition on Seth's exposed arms. Abaddon knew his kind—arrogant men always having others doing their dirty work for them. Abaddon always knew whose hands were stained with blood regardless of who committed the crime.

Men like Seth brainwashed their society to fight and die in petty, personal feuds. It made Abaddon sick deep down in the pit of his stomach.

Seth stood before Abaddon wearing a black Egyptian kilt, and a gold chest plate for a shirt. His calmness made Abaddon uneasy. He would have to change that.

"Then you probably already know killing you would be the easiest defeat I've ever had, particularly because you forgot how my arms and legs remain unchained. Even though your guards will eventually defend your honor by killing me, but, of course, not without a great loss on their end. It won't be until I've disemboweled you, and severed your head from your body. I see this taking place in ten, nine, eight," he said as he began to count backward. "Seven, six…"

Seth looked at him as though he were some lunatic who could not possibly be serious.

"Five, four…" Abaddon continued counting, unable to hold back the smile on his face when Seth started to shout at his men for help. He got to glimpse Seth losing some of his earlier calmness, a façade of composure, Abaddon now realized.

"Chain him, you idiots!" Seth ordered. When Abaddon got down to one, he simply stepped forward, closing in the distance between them, putting their faces only a few inches apart.

"Have I not given you the show you were anticipating? Is it not enough for you to force more blood on my hands, but then you insult me with your ignorance? Consider your life spared, Seth, and leave the dealings of the Underworld to someone like Osiris, who knows what they're doing."

Anger filled Seth's entire demeanor. Abaddon wasn't sure which thing he said that made the imbecile irate the most—the threat on his life, or the part about his brother, Osiris. If he had to guess, he'd call it a tie.

Seth's face transformed from anger to a canvas of calmness perfected, but Abaddon could still see the lingering fear in his eyes. "Have the Destroyer lashed as a reminder of his place here in the Underworld, not letting him forget that I, Seth, is the one ordering it done. Also, after he is bled in my name, put him back in his original holding, the dark and putrid surroundings will teach him better manners."

Abaddon didn't fight when four guards came to do Seth's behests. "One more thing before you go, you may act all honorable, but I don't think you mind having blood on your hands. In fact, I think you rather enjoy it. The difference between the two of us is I admit who I am, and what I am. Can you say the same? Who truly is the ignorant one here?"

Seth turned his back on Abaddon, and his men took him away.

* * * *

Once again, Abaddon was thrown into complete darkness, a solitude he resented. It was not so much the darkness that made him teeter on the edge of sanity, but the voices echoing around him in his cramped space threatening to push him over. War had already paid him a visit, who knew who or what else might come unexpectedly out of the darkness. Every now and then he could feel eyes on him, watching him, able to see him though he could not see them.

He got to his knees, and sat on his heels, straightening up as much as he could before his head found the ceiling of his prison-hole. The guards had thrown him in here, brutally tossing him into a tight space with sharp rocks uncaring if they tore his skin or if his head hit the hard ground. He had thought about overpowering the guards, and he could have, and then what? He would have been too weak to take on the guards who would eventually get word back to Seth about his escape. No, what he needed was to salvage his strength, and come up with another plan.

Abaddon reached out and felt his hands meet the iron bars. In order to get a better look, he brought his face closer toward the bars and found himself staring at a pair of glowing red eyes. He remained in a locked gaze until all at once, the eyes were directly in front of him attached to a gruesome pale face with sharp fangs that snapped out at Abaddon's throat.

He threw himself back as far as he could go, hitting his head on the low, rigid ceiling again. He recognized the creature at once as War's pet and Vampire. If he hadn't jumped back when he had, her pet would have taken a chunk out of his neck. Knowing War, she'd probably given it strict instructions to keep him in line.

Exhausted with the day's events, Abaddon stayed in the back of his prison and curled up into a fetal position on the cold, damp floor. In the morning, he would need to think up a better plan now that he knew War's pet was one of the creatures keeping watch over him at night, one of many he speculated. But it would have to wait until morning as he was unable to keep awake any longer, letting his mind take him to a place far away from Ryu and Seth's control, to a place warm and comfortable; a place where he did not have to kill even for a day. Where no blood would have to be on his hands.

CHAPTER EIGHTEEN

The Great Havoc

We ran to the cave as fast as we could, Riker gliding along right beside me. Having him here wasn't planned. I would have sent him away already if I hadn't thought he might actually come in handy later.

Somewhere along the way back to the cave, something caught a hold of my arm and a sharp searing pain tore my skin. At first I thought a rock or shrub snagged me, but when I could finally see the scratches in the candle-lit cave, there were three distinctive fingernail marks running the length down my forearm. Riker immediately came to mind.

I don't have time for a spiteful spirit set on torturing me! Hopefully he would use some of his hostility when it was actually needed. It was evident he couldn't make a connection for very long, otherwise I had a feeling he would make good on his promise right then and there. As soon as we returned with Abaddon I'd find a way to undo the dark magic and be free of Riker once and for all.

"Now what?" Pixie-girl asked once we made it back to the cave, taking the stone out of her pocket to hold in her hand. Blake was busy making sure the leather satchel he had packed with everything we needed was intact.

"I don't know. I guess we go to Ryu," I said, still slightly distracted by Riker's presence.

"How exactly?" Ebony asked, her voice sounding small, probably still affected by the nightmarish ritual with Scarlett.

"I thought you knew," I said. After all our planning, we failed to cover what to do should the ritual go bad. We needed to act fast now while the ward around Ryu was at its thinnest to let us in.

"My father didn't tell me anything. I assumed you already knew since it's your stone!" Pixie-girl said, sounding irritated.

"You mean no one knows how to use the stone?" Blake said, summing it up for us to hear how ridiculous this whole thing was. Just then, a voice at the entrance of the cave claimed our attentions. We had been followed.

It was the last person we wanted to run into tonight. We all stopped what we were doing to stare, momentarily stunned to see Kione.

"Shame I wasn't invited to this little party of yours. You have something I've been looking a long time for," Kione said, placing one hand out to the side and resting it casually against the cave wall.

The Moonstone is what Kione was after? I realized he was blocking our only exit, and began to frantically look around. Ace had tested me over and over again, trying to get me to find another way during what I thought was a hopeless situation. *"There's always a way out of any situation, all you have to do is be smarter than the others..."* Ace's instructions came to mind. It was something he had told me often during our trainings. *Gods, I wished he were here right now!*

Blake took one step forward in Kione's direction, and when I reached out and grabbed him by the arm to stop him, I could feel his body trembling with the aspect of change, his instincts telling him to shift. Not wanting Blake to fight Kione I quickly said, "Sorry, members only." Our greatest strength against Kione would be in our numbers, three against one. If we separated, each trying our hand at Kione, he could pick us off one at a time. Blake and Ebony had never seen what Kione was truly capable of, the way I did. Even so, Kione was bound to have a few more tricks up his sleeves, a deeply unsettling thought.

Just like that, an idea formed when I remembered how there was an extra knife in the satchel Blake had around his shoulder. *If only I could get to the knife without Kione realizing what I was doing.*

"And how do I become a part of this surreptitious group?" he asked, dropping his hands from the side of the cave so he could take a step forward.

"Can't. We're very selective and I'm afraid you don't make the cut," I said, trying to keep him talking and distracted long enough to get the knife. I stepped closer to Blake so our shoulders were touching, his covering mine so most of my arm was behind him near his bag. To Kione it would like look I was trying to unite with Blake, staying close and staying safe. Slowly, and without Kione realizing, my hand reached up to the bag. I found the hilt of the knife, and slowly started to draw it up toward the top of the bag when Kione took another step closer.

Blake was growing nervous and showing it when he leaned his head closer to mine so he could speak quietly between his teeth. "Whatever you're planning, you better hurry, or I'm shifting."

Kione raised both eyebrows at whatever Blake whispered to me. "That is unlucky now, isn't it?" Kione said, feigning hurt feelings by dropping his head slightly and squishing his lips to the side for a brief moment.

"Shame," I agreed, voice deadpan, finally able to safely conceal the knife behind my back without Kione noticing.

He smiled, smart enough to catch the sarcasm in my tone. "I'll pretend you actually mean that," he said, calling me out. "On the bright side, of this poorly-lit cave I might add, I found something I think belongs to you." He pulled out a beautiful blade, *my* blade that Scarlett's greedy hands handled moments ago.

"You mean stolen from me. That's mine, give it to me now, Kione!" I took a small step toward Kione, anger driving me forward.

"I could trade this one for the one you're holding behind your back as part of a fair trade, what do you say?" he said, a spark of danger flashing in his eyes.

The color drained from my face realizing I hadn't fooled Kione for a second. "Give it to me," I warned, not letting him see my panic rising. We were running out of time. This was our only shot to free Abaddon.

"Gladly, all you have to do is come and get it," Kione said, waving my knife around in front of him, watching the way the candlelight caught hold of the citrine gems and created dancing prisms on the cave wall all around us.

"No, Dess, don't. He's trying to bait you," Blake said reaching out and grabbing my arm.

Of course he was baiting me! We all knew it, if the satisfied way his lips tugged up at the corners of his mouth were any indication. The ramifications if Kione misused my knife outweighed my determination not to show him how his taunting efforts affected me. My gaze never wavered from where Kione stood, even with Blake's firm grasp on me. I didn't have to look back at Blake to know how his eyes would look while he pleaded with me not to go.

Kione's smile grew, he knew he had me cornered. "It belongs to me, I need it," I said, jerking my arm out of Blake's grasp and walking to him. Abaddon would understand that keeping the powers of my knife from Kione was more important for the time being.

Abaddon would have done the same thing. We would have to find another way to free my brother.

Kione's eyes sparkled in delight having gotten his way."You've made a grand decision," he said. When I was within arms distance from him, and a glimmer of anticipation in his every demeanor said he was about to get everything he'd ever wanted, that he had finally won. It became crystal clear how his motives were painfully obvious all along; the reason why he always seemed so interested in me, in my thoughts, in what I was doing, all the praise he'd always given me even when we'd first met: it was me and my blooming powers he was really after this entire time.

Everything in my body, my mind, heart, and gut instincts, screamed at me to turn around, it's not too late to go back to Blake and Ebony and stay far, far away from Kione.

He held the butt of the knife out to me—an anxious energy to his whole demeanor furthered my suspicions about his intent with me. I reached my arm out at my knife, ready to grasp it in my open hand, never having the chance when something hit Kione from behind, knocking him out cold and dropping him to hard-packed dirt of the cave's floor.

The King of all the Pixies stood casually as though what he'd done to Kione were no big deal.

"What the heck is going on here?" Blake said, running up to where I stood over the top of Kione's unmoving form.

"Sorry I'm late," the Pixie King said. "Though it appears late is better than never."

"What are you doing here?" Ebony asked, catching up to us at the mouth of the cave.

"Lending a much needed hand, daughter," the Pixie King said.

When the Pixie King and Ebony bantered, I slowly bent down and retrieved my knife from Kione's unmoving hand before lifting up the corner of my shirt and sticking it safely under my belt, using it as a knife holster before pulling my shirt back down to conceal it.

Turning back to where Ebony and her father continued to argue about why the Pixie King was here in the first place, I watched as realization crossed Ebony's features. "You knew we would have to find a Moonstone in order to get to Abaddon, didn't you?" she accused her father. After all of Pixie-girl's help tonight, I'd started thinking of her by her name instead of the nickname I'd given her. Thinking she'd be gone and out of our lives by this point. Since it was obvious Ebony was becoming a part of our dysfunctional group, she deserved to be rid of the pet name.

"That's crazy. How would he know we'd be able to get our hands on one in the first place?" I jumped in with questions of my own.

"Oh, he would know," Ebony said, glaring daggers at her father.

"I gave you the answer you requested. It is not my fault you did not ask the question properly," the Pixie King said, addressing all of us with a smile before doing a little gleeful dance. "Besides, I've been watching your little dysfunctional group, and have seen how resourceful you can all be, when you want to. Call it a leap of faith if you will."

"Why withhold details? Wasn't all imperative information a part of your bargain with Ebony?" Blake said, not even the slightest amused by Ebony's father. Clearly, what the Pixie King had hoped to get as a reaction from us.

"No, son, not withhold, I simply did not include you in this part of the plan, and if you recall, only promised to tell where and *how* to free the Destroyer," he said, correcting Blake. I could tell Ebony did not appreciate her father referring to the loose term of "son" for Blake. "I never promised to show you how to use this." he said, holding up the Moonstone between his pointer-finger and thumb.

Mine and Blake's gaze immediately went to Ebony who was patting her pockets, refusing to believe her father had somehow gotten his hands on the Moonstone. "You're right, you didn't say you would show us how to use the Moonstone, but you forget that I know how to word things in my favor too, father, and if you do not fulfill your end of the deal by making sure Dess actually frees Abaddon then I do not have to fulfill my promise either. Our agreement would then become void." Ebony spoke with a confidence I've never heard from her before.

All traces of joy disappeared from the Pixie King. Ebony did know how to play her father's game too. He looked unhappy when he said, "Indeed, and so I shall have to show you." Ebony held her chin high, not satisfied quite yet until he fulfilled his promise.

Holding the stone in his hands, he began to leisurely walk around the three of us, stepping over Kione in the process. I wondered how long we had before Kione would awaken, undoubtedly angry. "Did you know Moonstones are the most timeless pieces of magic? Severely undervalued in my opinion," the Pixie King went off saying.

"I don't care about your opinions, father, get to the point."

"Fair enough, daughter, though what I am about to tell you may come in useful someday. I suggest you pay close attention." He looked at all of us. "There are many types of Moonstones in many colors: Yellow, Blue-Cats-Eye, White, Peach, and my favorite, this Gray one, though if you look closely you can see every color of the rainbow in its depth."

"What's so special about the Gray one?" Blake blurted out, his love of knowledge taking over.

"That, boy, is the correct question," the Pixie King said proudly. Even I was starting to get uncomfortable with the fatherly term he kept using for Blake. "What sets this stone apart from the others? This one is a Travelers Stone, specific for moving persons, or things, into unseen realms."

"So now you're going to show us how it works, right?" I asked, cutting to the chase.

Moving slowly toward the farthest edge of the cave where the candles were lit, he continued, "If you look closely, you'll see how each Moonstone has a silvery-white reflection within running in a thin light, how clearly you see it depends on the light used." Once he was in front of the candles, he held out the stone and ran fingers across the surface, following the thin line. "That's called the Chatoyancy."

Light used? "It needs some special light to work?" I said, trying to understand. That made sense since its magic was derived from the moon's amber glow.

"Close, but you don't take the cake, my dear," he said, and then picked up one of the candles. "It doesn't need a special light to work. It simply needs direct contact with the light source." He tipped the candle toward the stone and while raising the stone upward, he touched the flame of the candle onto the stone's smooth surface.

The stone glowed from the inside out, lighting up in the palm of his hand. I could actually see the thin line he had mentioned, the *Chatoy, something*. "Now what?" I asked.

"Now each of you must hold the stone if you all wish to go."

"That's it?" I asked, not believing it was as simple as that.

"That's all. You must remember to think about the place you wish to be, and the person you wish to see for you to be taken there," the Pixie King said, walking over to me, encompassing the stone in his hands carefully before passing it over to me.

I held it gently in cupped hands. "Okay, it's time," I said to Ebony and Blake. Together they walked over to me. Blake was the first to put his hand on top of the stone, followed by a hesitant Pixie-girl. Ever since we were kids he'd always dove right in with me, no matter how crazy Blake thought any of my plans were; if I was there, Blake would be right there beside me. A luxury I took for granted.

Not sure what I had been expecting to happen, but it definitely wasn't a feeling of being electrocuted. At first it was a slight shocking sensation entering through my fingertips, followed by a humming sound, both only growing more intense the harder I thought about Abe and Ryu. Don't lose the Moonstone. It's your only way back!" the Pixie King's voice said from somewhere far away before we left our world and entered into Ryu, or at least I thought it was Ryu. It looked different than my imaginings and far worse than anything my mind could have conjured.

"Abe, we have to go find Abe!" I said, having to yell over the strong wind that was all around us. It was hard to see, and hard to hear. Finding Abaddon in this seemed damn near impossible. *And just when I thought we were so close too!*

CHAPTER NINETEEN

Caged Animal

"**I** can't see where we're going!" Blake yelled back at me.

"Me either!" I exclaimed, unsure of which direction to respond to Blake in, while taking a shaky step forward before losing my balance. This part of Ryu was surrounded by strong gusts of winds and some kind of fog or mist obscuring our vision. It was probably meant to deter others from entering, and possibly even meant to keep Ryu occupants from leaving.

Reaching out with both hands, I quickly grabbed hold of the first thing they touched. Lucky for me it felt like a rope lining a rickety bridge.

Carefully, while still holding on to the rope, I looked over the side of the edge, and couldn't see the bottom below us, no surprise there. The bridge was disorienting, and the constant swaying motion was making my stomach feel sick.

"There's got to be a better way!" Ebony called out. It became painfully obvious that if we continued on the bridge we weren't going to make it very far, and decided to try our luck with the Moonstone again. It was a Travelers Stone, so it had to be able to take us some place different. After deciding it was worth a try, I turned blindly around toward the direction of Blake's voice. "I'm going to try and use the stone again!" I yelled back.

Pulling the stone out of my pocket with one hand, careful to keep the other tightly on the rope for balance, I faltered. "Damn."

"We need a light," I thought I heard Blake say.

"Dessi," I heard Ebony call my name.

"I can't see anything," I yelled back to her.

"I know," she said. Her voice sounded closer, making her way toward me. "I have a light," Ebony yelled again, this time so close I bumped into her after taking a small step forward. The bridge swayed, and we almost lost our balance, struggling to find our footing and hold onto the rope, and for me, to hold onto the Moonstone. When the rocking dulled, Ebony shoved something small and rectangle-shaped into the palm of my hand. A shape I immediately recognized as a lighter. I was so relieved I could cry. Ebony must have stuck it in her pocket after lighting the candles in the cave. After waiting for Blake to get closer to us, I pressed the small flickering light against the surface of the stone.

It was the same electric shock as last time, starting in our fingers before snaking through our entire bodies. And as before, I pictured Abaddon, concentrating harder on what he looked like. This time envisioning him with more facial hair, maybe even a bit thinner after all this time he'd spent in Ryu. One moment we were standing in the wind and fog, and in the next, we were completely encased in darkness.

Well this is great, I thought cynically.

All three of us remained silent while trying to find our bearings. It was hard to say where we were, and most importantly, who we might have been there with.

"Blake?" I asked, in a low whisper.

"Yeah, I'm here," Blake whispered back. "Ebony?" he asked, feeling around with his hands, accidently catching his finger in my hair, not meaning to pull it.

"No, still me," I told Blake.

"Riker the Great Havoc can see," Riker said from somewhere nearby, reminding me I'd brought an evil spirit along to Ryu with us. I took a moment to thank the Gods he hadn't pushed me off the rickety bridge earlier, and then wondered why he hadn't since it seemed the perfect opportunity to be rid of me. Maybe it had something to do with our binding spell bond or something. "When I find you I'm going to—" he began to say when I shushed him, stopping whatever nauseating statement he was about to make about my impending death. He'd already unknowingly proved he couldn't do any real damage to me without probably damaging himself in the process, possibly chance staying in this state of limbo forever if he killed me.

"Go away!" I told Riker a little too loudly, afraid he'd scratch me again or try something worse. Maybe it had something to do with being in the dark and having other senses turned off, but I could feel something that wasn't there before; like an invisible string connecting me to Riker and the Underworld. When I'd banished him just now, I could feel a slight tug on our connection, letting me know he was no longer in this world with me.

"What did you say?" Blake asked.

"Nothing." *Oops.*

"Ebony?" Blake called again, this time a little louder.

"I'm over here," Ebony called from somewhere a little further away.

When I heard Blake's body start to make shuffling sounds, I quickly reached out and held onto him by his shirt, since it was the first thing I could feel. "Are you crazy? We need to stay together or we'll all be lost," I told him.

"That's probably a smart idea," he agreed. "Come on then, let's go find Ebony, and keep holding onto me." He began walking. While he led us through the dark, I reached my hand out and let it graze what felt like a stone or rock wall. We were probably in some kind of hallway.

"Blake?" Ebony said in a hushed voice.

"Ebony," Blake called back to her.

"You know, this is starting to remind me of playing Marco Polo in the pool," I said, poignantly.

"I think I hear something up ahead," he said, shushing me.

"Hey what if I just—"

"Shhh," he said again, and then stopped walking, which meant so did I. We both remained quiet, listening to what sounded like feet scuffing along the ground, getting louder the closer it got to us. Blake's whole body tensed, ready for whatever was ahead, and I felt the ripple of change read beneath my touch. They were close enough we could hear their breathing. Blake reached his arm back, wrapping it behind me in a protective stance, grabbing onto my waist as a result. I wasn't sure if he'd meant to do that or not, but there it was, his hand wrapped around my waist. It was probably just the dark but I was pretty sure Blake had never held me so close before, possible danger ahead or not.

Since Blake wasn't going to listen to me, I decided to take matters into my own hand. A little concentration on my part, and I was able to create two beautiful winged fire-creatures, putting off enough of the blue-hellfire's light we could see as Ebony strolled around the corner holding the lighter up in her hand. Ebony was using it as a mini torch.

Blake removed his arm from around my waist and went to her, hugging her.

"Did you see anything in that direction?" I asked her.

"Nothing promising," Ebony stated.

Turning to the right all I could see was a long, dark tunnel. It seemed to go on for quite a while. Everything was covered in black and gray stone. Turning to the left in the direction we'd found Ebony, all I could see was more of the same tunnel. "To the right it is."

We'd only gone about one hundred feet when I heard something up ahead. "Wait, do you hear that?" Not waiting for their answers continued to walk forward. I held the lighter out in front of me. "Did you see—" I started to ask.

"Yeah," Blake quickly said. "I'll go check it out."

Before he could take one step I interjected, "No, I'll go." Without a second thought, I walked away before he could argue.

Slowly, and while staying alert, I stalked toward where the light reflected. It could have been someone's torch or other light, which meant we were not alone in this tunnel. When I'd made it to the spot, I comprehended it wasn't one piece of metal catching light, it was a set of metal bars belonging to what appeared to be a mini cage-like holding cell of some kind.

Directing my two fire-creatures to come closer to the bars, I bent forward to have a better look, careful not to get too close. From what little I could see there weren't any occupants, and from the lack of breathing, or growling sounds, assumed nothing was in the cage. I began to relax some, and took one step closer so my face was right up to the bars. That was the first mistake I made.

Before I knew what was happening, something on the other side of the bars threw itself at me.

I flung myself back so it couldn't reach through the bars to grab at me, and landed on my back in the process. "I said get back beast!" it shouted at me, its voice sounding dry and raspy from either lack of water or from yelling too much. Whatever, or whoever, it was shook the bars wildly.

My breathing was accelerated from the adrenaline, and I could hear my heartbeat thudding inside my head. It was so loud it was deafening. Normally I would have reacted much faster, but I was frozen with the slightest possibility that it was him in there. I sat up and for the life of me, could not find my voice. It was obvious they'd been treating this person like some untamed animal, noticing the empty food bowl on the ground outside.

"Abe?" I finally managed to ask, having to repeat myself once again, louder this time so he could hear me.

All crazed movements from this person, this thing in there, quieted. I felt my eyes well with tears. The fact he wasn't throwing himself around like some animal, I could now clearly make out his disheveled features. It was him.

Abaddon was looking right at me, but wasn't saying anything. "Abe, it's me, Dess, um, your sister?" I said, as calmly as my excitement allowed.

"Desdemona?" he mumbled confused.

"Yeah, Abe, it's me. I'm here." I stuck one of my arms through the cage.

Abaddon jerked away before my hand could touch him. "It's okay, Abe, I've come to get you out of here." When he didn't move, an idea came to mind. With the hand holding the lighter, I brought it to my face so Abaddon could see me more clearly. "See, just me," I said.

Tears sprung to his eyes, followed by a look of relief. "I didn't think I would ever see you again," he said wearily, reaching his hand through the bars toward me. I didn't hesitate to take it, and then remembered I'd left Blake and Ebony a little ways down the hall.

"Hey, Abe, I need to go get Blake and Ebony, I'll be right back though," I promised him, reluctant to leave. He nodded in understanding and then relaxed back into a sitting position, appearing as though he was still trying to believe he'd actually seen me.

At the same time I turned to leave, I saw Abaddon shift his position spontaneously, a look of horror on his face when he called out to me, "Dess, look out!" he shouted. However, his warning was too late. Excruciating pain shot down my shoulder and collarbone when a hand reached out and struck me.

I screamed in pain, and heard Abaddon yell my name.

I managed to spin out of my attacker's hold, and in the process the lighter flew out of my hand. Another stabbing pain ran up my arm, it felt like someone's sharp claws were jabbing into me. I flung my leg out and kicked at it, hearing the grunt they made as the air whooshed out of them.

"Where are you, Dess!" Blake screamed.

"No, Blake, go back!" I said, not knowing what it was, or how many of them there were. *If I could find the lighter, the Moonstone could get us all out of here.*

"Dessi, get down!" I head Blake's voice echo from down the tunnel, warning me he was going to change, but I never had the chance when the thing I'd knocked down recovered, its hands wrapped around both of my ankles. Before I had time to scream, the creature jerked me away from

Abaddon in his cage and dragged me off before Blake could make it in time.

"Abaddon!" I screamed out while being dragged though the pitch-black tunnels.

* * * *

Somewhere along the way I must have hit my head hard enough to pass out, because the last thing I remembered was being dragged on my stomach, my fingers digging into the ground in my futile attempt to escape.

I woke up lying on my back in some place dimly lit. My mind was in a jumbled haze, unable to comprehend anything my eyes focused on for several breaths. Simple objects around me weren't making sense when at last I'd remembered being in a dark tunnel: things like the tall lamp in the corner, or what looked like the bottom of a leather sofa, or this cold marble flooring I laid on…I tried to sit up to make sense of things, only to lay back down when my head throbbed in pain.

"I wouldn't try to do that quite yet if I were you. You took a fairly vicious smash to your head," a male's voice said from somewhere above me.

Instinctively, my hand went up to my head to locate the source of the throbbing pain, wincing when my fingers found the tender spot on the back of my head above my ear. Pulling my hand back from the wound to look at it, I saw a patch of red staining my fingers. I wasn't exactly sure why I thought of this particular memory at the moment, but something about seeing my fingers colored crimson made me think of finger-painting when I was six years old and I'd gotten in trouble for painting a mural on the wall instead of on the paper in front of me. I remembered it was a picture of Abaddon and me flying over the ocean, and I'd given Abe a pair of magnificent red wings, drawing myself riding on his back. It was a silly painting, and a trivial memory to have right then. Somehow, it fueled my earlier determination to find Abe and get out of there.

"Where am I?" I asked, and immediately sucked in a sharp gasp in pain. My eyes were closed at first in order to help get past the overwhelming urge to vomit from the dizziness. Once it subsided some, though not completely, I opened my eyes and found a man standing in front of me wearing…*wait, was he wearing a dress?* A little voice in the back of my head corrected my thought and placed the term toga instead. I found it humorous how even with a head wound my cynicism never waned.

"You are in my command, the place I use to keep a close watch over the happenings of Ryu. What I'm interested to know, is how an unfortunate young girl managed to find her way here in the first place?"

"It wasn't easy," I said. "And I'm not a little girl."

This awarded me a laugh. "I've seemed to insult you, not my intentions. It is not every day we have a blossoming female amongst us, and no, I don't imagine it was." He stood from where he sat on the couch before walking over to me and extended a hand out meant for me to take.

I ignored his hand, not liking the way he spoke of about having a female in his midst, or the way the two guards next to him widened their eyes while looking down at me, and tried to stand on my own, feeling the need to puke. Eventually I managed to stand on my own.

He cocked his head to the side, giving me a strange look as though he were trying to decide something. He looked familiar, though I was certain we'd never met. He resembled someone else I knew, someone with the same sleek, black hair, golden brown skin, and slight body frame. After a few more seconds appraising him, I remembered who he reminded me of. Osiris, ruler of the Underworld.

Instead of having shoulder length hair as Osiris, he wore his short, and where Osiris' eyes were as rich as dark opals, his were the same blue as Lapis-Lazuli gemstones.

"You have something of mine, and I came to get it back," I said, not seeing the point in wasting time getting to know one another.

"What could we possibly have of yours that you would feel the need to risk your life to come and retrieve?" he asked, curiosity peaking.

"Release my brother Abaddon or I swear to the Gods you'll live to regret it!" I demanded.

His face conveyed understanding as all the pieces clicked together. "Ah yes, Abaddon. One of our finest guests," he said, sounding amused though his expression said he was anything but amused by Abaddon.

And I hoped by the tone he used, meant Abaddon had been making things hectic for him.

"Do you treat all of your guests like animals, Seth?" I asked, remembering at the last second the name I'd learned belonged to Osiris' brother. My lips sneered up in hate toward this man, this monster responsible for my Abaddon's somnolent state.

All traces of the feigned generosity vanished, replaced by a darker, more sinister mannerism. "I'm very busy and do not have the time nor patience to deal with children." He waved his hand out at me dismissively. "Your brother cannot evade his fate here, and it's a shame we have to kill unwanted vermin who show up uninvited in Ryu, female or not. Sorry, but rules are rules. If we let them slip one time, everyone will want to, and I cannot have chaos where it does not suit me." Seth didn't sound the slightest apologetic, in fact, he seemed mistakenly unworried by my presence.

Baring my teeth in a vicious smile, I said, "And it's a shame I'll have to kill you first. Sorry, it's my own rules I have to follow, but like you said, rules are rules." Seth's nonchalant face turned an angry shade of red.

Taking a step forward, I called out to further catch Seth and his guards unaware, "Riker, I may need you," I said, feeling the vibrations within the invisible string connecting the two of us, even though there was nothing he could do. Riker arrived in time for Seth to beckon to one of his Ryu guards, and with a snap of his fingers, a swarm of monsters answered his call.

One creature of every shape, size, and make, showed up in chains to keep them from wreaking havoc around the large expanse of the room.

Their eyes widened in excitement upon seeing me, some bared teeth while others growled or stomped their hooves or feet anxiously.

Perfect night this was turning out to be.

CHAPTER TWENTY

The Destroyer

I imagined the thread between Riker and I was similar to a guitar's string connecting to the air molecules that produce the high frequency of sound. At first, he was wearing an infuriated look on his face for being interrupted, though I highly doubted he was living it up in the Underworld. Once he saw me in my predicament, his look turned to one of delight.

"What is this, what have you done?" Seth asked. He felt I was enough of a threat that he stumbled back nearly losing his footing.

"Wait, you can see him?" I asked dubiously.

"Of course I can see that-that repulsive thing you've brought into my realm. Do you not know what you have done, child? You have thrown off the balance of the Underworld and all the creatures who inhabit it." He promptly gestured at one of his guards. "Banish them," he ordered. "Wait, stop. I have a better idea. Take this one to the pits first. I want her to watch when we execute the mighty Destroyer." The creatures around Seth growled and snorted in complaint, wanting to have had their chance to get to me.

"None of your monsters are greater than my brother. They'll never defeat him. Abaddon's going to kill you, and I'm going to help." The guards pulled my arms behind me. I didn't bother to struggle deciding to save my strength, clearly outnumbered. Looking at his guards and the way their eyes glowed a molten gold, whatever was beneath the armor, they weren't any creatures I'd encountered before.

He wasn't anything like Osiris I decided. Osiris wasn't *just* ruler and keeper of the Underworld—he acted like a God and held pride in his ruling by keeping order. It was clear Seth was only out for himself.

"Oh there are other ways to break someone. After all, with Abaddon gone, I'll need someone to replace him." His eyes lit up in excitement by this prospect.

"You're a monster!" I screamed, kicking and fighting to no use. "Why don't you just kill me yourself. One on one, what do you say, or are you a coward?" I asked before the guards could lead me away. "Or are you afraid you'd lose to a little girl?"

"I admire your energy, but if I were you, I'd try and save some of your strength. You'll be needing it," he said, with some hidden significant meaning I wasn't getting.

"There's only one fault in your plan." Abaddon's voice sounded from the entrance of Seth's headquarters, as he'd called it. "If you want her, you'll have to go through me first."

"Abe!" I whipped my head back to look at Seth with a vicious smile on my face.

Seth's face paled at seeing Abaddon unchained and in his headquarters. That's when I realized Seth really was a coward. He would not be able to beat Abaddon, or even myself in a fight.

"Riker, kill them," I ordered the evil spirit by nodding my head over at Seth and his guards. Riker glowered over at where the guards had me bound, but because of the power over him, he had no choice but obey. Riker looked like he was being dragged across the room by an indiscernible force toward the guards; it was either fight or die, forever this time. The keeper of Ryu let out a disgruntled scream and grabbed a sword out of one guard's hands before hiding behind the rest. Abaddon didn't have time to ask questions because after the one simple command I'd given, Seth's guards closed in.

Abaddon strode into the room, his sword in his hands and a new purpose moving him as he went for the guards containing me. I ducked in time for Abaddon to deal with the two guards who held me. Once released, I turned to Abaddon briefly, and said, "It took you long enough."

"Sorry," he said, kicking out at one guard while slicing through the armor of another, "I had to make a quick stop." He held his sword up at me. We didn't have time for me to ask where he found it or if he'd seen the others, Blake and Ebony, before we were swarmed by another group of guards.

"There's too many," I said, maneuvering away from a guard's fatal blow before spinning around and kicking out at him, knocking him back and buying me time to summon hellfire to throw at him. He flailed around, trying and failing to remove the iron mask he wore before he burned to death.

"I might be able to help, how does one super tough Hellhound as reinforcement sound?" Ebony said. I gave her a wide-eyed look of surprise, grateful for her when a massive Hellhound with razor sharp canines, and blue and orange flames scorching down his back, jumped out over several guards' heads, before landing in front of them, tearing them to shreds in a matter of seconds. Ebony had brought Blake as the reinforcement.

All I could do was smile over at her before falling into routine behind them, all of my training from over the past few months resurfacing in my mind. My new main focus was on protecting Ebony, since whether any one liked it or not, she was less skilled in combat, though proving herself efficient on more than one occasion, all while trying to keep an eye out for Seth. Where was Seth, he seemed to have disappeared miraculously fast, I thought while setting another guard on fire.

While we fought I couldn't help sneaking a few peeks over to where Abaddon fought with a vigor and vengeance I'd never seen him do before. Granted, I'd only ever seen him fight once before. He was magnificent to behold, his brute strength, his speed, all of it. However, worry also struck me with his reprisal; he looked thinner now and had dark circles under his eyes. I wondered what they'd put him through here, using this thought to anger and fuel me further in fighting.

These guards were strong, and also fast. Really fast, and proved difficult to overthrow. Difficult, but not impossible, especially with our team of Hellions. When one of the guards came at me holding a strange looking staff with a metal ball covered in lethal spikes, I thought maybe I was in trouble. Hellfire didn't work on this guard either. He seemed much larger than the others, but its molten-gold reptilian-eyes the same as the others told me was the same creature, only behemoth sized. He managed to knock me back when I'd dodged the spikes, taking a kick to my side. I went down hard, landing on my shoulder which still hurt from the thing that got me in the tunnel. Looking to Blake for help did no good. He was too busy tearing into one of the guard's throat still in Hellhound form.

I was on my own.

I tried to get up, but couldn't move yet. I needed a moment to recover. A moment I unfortunately did not have. Right before the guard almost smashed my face with this spiked club, I called out, "Riker, stop him!" My shouting distracted the guard for a split-second, long enough for Riker to appear before him and rip through his armor and take his heart right out of his chest.

That was disturbing, I thought, rolling onto my knees in a feline position before finding my feet to stand. "Thanks," I told Riker, not expecting him to care, so it was no surprise when he turned to hiss at me.

I stood dizzily, searching through the chaos for Ebony, spotting her crouched down beside a large bookcase trying to go unnoticed. On my way to her, Abaddon reached out and grabbed my arm, nearly getting punched in the face until I recognized him. "Seth, have you seen him?" he shouted.

"No," I said, catching the fiery glare in his eyes. It was the same look I gave Kione every time I saw him. It was clear he wanted to make Seth pay.

We'll see who gets to him first.

"If you see him, he's mine," Abaddon said, confirming what I'd thought.

"Where's Ebony?" Blake asked, standing next to me. He changed back to his normal form when everything was under control here.

"There," I said, pointing toward the bookcase at her. "Do you have Ebony?" I wanted to go find Seth before Abaddon did, and now was as good a time as any. "Yes, go," Blake told me sensing the urgency. I left him with her and rushed to find Seth.

I'd only made it as far as the door, when out of the corner of my eye something bone-white and quick, as in shooting star, flashed in my peripheral vision. Spinning back around, I saw Blake fighting off one last guard and War's pet Vampire lunging for Ebony. Blake had shifted back too soon. I ran, springing back toward Ebony, already too late. War's pet had his bony-white hands wrapped around her neck while she struggled for him to release her, his bared teeth dangerously close to her neck.

Blake let out a long, meaningful whimper in human form. War's Vampire teeth mere inches away from her jugular, cautioning for me to not come any closer.

"Let her go," I warned him.

"Don't come any closssserrr," it hissed, squeezing Ebony's neck tighter with his arm. My eyes went to the arm holding her, noticing the long, and particularly sharp fingernails on his pasty fingers and abruptly I knew what, or *who* actually, had grabbed me in the tunnel. War and Seth were obviously working together. *Why?*

"If you don't want me to come closer, then let her go."

His answer was to spit at me, which was its first mistake; his second was turning his head and bared fangs toward Ebony's throat. I lunged forward, making it over to the Vampire faster than I should have been able to, and grabbed the revolting pest by the neck, twisting as hard and fast as I could. Its neck broke before it fell to the ground, releasing Ebony in the process.

"Thanks," Ebony tried choking out, her voice sounding raspy and winded. My mind was racing with what I'd done, and how I'd done it. War's pet Vampire was the first creature I'd ever killed in real life, and not just a simulation training, not counting all the hellfire I'd used to wound guards so Abaddon or Blake could finish them off. All the training in the world, or anything Ace had ever told me couldn't have prepared me for it. Even though War's pet was a malevolent monster, I still felt like puking for being the one to kill it.

"Uh, yeah sure, no problem," I said dizzily. War was not going to be happy about her pet getting defiled the way it had been. Thinking about War would have to wait until another time. I turned back toward the room, peeling my eyes off the lifeless Vampire.

Blake finished off the guard he'd been working on and ran over to where Ebony and I stood. "You okay?" he asked her. Ebony nodded while rubbing at the tender spot on her neck already starting to bruise.

Making sure there were no more guards hiding anywhere, I left to go find Abaddon, hoping I wasn't too late.

As soon as I stepped outside the room, Seth's cries as he pleaded for his life could be heard. Running out of the room I veered toward the left, and found Abaddon standing over Seth with his sword pointed firmly against his throat. Blood seeped the blade.

"No, I won't kill you. I've done enough killing *for* you, and killing you now would be far too lenient a punishment for what you deserve," he said scathingly.

It all made sense now. Abaddon had been forced to battle, forced to kill in cold blood. It explained everything.

"I was only helping you do what you've always done, what you were made to do. Killing monsters is what you do, is it not?" Seth asked brazenly, stupid of him since Abaddon had a sword aimed at his neck.

Abaddon leaned in and pushed the sword ever so slightly, enough to see Seth squirm on his knees, fear apparent on his face.

I ran forward and clutched Abaddon's wrist holding the sword. "Stop, Abe, you don't have to kill him. Think about what you're doing, what will happen if you kill him?" I said gently, trying to talk some sense into him.

But he wasn't hearing me, "He'll be gone if I kill him. He'll be thrown out of existence unable to plague anyone ever again. He deserves no mercy," Abaddon said through clenched teeth, his jaw muscles flexing.

It was probably true, but I didn't think telling Abe as much would help him now.

"I know you, Abe, I know you don't like to kill, and I know you will only punish yourself for it later. Seth is not worth it, Abe, he's not worth it," I said, feeling tears spring in my eyes wanting so much to help my brother, and free him from himself and all his sadness.

"You don't know the things he made me do," Abaddon said, his gaze remaining dully focused on Seth.

"None of that matters now. If you want to let him go you can. We can go home, Abe, you don't have to kill anymore."

"Home?" he repeated the word as though the meaning didn't quite fit in his vocabulary.

"Yes, home, with me."

Abaddon looked hopeful for a moment, before trying to shove me away. "The things I've done…I'm a monster," he said, and I had a feeling he wasn't talking about whatever it was Seth had made him do.

Turning my body to Abaddon allowed him to see my face. Pain he felt within showed on his, making me remember the first time I'd ever used the Fountain of the Lost and saw Abaddon fighting creatures of hell who escaped and were set on torturing the human world. But Abe wouldn't let them, and stopped them before they could wreak havoc. It came at a price though, some of Abaddon's humanity, (which was in us all, even Hellions and the most sinister creatures were capable of finding their humanity). Every kill haunted him.

"You are not a monster."

"You don't know what I've done," Abaddon said sadly.

"Listen to the Destroyer, I've seen what he's capable of," Seth said, struggling to get the words out.

Letting go of Abaddon's wrist, I turned and slowly walked over to Seth, bending down so my face was directly in front of his, and punched him.

I punched him as hard as I could in the face, and then once more when he said what was supposed to be an insult, "A family trait, it seems." He smiled up at me.

"Thanks for the compliment," I told him right before he passed out.

Dusting my hands as though I could brush off this whole night, I straightened up and turned back around, holding my hand to my chest tightly. I hadn't quite perfected the punch it seems. Abaddon did not look happy with me, nor did he look angry. Mainly he looked tired, tired of it all.

Blake and Ebony were also standing there beside Abe and I wondered how much they'd seen or heard. It took some convincing for Abaddon to put down his sword. "Let's get out of here?" I said, breathing a sigh of relief.

"You don't need to ask me twice," Ebony said from beside Blake.

"Are you ready for what awaits us?" I asked Abaddon.

Abaddon sighed, wrapping one arm around my shoulder. "Come on, little Starr is it? Let's get out of this Hell hole." He winked at me.

Taking the Moonstone out of my pocket and placing it in my open hand, I used the other hand to summon a small blue-flame.

"The Travelers Stone," Abaddon whispered in understanding. "Do I even want to know how you managed to get your hand on one of those?" He turned a concerned look down on me.

"No," I told him, holding my hand out for the others to gather around.

Picturing the Morning Star Institute wouldn't work since Abaddon would not be a welcomed guest, instead thought up the safest place I know. Our mother's garden. Images of blossoming roses in all sizes and colors filled my mind as did the lion-head fountains, and felt the effects of the stone start to take place. Hopefully it worked and took us to my last thought and didn't land us in the middle of the Institute.

At the last second, I thought about warning Abaddon about the electric shock, ultimately deciding he'd survived worse, and could undoubtedly handle a little zap.

It worked because the next thing I knew, botanical bliss filled my senses. Before I could see our surroundings, I heard water steadily streaming from one of the nearby lion-heads.

One quick glance around told me we were all there and accounted for. Good, I thought. But we weren't alone.

"Hello again," the Pixie King said. "I see you've all made it back, and in one piece. What a lovely surprise," he said, eyes stopping on Ebony who was his main focus, and I wondered if he was here to collect his debt.

"What's he doing here?" Abaddon said, unaware of his helping hand in his rescue.

"He's here for me," Ebony spoke up, coming out from behind Blake's protective stance.

"Yes, well that's not entirely true," he said, walking leisurely through our mother's garden, stopping to smell a rose, like he had all the time in the world.

"What else is there?" Ebony asked, confused.

"You'll be happy to know that I have taken it upon myself to make arrangements for our little fugitive here. I have an unsuspecting place for him to stay," he said while eyeballing Abaddon.

This time it was my turn to speak, "Why would you do this for Abaddon? What's in it for you?" I had a notion he wouldn't do this out of the goodness of his heart.

"Because," he began to say, turning toward me with his hands clasped behind his back, "I know my daughter here,"—he looked back at Ebony

—"would be much happier if she knew her friends were taken care of first before fulfilling the promise made to me."

"What exactly did you have in mind?" Ebony asked, sounding unsure.

"What I would like to know is if he can be trusted," Abaddon quickly chimed in, crossing his arms over his chest.

I thought about it for a brief moment before I answered, "No, but what choice do we have?"

"Fine. You can take us there. When I do go with you, you'll need to do me one more favor," Ebony said. I could tell by the look on Blake's face this was the first time he was hearing about Ebony going anywhere. Ebony never told him about the deal they made, I realized, frowning.

The Pixie King looked abashed to hear Ebony making a request. Too curious, he could not deny her the opportunity to ask, "I'm listening?" he said.

"Allow me to stay until after the dance." Ebony glanced sadly over at Blake.

The Pixie King laughed at her absurd request, clearly catching him by surprise. "Fine, though no later. We do not have much time. Word of Abaddon's escape has already circulated. We need to depart now."

Turning to Abaddon, I hugged him as hard as possible. "I'll see you soon," he whispered in my ear, and then walked over to the Pixie King. Before they left he turned back to look at me and said, "Hey, Dess."

"Huh?" I asked.

"Thanks for rescuing me," he said around a wink.

"You'd have done the same." I smiled. And as before, one second the Pixie King was here doing oddball Pixie-stuff, and in the next he had vanished into thin air with Abaddon at his side, leaving a trail of pixie dust in his wake.

CHAPTER TWENTY-ONE

One Perfect Night

After leaving the garden, I practically dragged myself to my room to seek out some much needed sleep after the exciting night we'd had.

Looking up at where the pre-lit dawn filtered through the windows at the top of the hallway on my way there, I had to squint against the headache the light caused.

I'd made it to my room to find Ace sitting on the floor with his back against the door. At first I wasn't sure my weary mind wasn't conjuring an image of him. After seeing the exhausted look on his face mimicking my own, I knew he was real. "Ace, hi, what are you doing here?" It was early for him to be up let alone waiting for me at my room.

Ace stood. "I came by after my assessment but you weren't here, or anywhere else I went searching," he said. *Oh Gods, his assessment was last night, and I'd missed it. Damn.*

"I completely forgot, I am so sorry. I swear I didn't mean to," I quickly told him, feeling terrible for missing the most important day of his life.

His mouth opened and then closed again, wanting to say something, and changing his mind. "I guess it doesn't really matter." He brushed off my apology, making me feel even worse. "It seems I'm the one who missed your big day. Don't take this the wrong way, Dess, but you look like the creature who possessed you," Ace said, taking in my appearance for the first time since seeing me.

I held my arms out for me to examine, and noticed the dirt, blood, and something else I didn't recognize, covering my hands and arms. I laughed. "Yeah, I guess I probably do. It's sort of been a long night, and actually I should probably go take a shower," I said, pointing at my room.

Ace blocked the door, not letting me pass, his eyes further scrutinizing me as everything began clicking into place for him. I huffed annoyed, already feeling on edge with everything else. "Is this really necessary?"

"Shit. You did it, didn't you?" Ace asked, eyes wide, waiting my response. I didn't have to question what *it* meant to know he was talking about rescuing Abaddon.

"Yes, now shhh, keep your voice down," I quickly told him, glancing about, making sure no one was around to hear. An infuriated look rippled across his face, making the muscles in his jaw clench and unclench.

He took a deep breath and then released his arms down to his sides from where they'd been tightly crossed over his chest. "How did you do it?"

"We shouldn't talk out here." I bit my bottom lip nervously.

"Okay, let's go inside." He reached one hand behind him and opened the door, not taking no for an answer.

"Fine," I said, walking past Ace, inside my room and immediately eyeballed my bed affectionately. "I'll tell you everything, but first things first." I walked over to my bed and all but threw myself down on top of my covers, stomach first, letting the down-filled comforter swallow me whole. "Like lying on a cloud," I said lovingly.

"Okay, let's talk," Ace said, disrupting my moment.

I exhaled loudly before sitting back up to face him. "It was amazing, Ace, I mean it was completely terrifying, and it looked pretty hopeless at times, but we did it, we found him," I said, dreamily with the memory, and then started at the very beginning with Ebony's brilliant performance during the ritual, speeding through the part about Kione following us back to the cave. Then I told him about what a nightmare Ryu and Seth had been, voicing my concern about War and her pet's involvement, before finally getting to the part where the Pixie King left with Abaddon after meeting all of us in my mother's garden.

Ace did not respond the way I'd been expecting; he wasn't impressed, or relieved at all. "You could have been killed, do you get that? Why didn't you wait for me, I could have helped?" he asked angrily.

"We survived, why are you getting so angry?" I said, unable to keep the annoyance out of my voice with Ace's dismissing demeanor. I stood up off my bed.

Ace stepped closer, putting us only a few inches apart. His hand reached out to the side of my face, his fingers curling behind one ear as he tucked hair behind it. My eyes closed naturally, enjoying the comforting feeling of his hand on the side of my face, leaning in further. "I'm not angry, I care about you, so please don't go running off again somewhere so dangerous, not without first telling me so I can at least try to stop you, or join you since you probably wouldn't listen to me anyway," he said, sounding exhausted.

Exhaling heavily, I forced myself to let it all go, deciding he had a right to be worried about me, after all if the situation were reversed, and he did something reckless without me, I'd be upset too. "I really am sorry I missed your big assessment."

"I wished you could have seen it," Ace said, his eyes crinkling with excitement.

"Me too. I bet you were amazing to watch."

He smiled at me. "Yeah well, it's all over with now, for *both* of us."

"Yeah, I guess you're right." *Except for figuring out what happens next with Abaddon, or Kione, since it was clear Kione was after more than just ruining my brother's life, showing way too much interest in me.* We'd have plenty of time to go over everything tomorrow.

After a very hot, much needed shower, I all but collapsed back down on my bed.

"We can move forward now, with us I mean," Ace said, reminding my tired mind he was still here in my room, dragging my thoughts away from everything we still had to figure out, and back to him.

"Hmm?" I asked tiredly, forcing my eyelids to stay open.

"Promise me no matter what happens; whether I passed Hell's guardian test and they offer me a spot here at the M.S.I, or not, we'll figure it out together." He sounded more earnest and pleading than I'd ever heard him speak before. It told me how much he meant it, how much we wanted for us to finally be together.

Watching Ace stand in front of my bed looking down at me with deep, pleading eyes, and his heart on his sleeve, there was only one answer I could give him.

"Yes, I promise, whatever happens, we do it together." I sat up onto my knees where I half-crawled half-walked on my knees over to the edge of the bed. He met me the rest of the way, reaching his arms out toward me at the exact same time I reached for him. Both of our arms wrapped around each other, drawing our bodies together as close as possible. Our lips met swiftly, but the kiss was not one filled with rushed movements. Instead it was slow and gentle, giving us the false sense we had all the time in the world together. I could feel his heart beating against my chest. It too matched our kiss—steady and controlled, and completely content.

When the kiss ended, we both breathed a happy sigh before sitting on the bed next to each other. Leaning my head over onto his arm, I asked a question I'd been thinking since we returned from Ryu. "What do you think is going to happen when Apollyon finds out Abaddon is not in Ryu?"

Wrapping one arm around me, leaning his head on top of mine, he said, "I'm not sure. All that matters is I'll be there this time,"—and then kissed the top of my head.

"Yeah, you're right. Things are a little easier with you around," I admitted. "Mostly when you're in your big, bad slobbery Hellhound form." I laughed.

"Very funny. Gods, I love you, Dess!" He nearly made me choke on the air I was breathing. It was the second time Ace had ever told me he loved me, and this time we weren't in the middle of fighting or taking a break from each other. When I was rendered speechless he went on to say, "The way I felt today after acing my final test is nothing compared to you. The way I feel when I'm with you."

"I can't believe you just said 'acing'," I said in response, mostly because what he'd said made my heart do crazy things inside my chest. Ace telling me he loved me made me think of something else. "You still want to be with me, even after knowing how I could be in some serious trouble if anyone finds out it was me who freed Abaddon. Even after knowing I'm some ticking time bomb who not only sees ghosts, but has a ghost set on tormenting me?"

He looked down at me like my question caught him off guard. He quickly recovered, smiling when he said, "Believe me, little Starr, it's still a mystery to me too most days." He grinned. "You're the one constant thing in my life, and certain I will always need you."

All of a sudden, all was right in this messed up, malicious world we lived in again.

"So wait a second. Remember how you said you wanted to be together again, no matter what we'd be there for each other?" I asked, thinking about something he'd said earlier.

"Yeah, I remember," he said carefully, knowing I was up to something.

"If that's true, we need to be together again, and I mean all the way, no more of this halfway-business."

Ace's eyes moved from my eyes down to my lips where they stayed. He didn't need to tell me in words he agreed because a hunger drove him in answer. And this time when we kissed, it was all-consuming, hot breath and cinnamon. "It's about time," I breathed heavily in-between kisses.

* * * *

One heated moment of passion can have dire consequences in the waking hours.

My mind kept spinning with what happened last night. *I did it. I rescued Abe, and then Ace spent another night, here, in my room.* Every detail from last night came crashing back to me: thoughts about his lips on mine, his strong hands laced within mine, hands that seemed perfect for each other, like two matching puzzle pieces.

Distracted by my night with Ace, I'd forgotten I was supposed to meet up with Blake and Ebony later today in the garden. We'd made the plan yesterday after the Pixie King left with Abe. It had nearly killed me to leave Abaddon when I'd barely gotten him back. After Abe and the Pixie King left, I started questioning whether or not it had been a good idea. Blake reminded me at the time how if I had gone with Abe, my helping him would have been too obvious. Lucky for us, Apollyon was away from the Institute, and hadn't been seen or heard from for days now. Hopefully our luck would continue, and it would still be several days before he made it back to the Dark Manor.

Quickly getting dressed, throwing on a pair of my leggings, my favorite pair in a cobalt-blue shade, before pairing it with a white, spaghetti-strap shirt, and my usual black combat boots. I took a moment to brush my hair in front of the vanity mirror before heading out to meet Blake. Changing up my usual hairstyle, instead of wearing it down, I pulled it all up into a smooth, high-ponytail, unconcerned if my markings on my upper back were exposed or not. Last night had given me a new perspective on all these changes coming over me. They allowed me to do things no one else could do, to help others and get us out of some tricky situations. *Maybe they weren't all bad.*

Ace snuck up behind me while I was examining myself in the mirror. Until now he'd still been asleep in my bed. He stared at me with longing in his eyes. I turned around in my seat to face him. "Hi, sleepy-head, I thought maybe you were going to sleep all day."

"Hi back," he said, bending down and grabbing my chin before gently kissing me.

When our lips parted, and his hand fell back down, I noticed the dark circles under his eyes, suggesting another restless night's sleep. "Are you still having those odd dreams?" I asked in concern.

He shrugged. "I'm starting to get used to them. Besides, you'd be surprised how much stuff you can accomplish when you never sleep," he joked.

"What are they about?"

He shifted uncomfortable on his feet. "The point is not what happens during the dreams. What bothers me is how sometimes it's hard to recognize what's real and not real; and when finally I do sleep and wake up, it feels like I'm still dreaming. I guess I'm not making much sense right now," he told me, before placing a quick kiss on the top of my head, "Weren't you headed somewhere this morning?"

Ace needed to change the subject I realized and decided to ask something I'd been thinking about since last night. "When you said that you want to be with me again, really be with me, did you mean it?"

He smiled as though he found my question funny. "Yes, of course I meant it."

"Okay, but you're going to have to find a way to keep your new title as an official Hellhound Guardian and be with me because I'm not going to be the reason you give it all up," I said, in a no-nonsense tone.

"You won't be. What if we could make it work, somehow."

"How?"

"Well for starters, to avoid any whiplash you could tell me when I'm being an egotistical jerk, and I'll tell you when you're being a Dark Princess brat who, by-the-way, is a constant pain in my ass."

"A Dark Princess brat, huh?" Ace gave an innocent shrug that made me smile. "I guess we do push each other quite a bit."

"It's what we do. I push you when you start holding back, and you push me to be a better person."

I'd been waiting a really long time to hear Ace say all this, maybe in less words. There were still bigger issues at stake. "Sounds great. What if, um, I can't control whatever is happening to me, to control this thing inside of me constantly reminding me of the darkness I'm capable of, constantly reminding me of being Apollyon's daughter? What if I lose myself?"

Ace reached out and grabbed my hand, pulling me up to stand, and said, "You won't, I'll make sure of it. It's not too late, for you, for me, for us."

"No, it's not too late," I echoed him.

"There might be one more concern we haven't addressed," he said, slowly rocking us back and forth as though we were dancing to some invisible song. He was as happy as I'd ever seen him.

"What haven't we talked about yet?" I laughed, curious to hear what he was going to say.

"Will you go to the dance with me?" he asked, catching me off guard.

I couldn't help but laugh. Asking me to the dance seemed completely mundane in light of the recent state of affairs. I faced him and stood on the tip of my toes where I then kissed him as my way of an answer. "Just don't bring me flowers or anything lame like that," I warned upon seeing his arrogant smile.

"Yeah, yuck, who likes flowers? I wouldn't dream of it." His grin accented the mock tone.

"Good."

Ace laughed. "You are the strangest girl I've ever known. Devil's daughter or not."

"And you, Alcander, are getting better at complimenting."

CHAPTER TWENTY-TWO

Dresses, Blood, and Betrayal

"**W**hy did I have to say yes? Now I have to go to this stupid dance and I have nothing to wear!" I said, feeling frustrated.

"Because you love Ace and you want to see the look on his face when you're all irresistible," Ebony said from where she lay sprawled out comfortably on her stomach on my bed. Ebony didn't bother to look up from the magazine she was flipping through. After Ace had left this morning, claiming he had something he wanted to check up on, I called Ebony over in a panic to help me pick out something to wear to the dance.

"It was a rhetorical question," I said dryly.

"Sorry, it sounded like you needed an answer," Pixie-girl said, reminding me of something I'd say if the situation were reversed. It matched my own feelings right then, exasperated and unsure.

It was too late to order something off the Internet or even make a quick trip to the mainland. Whatever I was going to wear would have to come from the few dresses hanging in my closet, and none of them seemed right, not when the dress I'd seen in the creepy old lady's shop kept coming to mind. Everything else was dull in comparison.

"Go with the red one, the color compliments your amazing tan skin," Ebony said, before closing her magazine and coming to a crossed-legged sitting position.

Bending down and sifting through the mound of laundry on the floor in front of me, I retrieved the dress she referred to. Holding it out in front of me with my two fingers in disgust, I said, "You mean this maroon one?"

"Red, maroon…it looked great on you."

My gaze raked up and down the dress feeling repulsed by the idea of having to wear it. The straps were too thin, the polyester material too casual, and the hemline too short coming a few inches below my knees. Opening my fingers wide, the dress fell back down on the pile of clothes. "This sucks! It's my first dance where I actually have a very hot date, and I'm way over my head."

Pixie-girl sighed and crawled off my bed. I watched as she walked across the room and over to where her dress hung from a hanger on my vanity mirror. That's how all this started, the disaster that was now my room; she had come over to show me how the dress she'd be wearing for Blake at the dance looked on her. After trying it on, and we both gushed over how beautiful the blue topaz dress looked on her, and the way the pink, almost iridescent jewels sparkled all over it. That's when it hit me: I didn't have anything to wear for the dance.

"You can wear mine and I'll wear the red-err, maroon one," Ebony said.

At first I didn't know what to say, finally my mouth remembered how to work. "You'd let me wear it to the dance? But you look so beautiful in it," I told her, striding across the room, nearly tripping over some clothes in the heaping pile. I caressed my fingers over the dress.

"Going to the dance with Ace means a lot to you, I can tell."

"But Blake—"

"Blake won't know the difference. He hasn't seen this one yet. He probably wouldn't even notice what I'm wearing." Ebony laughed, pushing the dress into my hands.

It was beautiful, and a much better choice than anything I had in my closet. Yet, as I watched the way Ebony eyed the dress with a longing expression, she absolutely had to wear it. Grabbing her hand in mine, I gave her the dress back. "Blake *will* notice what you're wearing because you look stunning in it," I told her.

Ebony took the dress back, confused. "Are you certain?"

"Yes. I'll wear the red one," I said, and winked at her. "Maybe I can sew on some new straps, and add a slit to one of the sides and embellish it with some rhinestones from my throw pillows."

"Did you say you were going to sew something?" Blake stood by my door. I'd been so busy rummaging through clothes, obsessing over what to wear that I didn't hear him open the door. He knocked as though it would do any good now, before opening the door further and stepping inside.

"Hey, Blake," I said, and then noticed Ebony was still holding out her dress. Quickly, I stepped forward in front of Blake to block his view and hopefully distract him from what Ebony was holding. "What's so funny? I have a sewing machine. It's right over there." I pointed toward a box sitting beside my nightstand.

"Ah...I can tell you use it a lot," Blake said, sarcastically.

"Hey, I use it! Sometimes, or I would, if I knew how," I said when he didn't look impressed.

"Okay." He smiled at me, totally not buying it. "It's never too late to learn something, um, practical," he said, before shoving his hands into his pockets, gazing around my room for the first time since being there. "Doing some spring cleaning I see."

"Cleaning, me? Not a chance. I was trying to find something to wear for the dance."

"You don't know the half of it. Dess tried on everything she owns," Ebony said.

Blake smiled before walking over to Ebony and giving her a small kiss. It was sickly-sweet to witness, and I was afraid I'd form a cavity just by watching it. "Hi," Blake told her.

"Hi," Ebony said back, flustered to have been caught off guard by his kiss; Ebony didn't seem the public display of affection-type. It was a shame she had to leave in a few weeks to fulfill her promise to the Pixie King. I wondered briefly how Blake would take her absence. Not good, I imagined.

A quick glance at the clock reminded me it was almost time to go meet the Pixie King so he could report back on where Abe's being kept, and also so I could give him the Moonstone; I couldn't wait to get it out of my possession. "We better get going. Has anyone seen Ace?" I asked.

"Sure, I ran into him this morning, he was on his way out, somewhere, I'm not exactly sure." Blake shook his head. "Wherever he was going, though, he was in a hurry. Hmm, now that I think about it, Ace seemed strangely anxious about something." Blake's face transformed into a look of growing concern.

"Strange how?" I asked, a nervous feeling churning in my stomach, bringing back a feeling of unease I'd felt this morning when Ace talked about his sleepless nights, and how he needed to take care of something.

If something was going on with Ace how could I have possibly missed it? He was right there in front of me telling me how he felt and I threw it away like it was nothing. I stepped forward and reached out toward Blake, wrapping one hand around his forearm tightly.

"Tell me everything you saw that Ace did this morning," I demanded, the urgency clear in my tone.

Blake's bushy eyebrows creased, deep in thought. "To start with, he looked tired. To put it lightly, his hair was a mess, and he had dark circles under his eyes. He was definitely agitated about something."

"What do you mean by agitated? You know, like Ace's usual grumpy, caustic attitude, or did he seem afraid?" I prodded Blake to explain further, sounding desperate.

"Afraid? I've never seen Ace afraid of anything," Blake said, confused by my question. Exactly why Ace's behavior worried me. "Hostile, not afraid. When Ignacio and Warren were playing with the football out in the hall and accidently bumped into Ace, I thought maybe Ace was going to bite their heads off or something, literally. I mean we all know Ace doesn't have a lot of patience and sometimes says some pretty messed up stuff, but his reaction was strange, even for him," Blake said, and I wondered exactly what Ace said to Ig and Warren.

"An odd response for such an insignificant accident for sure," Ebony agreed, joining Blake's and my concern. Nothing came to mind to say until Ace suddenly spoke from the doorway.

"Who doesn't get a bit cranky every now and then." Ace waltzed into my room nonchalantly. I wondered how much of our conversation he'd heard.

"Cheese and rice, Ace, you scared the shit out of me!"

"You know, the point of saying something cheesy in order to avoid cursing means you can skip the cursing part," Ace said, flashing a dazzling white smile over at me.

Even though there wasn't anything different with the way he spoke, there was something off about Ace. About his stance, his facial expression, even the way he smiled felt foreign to me. Unable to put my finger on it, I forced myself to smile back at him while keeping a watchful gaze. Out of the corner of my eye, Blake's expression showed he'd come up with the same conclusion as me. "I was wondering if you were going to make it before we left." I tried to hide the unease which grew every second Ace stood there, a stranger in my room.

"You know how I like to make an entrance?" Ace walked over, stopping directly in front of me, ran his hands up the base of my neck before wrapping them on either side of my head, his fingertips curving up behind both of my ears. The moment didn't initiate this kind of display, and ended up feeling off and out of place. Ace oblivious to my discomfort continued to hold onto me, going so far as to lean his head down and kissing me fervently, uncaring of Blake and Ebony being in the same room. It was the type of kiss that Ace would have normally savored for just the two of us.

This kiss had taken me by surprise, unable to stop it once it began. Normally I wouldn't have wanted a kiss from Ace to end, but this didn't feel right, and I was relieved when he finally stopped. "There, I've been thinking about doing that all day," he said, with a buoyancy that bordered cockiness, before dropping his hands from my face.

Ace stood back, looking down at me satisfied with his handiwork before giving Blake an arrogant expression, contrite with himself. If I didn't know any better, it almost appeared as though Ace intentionally tried to arouse a reaction from Blake. After all, he knew about Blake's feelings for me, or his old feelings for me anyway, and kissing me in this manner was meant to be cruel and unnecessary torment for Blake. It left me feeling dirty and angry.

Ace clapped his hands loudly together out in front of him. "Well, are we leaving or are we going to stand around in Dessi's room all day?" he asked, impervious to the three of our shocked expressions.

"We are as ready as we'll ever be. Right, Dess?" Blake was the first one to speak, turning his questioning, and worrisome gaze on me.

I wasn't sure. *Were we?* I had to blink several times before I could speak again. "Um, right. Ready."

After the humiliating display in my room, the four of us left, making our way to my mother's garden. It was the safest, most secluded spot I could think of where we wouldn't be interrupted by Apollyon's guards or noticed by other Hellions passing by.

"Kaj, we're here so you can come out now," Ebony said to the empty air. It was the fifth or sixth time she'd called his name now.

"You don't think he has changed his name on us, do you?" Blake asked what we were all thinking. Before Ebony had a chance to answer, a thin gust of wind picked up all around us, making my hair fan out around me. It brought with it the smell of the changing leaves in autumn, even though it was spring outside. Tiny molecules of gold floated down in a thin dust while Kaj began to materialize with the calling of his given name. It wouldn't have surprised me if we heard the twinkling of bells chiming along with the pixie dust and magical atmosphere of the Pixie King's arrival.

"The only thing missing is fireworks," Ace said, eerily on the same mental train. He was right though, the Pixie King could probably appear without all the glitter and drawn-out theatrics.

"Where would be the fun in that?" the Pixie King said, answering both mine and Ace's thoughts. All of us turned toward his voice to see him sitting on top of one of the lion-head fountains.

Ace and I both shared similar facial expressions, questioning whether or not the Pixie King could read minds, a rumor never proven. It didn't really bother me if he could or not, I spoke my mind most of the time, but then again, so did Ace.

"Running a bit late, father. As usual, you only care about your own plans and not thinking about the fact anyone else could have better things to do than sit and wait on you," Ebony said.

He did his weird glitch-thing and jumped down from the lion-head, and appeared directly in front of Ebony. "I am only here because you have asked it of me. I too have better things to do with my time than to help children play their little foolish games," he said, using their conversation as a chance to rattle on. "Your cousin Carrick has been raising Hell, pun intended," he quickly said to me, "for our kingdom."

"*Your Kingdom*, you mean," Ebony said, correcting her father.

"It is still yours whether you claim it or not. As long as I live, it shall remain ours, though Carrick would gladly wish my death to see our name vanish in the wind while he, in all his selfishness, thinks himself fit for the job. Even you would make a better ruler than he." The Pixie Kind held a look of disgust, his mouth into a severe sneer.

"Thank you for the vote of confidence. You know I did not bring you here to talk about *your* kingdom's quandaries," Ebony said. "All we need is for you to show us the way to Abaddon, and nothing more."

The Pixie King looked genuinely crushed by his daughter's lack of concern for a place that was once her home. "As you wish. First, the stone please?" He held out his hand toward me, never taking his eyes off his daughter.

I stuck my hand in my pocket and then hesitated. "Wait. How did you know?" I asked, and then decided I really didn't want to know if he could read minds or x-ray vision. "You know what? Never mind. Here, take it, it's yours." Pulling my hand out of my pocket grasping the stone, I held it out to the Pixie King. He had barely laid one finger on the stone when his head whipped in Ace's direction, and a small sad sigh escaped his mouth. That's when all Hell broke loose, and everything I thought I knew shattered right in front of me.

The Pixie King never had a chance to say whatever he was about to because Ace had pulled his hand out of his own pocket so fast that none of us had time to realize what he was about to do. There was no way any of us could have seen the knife in Ace's hand; I didn't have time to finish screaming Ace's name before he lunged forward and held the Pixie King in a tight hold, plunging the knife straight into the Pixie King's heart.

202 | Alissa T. Hunter

CHAPTER TWENTY-THREE

Black Sea

Ace took the Moonstone from the Pixie King's hand and then removed the knife from his chest by shoving his limp body forward all in one motion, discarding him to the ground. Gold glitter scattered out all around the Pixie King's body where it littered the soil of my mother's garden.

"No!" Ebony cried, falling to the ground beside her father, Blake following her, reaching out to the fallen Pixie King.

"Ace, what have you done!" I screamed in horror.

Without looking up at me, instead too busy watching the knife as he cleaned the blood off, he said, "Something that must be done."

Okay, who the hell are you and what did you do with Ace? "What do you mean by doing what must be done? He's the Pixie King and Ebony's father, not to mention our only way to find Abaddon!"

"Not my problem," Ace said, and I felt as though he stabbed a knife inside my chest as well.

"I-I don't understand?" I tried my best not to lose control of my emotions when nothing was making sense.

I hadn't realized I'd been slowly moving toward Ace until he put his hand, motioning for me to stop, and not come any closer, "You don't need to understand," he told me forcefully.

Planting my feet on the ground, feeling as though I were standing on legs made of wood, trying my best to keep them from wobbling, I said, "Then can you at least tell me why?" My hands balled into tight fists by my sides in order to keep them from shaking. I tried telling myself this person in front of me was not Ace because *my* Ace would never kill unless he felt we were in danger, which we clearly were not.

"There is an answer to your question, though I'm afraid you will not appreciate it," a new voice suddenly entered my mother's garden. My head turned to the side to see Kione pacing over to where Ace stood, only a few feet from me. Glancing back to where Blake and Ebony were still kneeling down beside the Pixie King, I saw Blake's face drain of blood when seeing Kione.

"You. I should have known you were behind this," I growled, taking an involuntary step toward Kione.

Out of the corner of my eye, Ace shook his head ever so slightly at me, warning me not to do whatever I was thinking of doing, remaining next to Kione. Ace's concern contradicted his new attitude; it was obvious Kione was behind all this, maybe even somehow controlling Ace, but with that one, miniscule show of concern had me thinking Ace was in there somewhere, trying to fight it off.

"Are you working together?" I asked, forcing my voice to leave me, and hating the taste of what I'd asked.

Ace shrugged, not giving me a direct answer.

Kione smiled.

"Ace, is Kione behind this—was it his idea to murder the Pixie King? Because if he did, we can help you, none of this will matter," I said, taking a step forward anyway, despite the look of unease on Ace's face pleading for me to stop coming closer.

When Ace didn't say anything, instead remaining Kione's silent sidekick, Kione spoke for him. "Actually, little Starr, killing the Pixie King was your Hellhound-lover's idea."

"You're lying!" I screamed, my mind not willing to believe it could be true.

"I know this is all still so confusing to you, and that you're having a hard time believing your Hellhound leader could do anything wrong, but I assure you, he acted on his own."

"Why would I believe anything you say? Especially after admitting to framing Abaddon's involvements in the attacks on the Institute? You could be lying now." I felt my nails bite into the soft flesh on my palms, and thin lines of blood being released.

"You can't," he said, plain and simple, before turning his attention back on Ace. "Do you have the stone?"

"Yes, I have it. You could have warned me the Pixie King could read minds," Ace said to Kione, irritated.

"If I had, you would not have been able to keep your thoughts to yourself. Like I told you, have a little faith in me and I'll be sure to make good on my promises," Kione responded. My head felt like it was about to explode while watching their display in disbelief.

"What did he promise you, Ace?"

Ace gazed right though me, indifferent of my worried tone.

"You know you can't trust anything Kione tells you, right?" I asked Ace, trying to ignore Kione's presence all together.

"You don't know Kione, he's not like we thought," Ace said, his tone going softer, willing me to understand. *He actually means it! Somehow Ace has been fooled by Kione.*

"Of course he is, he's exactly like we thought. Are you even listening to yourself right now, Ace?" I took another step forward, sounding completely outraged. He wasn't fazed by my anger so, instead, I decided to try a different approach, a gentler one. "Look, whatever he has promised you, it doesn't matter, you don't need it. But I-I do need you." I pressed my hand to my heart, trying to get him to remember all that we have together. "We can forget all of this, everything that's happened tonight, all you have to do is come with me, Ace. Just take my hand. Here," I said, holding one hand out to him, begging him with my whole being to take it and come away from Kione. His face twisted in conflict.

When he took a step forward, looking as though he were about to take my offered hand, Kione stepped in front of him, blocking me from his view.

"Desdemona is a Starr, and can offer you nothing. Come with me and I can give you everything," Kione said to him.

Ace blinked, and what I said to him didn't matter anymore. *I* didn't matter anymore, only Kione's persuasion over him did.

"You son-of-a-bitch! What did you do to him? I'll kill you!" I screamed, lunging myself at Kione, hitting and clawing at him. Hands and arms stronger than mine pried me off his back, but it didn't stop me from trying to kick and hit him all the same.

"Stop, Dess, you need to stop. You can't prevent any of this, it's already started. There's nothing you can do now," a familiar voice spoke to me as he continued to pull me back and away from Kione. I was seeing red with rage and couldn't make sense of what he was saying or who was saying it. Only when he put his lips right up to my ear and began whispering, could I comprehend who it was trying to talk some sense back into me. "Please, Dessi, you need to forget about Kione, it's too late, you need to let me go," Ace said.

My head shook back and forth, unwilling to do as he asked. "No, it can't be too late. I'll kill him for what he's done to you. This isn't you. Kione is the only monster here," I said, my whole body wracked with anger and despair.

"Yes, you have to. You can't win this one," he said. "If you love me, you need to forget about Kione, forget about me, forget everything."

I turned around and looked into his eyes, and for a moment I could see the Ace I loved buried somewhere inside this new cruel Ace made by Kione.

My entire body stilled. "I can't, Ace, I won't!"

"Yes, you can. Please, you have to," he pleaded. "I have to know you're still here, even if I'm no longer a part of your world anymore."

Ace no longer a part of my world anymore?

Throwing my arms around his neck, I sobbed into his chest. "You have to fight this, Ace, don't stop fighting Kione. I know you're still in there somewhere, you have to be."

"The Ace you knew is dead, Dess, this is me, the *real* me is right here in front of you now, the way I was always meant to be, I know that now. He," Ace said, meaning Kione, "showed me that. If you keep fighting, he'll kill you," Ace whispered one last time before reaching up and removing my arms from around his neck. It was evident he still cared for me, even if he didn't want to admit it, he still loved me. Kione's persuasion could never take away what Ace and I had. I would remind Ace of this fact, only not today. Nothing I said would make any difference today.

My body sagged in defeat, and I let Ace push me aside. "I'll stop fighting him, for now," I said throwing a look of daggers over at Kione who stood watching us with a look of boredom, "but I won't stop fighting for you, for us, even if it does kill me." I felt the hot stream of traitor tears running down both sides of my cheeks.

His reply was cold and sent chills up my spine. "I did my job warning you. You go ahead and do what you want, since you do most of the time anyway," he said, grabbing me by the shoulders and passing me off to Blake.

"If you don't want her getting hurt, you better keep a tight chain on her," Ace warned Blake.

"You and I both know, Dess doesn't do well locked up, it will only fuel her, and if it's a fight Dess wants, what kind of friend would I be if I didn't help," Blake growled back at him.

"I'm counting on that one, small detail," Kione said, reminding us he was to blame for it all, motioning for Ace to come to him. Ace obeyed without question, turning his back on us to stand beside Kione.

They turned to leave together, Ace with an unreadable expression on his face, maybe one you would wear to your own funeral since Ace declared today as the day he died.

They were gone, and Blake and I were left behind with the biggest mess of both our lives strewn around us. "I'm going to be sick," I said, feeling the world spin around me.

"Here, I've got you." Blake's hands clasped around my wrists to keep me from falling.

The sick feeling only intensified when a shining white light began to appear before us, temporarily blinding us. The three of us who remained, Ebony still kneeling by her father on the ground, threw our hands in front of our eyes to shield them from the brightness. When the light finally dimmed enough that it was no longer painful to look at, we glanced up to see the Angel, Lain, standing before us.

He was staring at the body of the Pixie King, with a pained expression. "I'm too late," he said, before exhaling deeply, his shoulders slumping in sorrow. "Is Lilith's daughter hurt?" Lain asked Blake.

"What?" I asked, confused. Of course I wasn't all right.

"No, I don't think so. How could she be?" Blake told him. *Not physically?* What other kind of pain would the breaking of a heart be considered? I wondered inwardly.

"Good," Lain said, sounding relieved.

"I feared when the hound sided with the drifter, Desdemona would not fare well," Lain said, gently.

Of course Lain already knew about Ace. Sometimes I thought it was unfair Angels had the knowledge of our actions before we did. He should have told me if he knew Kione would get to Ace. I could have tried to stop him before he even knew he needed to be stopped! I fixed an icy glare toward the Angel. Lain was not affected by my hostility, instead he remained looking sadly over at me.

A black sea of thoughts flooded my mind, and then all at once everything inside me hurt: every nerve, every vein that pumped blood dutifully to my broken heart, felt like it'd been set on fire. A strangled scream left my lips and my knees buckled out from under me. Luckily, Blake was there to catch me. Somewhere deep down I knew Blake needed to be there for Ebony too. A selfish part of me was glad he was here for me first.

"We need to take her someplace safe," Lain told Blake.

"We can take her to her room," Blake said.

Blake only got a step or two in before he stopped to look back at Ebony. "Maybe you should." he began to say, motioning for Lain to take me. "I can't just leave Ebony."

Lain hesitated for a moment before conceding, reaching out and taking me from Blake's arms. Little waves of what felt like static electricity swarmed through my body with his touch meeting mine. I knew he had felt it too, the same way we both had the first time it happened in the library when our legs accidently bumped. It wasn't exactly painful, in fact, in a weird way it felt quite pleasurable, and definitely uncomfortable.

A morbid thought came to mind as I wondered if I would mourn over my father if it was him lying there in my mother's garden instead of the Pixie King.

No.

The answer flitted across my mind before Lain crouched and then sprang up into the sky, me still nestled safely in his arms. I looked down to see my world grow smaller. It seemed fitting now that Ace was no longer a part of my world, as he'd put it. My world was smaller, mimicking the way I felt about myself: small, miniscule, non-existent.

For a moment, I wished I no longer existed in a world where I couldn't be with Ace and simply exist to punish him. I wanted to make him hurt for turning his back on me, to make his heart ache the way mine did now.

Smaller and smaller the world grew. I closed my eyes and wished I could stay right here in Lain's arms, high above the earth and sea, where, for a moment in time, I did not exist anywhere.

CHAPTER TWENTY-FOUR

Descent

Descending back down to earth took a lot longer than I thought it would. I think Lain knew I needed the extra air to clear my head and took his time while flying us.

Eventually we did have to come back down, because no matter how much I wanted my problems to disappear, they would remain there waiting for me.

Lain landed on my balcony outside my room after coming to a smooth stop. "Can you stand?" he asked me.

"Yes," I replied with effort.

He lowered me and held on until he was certain I wasn't going to topple over or something.

"Thanks," I said, sighing because it was the only thing I could do. My legs felt unhinged and not belonging to this body, trembling as I walked clumsily over and sat down on the bench nearby, remaining outside on the balcony.

Lain looked around us, uncomfortable, trying to decide something before at last he decided to sit down next to me, careful we did not touch again. For that I was grateful. "How did I miss it?" I asked, looking down at my hands, which I had splayed open in front of me, palms up as though they held all the missing pieces.

"He deceived you," Lain stated.

Yeah, that was an understatement. "He was right there in front of me, how did I miss it? How long had Ace been gone, and how long ago did

Kione steal my Ace?" I asked, thinking out loud, and hearing how jumbled it all sounded. I hadn't been expecting an answer, so it didn't surprise me when one didn't come. Remembering how Lain knew something was about to happen, and then showed up too late, came back to mind, along with a new thought. "Can you see things the way you could before, um, before you were cast out of heaven or put on probation, whatever you Angels call it?" I asked, realizing how that question might not make sense to many people, but Lain understood it perfectly.

"No. I cannot," he said, looking as miserable as I'd ever seen bird-boy look before. "When I heard reports of what Kione was planning, I knew I needed to find you. I did not know his plans would involve killing the Pixie King or using your, your..." Lain stumbled to find the right name for what Ace was to me.

"Boyfriend, lover, comrade, leader?" I said, trying to throw him a bone even though saying all those things twisted my stomach into tighter knots.

Lain ignored all of my suggestions and found his own name for what he wanted to call mine and Ace's relationship. "Hound companion," he said, at last. I felt my heart give a tight squeeze inside my chest with the term companion; in a weird way though, it worked to describe us. We worked better together as team than we did apart.

"I've lost him, Lain, I've lost Ace; and Abaddon is only Gods know where. I'm alone, and Ebony, she's alone, her kingdom or homeland probably in disorder now. How did things get so messed up?" I said, more to myself.

Lain turned his body toward me with a determined expression on his beautiful, baby-faced Angel features. It was times like this, when he was filled with determination that made him look like the glorious warrior of heaven he is, or used to be before I got him in trouble and sent away.

"You are not alone, Starred One," Lain said, reaching out to touch my face when he saw one lone tear running down the side of my cheek. At the last second before his finger could touch my skin, he hesitated and pulled back. "Do not give up hope. A much bigger challenge is yet to come for you. You are superior, Desdemona Starr, and you are not alone. I am here, you have more following you, believing in you, than you can ever imagine," he said.

His total faith in me only made me feel worse; the part about followers was lost on me. I didn't let him know how his words affected me though. I stood tiredly and said, "You shouldn't be here. You've probably already been seen by Kione." Or Ace who also can't be trusted now, my mind added. "I wouldn't be surprised if he already informed Apollyon's guards of your presence. You need to leave." The last thing I needed was for bird-boy to get caught and weigh on my conscience.

"Your worry for me is unnecessary," he said, giving me a curious look, making me think I'd surprised him by my concern.

"You're not riding on some invincible cloud, Lain, you're vulnerable to my father's tortuous ways the way anyone else is. If anything happened to you it's on me," I told him, running my hands through my hair and walking over to the iron rails of the balcony, leaning my arms on it and looking out at the dark waters of the Aegean Sea.

"I cannot avoid my fate any more than you can avoid yours, Eve's Beloved."

"Eve's Beloved?" The name rang a bell. I looked over at Lain and saw him holding his breath in anticipation, waiting for me to put it all together, close to whatever it was he was trying, but couldn't tell me because of his Angel oath. Eyebrows furrowed in deep thought, I started playing around with different sayings, trying to recollect the riddle he'd left me with right after Abe was taken. Something about Evil's purest light, Angels weeping, and Eve's Beloved conquering the night, I tried remembering correctly.

Lain started nodding his head at me in encouragement wanting me to understand everything that was happening: my phasing, or blossoming as Apollyon called it, into something unrecognizable in the mirror, and why demons, and drifters, like Kione, were after me, all of it.

"I still don't understand any of this!" I said in frustration, spinning my body around, hitting my back hard against the iron railing.

Lain's face fell. "You will, in time," he told me, and this time when he reached out grabbing my hand in his, he didn't hesitate. Currents of electricity ran through our joined hands and up our arms. It felt both painful and wonderful at the same time. Normally my eyes closed against the striking contrast, but this time I kept them open. Lain's eyes were already open and watching me, his gaze focusing on our hands. My eyes followed his to see a bright gold light shining from within my veins, surging up my arms. His light, every essence of his soul flowed through me. I could feel how flawless Lain's soul was—he was so good, truly the perfect descendant of Heaven. The exact reason for why he should stay as far away from me as possible.

Lain ground his teeth against the pain that threatened to overwhelm him. Where my veins were flowing with gold light, his were becoming thicker with obsidian-black; his blood becoming tainted with the darkness inside me. The thorny creature I kept buried and hidden away on the base of my spine woke its snarling head and began to slither beneath my skin. Frightened it would make its way to Lain, I began pleading for him to stop, struggling to take my hand from his.

"Lain, stop, I'm hurting you." I watched his face twist with pain, still he did not let go. Lain had an unworldly strength I'd only now realized, fighting against his hold was hopeless.

"To understand, you need to feel their cries," Lain told me, having to choke out the words through the agony.

Words I did not form on my own began pouring from my mouth involuntarily as some great force using me to send a message:

"Evil's purest light shall break through desire,
as Angels weep, in fear and love, through flames of fire,
the pits of Hell quake before her,
even the strongest of the fallen shall fear her bending their knees in
fright of her power.

Creator of the darkness shan't bend the light, while Eve's Beloved, shall conquer the night."

The verse I'd been trying so hard to remember spilled out around us, all the while I kept looking down, horrified, with large, frightened eyes as the thorny beast traveled down my arm, and headed straight toward Lain.

He let go of my hand in time before the ominous creature had a chance to reach him and then watched as it recoiled back to where it came from within me. Sometimes it scared me to have no control over my demon.

"Everyone is capable of having a demon if they allow it. You must remain stronger than it," Lain said, understanding the horrified expression on my face.

I breathed a sigh of relief, and then immediately felt dizzy and had to go sit back down on the bench. Lain did not follow this time, and chose to remain standing where he was. An emptiness at having felt such glorious light pour through my veins and have it stop too soon, filled me.

"Why did you do that? Why did you risk yourself to the darkness inside of me?" I asked, outraged.

"You needed to remember. It was the only way I knew how to help you remember," he said, exhausted, swaying slightly where he stood, and I wondered exactly how much energy it took from him.

"You shouldn't have done it. What if I couldn't have stopped it? Did you ever think of that?"

"I allowed it to work properly," he said, wiping sweat from his brow.

Lain was missing the point here.

"I didn't want to stop. It could have easily overtaken you."

"You would have if you truly wanted to. It was a test you passed. You are stronger than you know, as I've told you before," he said.

I opened my mouth to argue more, and ended up deciding it would do no good. Lain may have been naïve, and maybe even stupid to put so much faith in a creature of darkness only just learning her capabilities. Lain's stubbornness would surpass anything I said. Really, the Angel wasn't capable of having regrets since he believed everything he did was part of this fate he kept talking about.

A knock at the door hindered any more conversation. I got up to answer and thought better of it, turning back to Lain. "Don't go anywhere." I said, waiting for his reply which was slow coming. He nodded tentatively he'd stay.

After answering the door, and turning back around to face my room, I held out a garment bag in my hands, bewildered where it came from and why it was delivered to my room. Lain slowly walked into the room, watching me, concerned by my uncertainty. "I think it's a dress," I said. Lain didn't say anything, and instead continued to watch me as I laid the bag down on the end of my bed, unzipping it first, and then pulled out a beautiful dress the color of midnight. Without thinking, I held the dress made of Victorian satin up to me, positioning the one angled sleeve across my shoulder.

"The dress suits you," Lain said, reminding me I was not alone.

Running my hand over the lace that was the same color as the dress, I said, "Yes, it doesn't matter now, I have no one to wear it for." Sadly, I placed the dress back down on the bed and faced Lain.

He turned his head to the side, listening to something only he could hear. "I would not be so sure of that, yet."

"You know this knowing stuff before it happens business is starting to creep me out," I said to a smiling Lain, before turning my back and answering the door, again.

Blake stood on the other side, looking as weary as I felt. "Blake, hi, come in," I quickly said, surprised he was here and not with Ebony.

"Thanks," Blake said, and stepped in.

"You know Lain," I said, gesturing behind me.

"Yeah," Blake said, suspiciously. "Why?"

"Of course he's gone." I said out loud to the empty spot Lain had been standing in mere seconds ago. "Never mind."

"Ebony's gone," Blake said, wasting no time.

"What do you mean gone?"

"I mean she's gone. After you left with that Angel, these two other Pixies showed up, and they were talking to her all urgently, and I wasn't really able to keep up because they were saying all this stuff I didn't understand and then she left. Ebony is gone."

"Whoa, Blake, slow down. Tell me exactly what happened. Ebony wouldn't have just left without a good reason." I crossed my arms over my chest, willing myself to keep it together for Blake's sake.

"They were talking to her about her father's kingdom, throwing out words like new successor and rightful ruler, and how they didn't want her cousin ruling their people, Carrick? And then Ebony said something about needing to take her father back to her home so they can give him a proper procession with a pyre or something," he said. "After they took the Pixie King's body away, Ebony explained how her people needed her. She kissed me goodbye, and then left. I tried reminding her about the dance, which seems a silly thing to be worried about after everything." Blake gave a small, sad laugh.

"I'm so sorry, Blake," was all I could think to say.

Blake shrugged. "I get why she left, even after I told her not to go, and she insisted it is the right thing to do and she needed to keep the promise made to the Pixie King. She said she needs to do the right thing. Dess, I don't even know what's right or wrong anymore," Blake said, starting to come unglued.

"Here, I think you should sit down, and maybe try breathing," I told him, grabbing hold of his shoulders and leading him to the edge of my bed, where he sat down robotically.

I didn't blame him; all of the events of the last twenty-four hours seemed a distant, horrible dream already. At least it was the real Ebony who kissed Blake goodbye, and not some corrupt version of her, the way Ace had been. My lips still felt the slightest tingle of betrayal on them, and I had the inkling to go wash my mouth and get it off.

Being reminded of the dance made me glance over at my clock on my bedside table. The dance had just started.

"What are we going to do now? There has to be some kind of plan we can come up with, right?" Blake asked, lifting his head to look at me for some kind of genius answer.

If Ebony needed to be with her court right now, I didn't think any kind of plan would work on getting her back. "I'm sure there is," I lied. "Tonight's probably not best though."

"Yeah," he said, dejected. "What do we do tonight then?"

"I have an idea, granted it's not a very good idea, still it's something." I said, thinking it best we don't end up alone, in our rooms, drowning in self-pity.

"Whatever it is, it's better than anything I can come up with at the moment," Blake said.

I doubt it.

I cringed, almost changing my mind about telling Blake my idea. "We go to the dance," I said, and then waited for him to refuse with good reason.

When he didn't immediately start yelling or shaking me angrily in order to talk some sense into me, my shoulders released from where they were shrugged anxiously. "I don't know, do you think we should?" he asked, uncertain.

"No, not at all. You said it yourself, what else are we going to do?" I got off the bed to stand in front of him, holding my hands out for him to take. He took them and stood.

"This could be one of your worst ideas yet," he said, unconvinced.

"Let's hope so." I so needed this distraction.

CHAPTER TWENTY-FIVE

The Dance

The moment before your whole world crumbles down around you, all you can do is brace yourself and hope you come out a survivor, with most of your dignity and self-preservation still intact.

I would not be so lucky regarding either of those things.

By the time this night was done with me, I would be lucky enough if there was any shred of hope left in me; hope in helping the people I loved, and not lose myself in the process.

The night started as expected, sad and really pathetic. Blake and I agreed to meet at the dance instead of meeting in one of our rooms.

"You look as beautiful as an Angel," Zola told me around a proud smile, after tucking my hair behind one ear so she could admire my earrings.

"Thanks." I said, finding her choice of words ironic. "Do you think I should wear it? The crazy old lady sent it to me because she's scared of having it in her shop or something."

"Or because Ace is not here to see you in it?" Zola said, knowing my real reason for being upset.

"Well he's not," I said, running both of my hands down the bodice which fit nicely over my waist and hips.

"The dress is meant for you to wear this night," Zola said, finishing her last touches on my hair, placing the curls just so around my shoulders and collarbone.

"Are you sure you've never met creepy dress shop lady?" I asked sardonically.

"Don't fret, child, he could never truly be lost, not when he holds my girl's heart with him," Zola said softly, giving me a quick sideways hug over my shoulders, before stepping back to admire her handy work.

I'm not so sure my heart is enough for him, I thought, frowning.

Taking a deep breath, I shook all thoughts of Ace away. Blake would need my strength to help get him through the night, and I couldn't be strong while dwelling on what Ace was doing tonight instead of being here with me. Zola wished me good luck and sent me on my way.

Hellions eyed me as I sauntered into the crowd, trying to find Blake, and I found myself wishing this dance had been a masked ball to hide from prying, condemnatory eyes. *Word about Abaddon's escape had gotten out I see. No doubt people are probably suspecting me.*

Farther in, the dining room turned into a dance floor led me to find Blake leaning against a wall. He was sort of sticking out like a sore thumb and was lost on me why I hadn't spotted him sooner. His shirt was loose around the waist, his hair disheveled, though I couldn't be sure if he'd done it on purpose or not. "Could you look any gloomier?" I asked, once standing in front of him.

He blinked at my approach, needing a second to comprehend what we were doing there. "Oh hey, Dess, you look…nice," Blake said, his eyes going wide once he finally noticed me.

"Oh, um, thanks, so do you."

"You don't mean that," he said around a small, forced laugh.

"No, I was trying to be nice. You look like Hell. Are we pathetic or what?"

"Definitely," Blake agreed, shoving his hands into his pockets.

"So, no word on how Ebony's doing yet?"

He shook his head.

"Ebony will get word to you as soon as she can. I'm sure of it, Blake."

"Yeah, maybe," he said. "Well since we are here, and both equally pathetic, did you want to make the most of it. Dance with me, Desdemona Starr?" He bowed at the waist before offering me his arm.

It was completely clumsy and ridiculous, and exactly what I needed; plus there wasn't anything better, and I didn't want all this work Zola did on me go to waste. "Why not? Let's see your moves gloomy-boy," I said.

"If I'm gloomy-boy you're gloomy-girl," Blake said, straightening up and taking my hand.

"That goes without saying." I let him lead me out to the middle of the dance floor.

Blake wrapped his hands around my waist, gentle where they sat above my hips. Even though the song playing was meant for faster dancing, Blake and I slow danced it as well as the next few songs. We'd been enjoying ourselves, to our dismay, until a girl wearing her hair in a short bob-cut, ran by laughing and not watching where she was going, and ended up bumping into Blake.

Blake's eyes went wide and hopeful when seeing the back of this girl who resembled Ebony perfectly from the angle she was in. When the girl turned around and Blake realized it was not Ebony, his whole world shattered right before me.

His gaze cut through me and broke my heart. Out of reflex, I reached out and grabbed his hand, squeezing it in mine; the look he wore now reminded me of the time I'd broken his heart after telling him I couldn't love him back the way he wanted me to.

Only now he wears it for Pixie-girl.

We'd stopped dancing when the girl bumped into us. Blake looked down at my hand on his before pulling me into his chest and continued the dance. "Thanks for doing this for me. I know you didn't really want to come," he said, his mouth somewhere near my ear.

I hesitated before speaking, "I did want to come. I thought it would be awkward. Glad I was wrong about that." We both laughed. This night had been totally awkward in every sense of the word.

"What are you thinking?" Blake asked, a few moments later.

I'd just been thinking about the time when Blake and I were younger, and we had tied sheets around us while jumping off my bed. I decided to tell him the truth. "Do you remember that time in my room when we were trying to fly?"

Blake looked up out of the corner of his eye as he tried to recall the memory, his head turning back down to mine with wide eyes and a smile to match my own. "Oh, I remember. You wanted to see if the wind was strong enough to carry you. I suggested we try jumping off your bed first before you tried jumping off the balcony."

"That's right," I said, not remembering exactly why we were jumping off my bed. "You probably saved my stupid life. It wouldn't have been the first time either."

"And probably won't be the last." He smirked.

"Aww, well thanks for the past and for the near future," I joked, liking where we were at keeping things simple and light.

"Truth is, I'll never stop trying to save your life," Blake said, on a more serious note, though the gleam in his eyes remained. *So much for simple.*

"I wanted to fly away from the Institute that day."

"Huh?" Blake asked, not quite keeping up with my sporadic thoughts.

"That day with the sheets was the day Abaddon had left after fighting with our father about why my mom left. Abe left me all alone to deal with our father, so I had this bright idea to fly away. Apparently hitchhiking didn't come to my young foolish mind, yet a theory about flying away did. First, for this theory to work I needed to make myself wings."

"I didn't know any of that," Blake said, looking at me intently. "Why didn't you tell me you needed to leave?"

"Because as much as I hated Apollyon for making Abe leave, the thought of leaving you was worse. I didn't want to say goodbye, and I probably figured you would want to come with me, but didn't want to get you in trouble," I told him softly. Our swaying had nearly come to a standstill.

Blake took a few seconds to absorb this information. Finally, he said, "I wouldn't have let you leave."

"I know you wouldn't have—" I began to say when Blake quickly interrupted.

"I wasn't done. What I was going to say was: I wouldn't have let you leave, by yourself, and instead insisted on going with you, all while coming up with a better, less dangerous plan, of course."

"Even if my plan was reckless and could have killed us, you still would have gone with me?"

"Yes, even if," Blake said, and I could tell he meant it. Even as children, Blake had loved me so much he was willing to jump off a cliff after me, so to speak.

"Why?" I had to ask.

Blake exhaled a heavy sigh. "I think you already know why."

"Blake—"

"No, don't, you don't have to say anything, Dess, I already know. Besides, I'm pretty sure I love Ebony now too. No, actually, not pretty sure, I do love Ebony, and if I thought making wings out of a sheet would take me to her, I would," he said.

I wasn't sure how his declaration for Ebony made me feel. It was a relief in many ways since Ebony could love Blake the way he deserved.

There was something else I realized right then; if Blake asked me to help him get Ebony back, I would do it for him, for the same reasons Blake was willing to help make me wings all those years ago. Leaning my head against his chest I said in no more than a whisper, "I do love you, Blake, I think I always have to be honest. You've always been there for me, and I've always wanted you there, even now, and I think it's because you were partly right before when you told me I did love you, only I didn't know it yet." I'd meant it, even though my love for Blake was not the way I loved Ace, Blake had been right in calling my feelings for him out when he'd declared his love for me months ago.

I felt his arms go tighter around me before he breathed a sigh of relief. I wasn't sure if he believed me. It felt like the right thing to say, what Blake needed to hear. "Thank you," he whispered in my ear.

A feeling of being watched had me straightening up out of Blake's arms. "What is it?" Blake asked, before a look of alertness crossed his features too, his Hellhound guardian instincts kicking into overdrive. "We have trouble," Blake echoed my thoughts.

Stepping back out of his embrace, I said, "I think I know where it's coming from,"—and then turned and walked out of the dining-hall/ballroom.

Blake ran outside into the courtyard after me. The night air was cooler than usual for May. The brisk winds making the cold settle into my bones, and giving me goose bumps. The sound of the sea's angry waves crashed against the cliffs, resonating with the stir of dark emotions I felt inside upon seeing *him*. My feet froze in their place. Unable to take another step, my knees were about to buckle out from under me if I didn't control their trembling. Ace was sitting casually on the stone bench near the fountain.

Seeing him sitting in that particular spot made me remember an incident which took place only a couple of months ago when we were both sitting on the bench under the same fountain while the school was under attack by the Lamia-demons. Ace had protected me then, he would have done anything for me, and not merely because Apollyon had told him to, but because even then Ace unknowingly felt something for me. We *both* had felt something for each other, only we'd been too damn stubborn to realize it quite yet.

Looking at the smug expression he now wore, I knew any trace of lingering feelings he might have had vanished along with my former protector.

"What are you doing here?" Blake growled before I had a chance to say anything.

Ace stood and took a step forward. "I was invited, well technically I invited her to the dance," Ace said, pointing at me.

"My bad. You see the way I figured, Dess was allowed to go back on her invitation the moment you stuck the knife into the Pixie King's heart!" Blake said, irate.

Ace's eyes glowed a shade that could only be described as violent. "Ah, I see what's going on here," Ace said, his head turning back and forth from Blake's face to mine and then back to Blake again. "You just couldn't wait for your moment to swoop in and steal my girlfriend away from me." He took another step forward.

Blake didn't speak, and he didn't think twice when he strode past me at Ace, rage filling his entire demeanor. "No, Blake, don't," I said, racing forward and grabbing Blake by the arm to stop him.

"Can't argue with that reaction," Ace huffed, "It's exactly the way it looks, usually is."

"Shut up, I'm not *your* girlfriend," I said, turning to glare at Ace.

"I've been gone for less than forty-eight hours and you fall for this mutt?" Ace said it like a question but meant it as a joke obviously as he started laughing.

"What I meant was I'm not your girlfriend, I'm Alcander's, the hound who comes first in everything, especially the things he believes in which includes leading his hound comrades, including Blake. Let me know if you see him around, will you," I said, bitingly.

"Nope, this is all me, babe. This is as real as it gets," he said, spreading his arms wide as if to showcase what *all this* implied.

"Why are you here, Ace?" I said through clenched teeth. It took all of my strength to keep my voice from shaking when I spoke.

"I couldn't miss a chance at seeing you all dressed up now, could I?" He walked closer to me. Blake made way to take another step forward before I stopped him, ensuring him it would be all right. My gut instinct was telling me Ace, or um, whoever this person in front of me was, wasn't going to hurt me, not physically anyway.

Putting his hand to his chin in an inquisitive stance, he then began circling me, taking in every detail of my appearance; appraising me as though I were some kind of precious piece of art he was carefully examining for flaws. A week ago I would have killed for him to look at me with such keenness, but something about the way he was doing it now felt all wrong. There was something vaguely familiar in the way he gazed at me, another who always fixed me with a similar gaze, only my mind was too distressed to put the pieces together.

I hated every second of it, "Satisfied?" I asked.

"Almost, though not quite," he said swiftly. Not worried about coming across as offensive, he added, "But I will be soon enough, once we're done getting everything we're after, then maybe I'll steal a moment in our busy schedule to come back for you." He reached out and ran the side of his forefinger down my cheek. Even his touch felt wrong.

After they got everything they were after—who were they? Kione?

Unsatisfied with the holes in the clues Ace dropped left and right, and needing to keep him talking some more, I said, "Why don't you take me now? I mean I'm already right here in front of you,"—trying to keep the sick feeling in my stomach under control, and sound as though I'd actually meant it.

Ace paused, thinking about my offer, looking like he wanted to take me up on it, and for a brief moment, I could swear I'd seen the old Ace, *my* Ace, flash across his features, but only fleetingly before something else won over, and it was gone. "I like my idea better, just knowing you're here waiting for me is all I need," he said, turning his back on me and walking away.

For some reason I couldn't quite let him go yet. What can I say...I'm a glutton for punishment. Figuring there was nothing else to lose and only wanted to know one thing. "When you said you loved me, did you mean it, or was it some twisted way to keep stringing me along for your entertainment?" I asked. Really, I wanted to know if imposter Ace was the one who told me he loved me that day in the library.

Ace stopped walking, only turning his body halfway back around to look at me, enough so our eyes could meet. There was a split second where I thought I'd seen regret flash across his eyes. As fast as it was there, it fled, replaced by a glare edged in cruelty so tangible it could have cut glass. "I can't love anyone, not anymore. I know that now," he said with conviction.

I couldn't help it when his words tore into my heart as deeply as if he'd physically sank his sharp canine Hellhound teeth into me. Though it was Ace's mouth the biting words had come out of, it was not his voice I heard.

This time when he turned around, he was gone for good.

Unable to move, or breathe, anger filled my entire body like a red-hot wire, from my feet up through my vertebrae and to the nape of my neck. The whole world was threatening to crush me and I had two choices: to stand there and let it break every bone in my body, or let the anger fashion a new person in place of the old Dess. If Ace could change everything he believed in within a blink of an eye, then so could I.

Angel Lain once told me how, "The sun brings us closer to Heaven." Lain wasn't talking about his kind of Heaven, the one where you might imagine Angels dressed in white robes, where everything is made out of gold, and Cherub babies are frolicking through the clouds. No, the kind of Heaven Lain was talking about was the subjective kind where everyone finds their own kind of peace. He also told me, so long as I believed there was a little light left in my heart, there would also be peace. But that would be taking advice from someone who had a strange obsession with green food.

Right now, my heart was full of so much hurt and regret, there was no room for any amount of warmth and light.

Despair.

That's all I could feel right then. So much so, the hole inside my chest began to grow and expand resembling some black void, letting in all the hurt and angst I'd tried so hard to repress and keep at bay until now. For the first time, I let the thorny creature on the base of my spine swim up my vertebrae until it coiled around the base of my neck, just before it raised its ugly head, hissing in excitement as it entered my mind.

Kione had said I wasn't using my full potential, and now he would see what Desdemona Starr was really made of. I only hoped I wouldn't get so lost and lose my way back.

Whatever happens, it will be worth it if it means getting Ace back.

Clouds of darkness began to shade my mind. I felt the surge of power burn a fire through my veins. There was no turning back from this point on. I had one last thought before the feeling of ecstasy, brought on by the thorny creature of darkness and despair, consumed me.

Maybe I shouldn't be worried about Kione's corruption over Ace. Maybe the only real thing I should be scared of is me.

Epilogue

Apollyon

Stuffy city air and the smell of a fat man sweating before Apollyon made his nose wrinkle in disgust. He wouldn't have been there in the first place if it wasn't for *her*; he always did things he wouldn't normally do for her…his Lilith.

The train arrived not a moment too soon. Following the crowd inside the train, Apollyon found a corner to stand in, refusing to sit in one of the filthy chairs. He watched as the fat man picked his nose before admiring his winning prize, wiping it on his own pant legs after.

Mortals were such revolting creatures, Apollyon thought, making his way through the crowded train. One of his hounds, the one he'd made his own personal private investigator, had gotten a lead on Lilith's whereabouts, something Apollyon had been trying to find for years. He refused to believe a woman who was as magnificent a creature as Lilith could simply perish from his world or any other. What he could believe, however, was Lilith's desire to escape a romance deigned to be doomed from the beginning. She'd been sighted at this train station outside Rochester, New York, one year ago. He knew the chances of her being here now were slim, but it was the only lead he had in years. He'd felt the obsessive string that attached him to her, the only woman he'd ever loved, tug on him, begging him to follow. Lilith could be anywhere in the area now though, if she was even here: New York City, Buffalo, Yonkers, Syracuse. All big cities, making it impossible to find her.

The woman next to Apollyon began nit-picking at everything her husband was doing, loudly and frenziedly, in turn breaking Apollyon out of his deep contemplation.

Temptation to reach out and grab the woman with the incessant chatter by the throat and cut off her air supply arose. He felt the thorny creature which lived on his spine wake, hungry to satisfy Apollyon's needs. It slithered beneath his skin and up the length of his vertebrae, before it nested into the nape of his neck; it was his Demon, the essence of subliminal dark thoughts. Everyone was capable of having their own Demon, only few beings were aware of their presence. Luckily for the woman, the train arrived at their stop, and Apollyon resisted, against his better judgment, to do the world a favor by ridding it of the pest of a woman.

Apollyon left the train, and searched for the hound that should have been waiting to assist wherever he needed him to. Long ago, before he had made the Morning Star into what it was now, a place for younglings to learn their place in this world, he had used Hellhounds as slaves, chained and always in beast form. It wasn't until Lilith had suggested a different way to use the hounds which let them shift back to their original human forms. Apollyon thought it was a waste of their potential, and he was afraid they would get too comfortable in their human form and forget their proper place in Hell.

Over time, Lilith's plan had proved useful. What Apollyon couldn't foresee that Lilith could, was the degree of respect and loyalty from the Hellhounds that would follow naturally; eventually the hounds became faithful servants on their own accord.

There was something fulfilling about having them flock to him without the force of his hands, or chains. It only proved to Apollyon how he was a God of his own decree.

There, Apollyon spotted Quintin, one of his oldest and most trusted Hellhounds standing next to the car they would use as their next transportation to delve deeper into the city. He was holding the door open and ready for Apollyon.

"Quintin." He nodded at the large bulk of a man-beast in greeting. "Come, it's time we find Lilith and bring her back where she belongs."

"Lilith has been gone too long," Quintin said, agreeing.

Yes, far too long, though Apollyon wasn't certain Lilith hadn't planned on keeping it that way, intending to put a sizable distance between her and the Dark Manor.

"And distance from you as well," the thorny beast said. His Demon spoke to him often.

"Shut up and be gone, you insolent pest," Apollyon spoke out loud to the thorny beast sitting comfortably on the back of his neck. Apollyon could feel his skin there become stretched as it spun in circles, like a dog trying to get comfortable in its makeshift bed. Its enlarged form made a bulge under his skin and made it nearly impossible for Apollyon to get comfortable.

Quintin, who Apollyon could see from his seat through the driver's window, did not pay any heed to Apollyon's sudden outburst. It would not have been uncommon for Quintin to hear Apollyon talking to his Demon. It was another characteristic trait he found himself fond of about the loyal hound.

Apollyon was disconcerted when his driver veered off the main road and onto a gravel driveway. He looked out of his window to see the road had a plethora of Angels carved out of white marble, lining both sides of the drive. His puzzlement only grew when Quintin parked the car in front of an old hospital institution: Saint Agatha's Hospital, and Rehabilitation Center.

Apollyon waited for Quintin to open his door. He exited the limo and stepped up to the curb and the set of stairs that led up to the entrance of

Saint Agatha's Hospital. It looked to be a cold and sterile place. Too cold and not somewhere he could ever picture his Lilith to be.

Anger stirred within him at Quintin for leading him there, along with the immense urge to lash out at the hound, because surely he'd been misled in his findings. Instead, he walked up the steps and pressed the button to buzz himself into the building. The inside was just as pristine as the outside. Every square inch of the institution was unsoiled by the outside elements. More of those oversized Angels, Apollyon loathed inwardly, stood as you first entered. They'd poorly chosen the largest one to greet people in the foyer, and Apollyon had to go around it in order to see the person behind the desk. If the Angels weren't in statue form or, Apollyon's favorite, hanging like a hunted animal and mounted on the wall, they were on the wallpaper, and the chandeliers.

"Can I help you?" the receptionist asked, in a voice far too nasally to be pleasing to the ears, not bothering to look up from the computer in front of her. Her appearance lacked the kind of appreciation Apollyon preferred. Her lipstick had only made it halfway on her lips, the other half colored her teeth in an outdated shade of bright-pink, the buttons on her shirt misaligned and hung crooked on her breasts, while her hair bore a dingy shade of blonde, and hung repulsively like soggy pasta down past her shoulders.

Apollyon squinted at her as a snake-like smile overcame his lips. He stepped forward, careful not to touch the desk and all of its holy reekness.

"Yes, I am looking for a woman whom by good authority I was told is being housed at your fine institution. I believe you have her down as Lilith," Apollyon told the receptionist, voice dripping in false geniality, taking on a quality most women could not ignore.

Like clockwork, her gaze found Apollyon, her eyes widened and her cheeks flushed a crimson-pink that grotesquely matched her lips and half of her teeth. "I'm sorry, sir, but our clients here at Agatha are not allowed visitors unless you are the responsible party," she said shyly.

Apollyon had to resist the urge to let his tongue push through his lips and hiss at her. Instead, he gave her a cool smile and forcibly said, "Hello, Martha,"—spotting her name tag—"I'm a dear old friend of Lilith's, and after hearing she hasn't been doing so well, traveled all the way down here. Couldn't you make an exception, this one time?"

"Really, I'm not supposed to," Martha said, and then creased her eyebrows together. "What was the name?"

"Lilith, Lilith Starr," he told her.

"Hmm, I think you have been mistaken. I'm sorry, but we don't have any one by the name Lilith Starr," Martha said.

Of course Lilith would use a pseudo name. She was a clever woman. Too bad for Martha, Apollyon's patience was beginning to dissipate at her incompetence. "How about I take a quick look around to see if my friend is here, that would be all right, wouldn't it?" Apollyon asked, losing some of the façade he'd been using.

Apollyon reached out and grabbed her throat, choking the life out of her. Her eyes looked like they were bulging out of her head, and when Martha could no longer make struggled gasps, Apollyon released her limp body, careful to keep her sitting in her chair, her body hunched over her computer. To anyone else, it would appear as though Martha was taking a catnap.

"Thank you for your willingness to help, Martha. It appears my self-control is lacking, and for that I apologize," Apollyon said, scathingly to the unmoving receptionist. Leaning over her desk, he snagged up a set of keys all labeled to their appropriate room numbers.

Stepping past her desk, Apollyon strolled casually down the hall. The smell of rose and white-lily was faint; it was Lilith's smell. Apollyon would never forget that fragrance which always marked her uniquely. Lilith left a bottle behind at his precious Morning Star, the only evidence she was ever there in the vacant room next to his. Lilith would not bed beside Apollyon in the same room each night, too ashamed of her love for him that she demanded to have her own room. Though obviously

Lilith had given into him more than once; their offspring were proof enough of how Lilith had once loved him. Her smell faded away from the still vacant room years ago. Apollyon could never forget her smell, even now.

He raged forward, feeling merciless to all, and unforgiving to whoever hid her from him. When he found out who it was, he swore he would make them pay in the most agonizing way possible.

Her smell resonated through the hall the farther down he went. Lilith was here, he could almost smell her sleeping somewhere here. Longing came over him in the form of chills running down the length of his spine, enough to make the beast grow hungry, anxious to feed on Apollyon's emotions. His world had been destabilized without his Lilith by his side; today he would set things right again.

Apollyon walked through the empty halls wondering if Martha had been the only staff here. He'd passed by several rooms until he'd gone the full length of the hall, and met with a dead end. Roses and a fine white-musk derived from lilies were at its strongest, yet there was nowhere else for him to go. Or so he thought. Apollyon spotted a leather handle on one of the ceiling's square tiles. There was a door someone had forgotten to close all the way. He reached up, pulled the handle and unfolded a set of attic stairs. She was there, Lilith was up there, he knew with every one of his being he'd finally found her.

Apollyon ascended the rickety stairs and paused once, standing at the top; there she was, sleeping on a bed with machines blinking colorful lights. Tubes invaded her body keeping her still. Anger grew at seeing her hidden away and restrained. Lilith was even more beautiful than he remembered, with hair the color of fall leaves burning a rusty-red. Caring for any one person or thing was not logical for Apollyon. He never understood how Lilith moved him so fiercely. But all the same he was standing before her again, knowing that she still affected him the same way. Lilith possessed a power over him no other could, he would do anything for her, even bow down to her should she ask.

He stared at her silently for several breaths. "Forgive me, my beloved," he said. "You have my assurance that whoever did this to you shall pay, repeatedly, and for all eternity in the most unpleasant, excruciating way I can imagine." His anger bubbled fiercely to the surface again. He could feel his eyes burning with rage, and knew flames were flickering in his eyes' reflections.

Apollyon's attention was diverted when he heard a car's tires crushing gravel. He looked out of the one window in the attic to see a black SUV making its way up the long drive. He needed to move quickly. Without a second thought as to what might happen if he unhooked the monitors and removed the tubes leading into Lilith's veins, he freed her from the institution's imprisonment.

He held Lilith in a tight embrace in his arms, moving in a hurried stride. His magnificent fallen Angel powers allowed him to glide effortlessly back down the stairs, dodging the edifice of Angel statues to carry his beloved out of Saint Agatha's. Quintin had the doors open and ready for their departure. Apollyon exited Saint Agatha's with Lilith, however he would not bring her home, yet. Not until he discovered who had put her there. In the meantime he would keep her safe, have his guards watch over her forever if he had to. Lilith was his once more, he would be damned if he let anyone take her away from him again.

* * * *

Kione

Kione hid behind one of the Angel statues at Saint Agatha's after spotting the Hellhound. Upon seeing one of Apollyon's hounds, he tightly clutched the Traveler's Stone. He had decided to test the stone shortly after the corrupt hound, Alcander, killed the Pixie King. What Kione hadn't been expecting was to find one of Apollyon's hounds guarding this place.

He needed to find another place to keep Lilith before Quintin reported back to Apollyon of her whereabouts. He almost had the stone take him

234 | Alissa T. Hunter

to the attic where he kept her, and hesitated. It would be rash of him not to assume Apollyon was already here, and perhaps even with Lilith at this very moment.

How did they find her? He'd had a Seer put a protection spell on Lilith, ensuring him no one would ever locate her. He found Lilith several years ago, or more accurately, Lilith found him. She had learned that there were younglings similar to Kione living out there in the world unguided. She'd taken him and the few others like him, under her wing to safeguard and explain what was happening to them. Lilith warned them about keeping their identities a secret and their impending demise should any of the higher beings, from either Heaven or Hell, get word about their existence.

Lilith also taught them to embrace their differences, not to be shamed or shy away from their fate, that they were just as important as any other creature in this world. And most importantly, Lilith taught *them* the fear of leaving their mark on the world; it would destroy their soul.

In many ways Lilith had been like a mother to him and the others, but her inability to stay long term affected them, him more so than the others. Lilith would always leave to go back to *them* at the Morning Star, choosing them over him and his kind. Kione tried to not let it bother him, he understood why she could not stay with him forever, having children of her own, and because he, Apollyon, would not allow her absence, but still, he couldn't help to grow jealous. Her time away from the facility grew each time she left before Lilith would return, until one of the times, she did not return at all. That was the day Kione put himself in charge of the others. He'd done his best to remember all she'd taught them, but when their hiding place was compromised, he hadn't been able to help anyone else let alone himself. He'd failed them all.

The way Lilith failed him.

Kione moved around to the other entrance, unseen by Apollyon's Hellhound; it was a back door closer to the attic's drop-down stairs. He'd had his suspicion that if Apollyon was already inside, everything he'd worked so hard for was now destroyed. Nothing mattered anymore. Kione would not be able to use Lilith if Apollyon was here to take her back. No, he'd have to wait, he decided. He punched out a hole in the glass big enough for his fist to fit through to unlock the door.

Once inside, Kione immediately knew someone had already found her—the stairs were still pulled down.

It was time for him to leave, to go back to the Morning Star; no more could be done here today. Kione only hoped the catastrophic turnout of the day would not interfere with his and his followers' imminent plans. Without the ability to keep Lilith in a sleep state, his identity was not safe should she tell Apollyon who was responsible for her absence all these years.

Kione clutched the stone in his hands, not needing a light to persuade the stone to take him where he desired: light was a part of his being as it is in all Angels or half-breeds. He pictured his guesthouse at the Morning Star and immediately felt the shock of electricity overcome him and take him away from Saint Agatha's.

When he got back, he immediately barked out commands to his two followers he kept close by. "Get everyone ready to move things along faster than we anticipated. We make our move within the month," Kione said, not slowing to the looks of shock and confusion following his orders. They didn't ask why, trusting Kione since he'd gotten them this far.

What was he going to do about not having Lilith around to get the blood supply he needed in order to make creatures like him stronger, and more powerful? Lilith's blood for a while helped complete other Nephilims' transformation. There was a certain potency to Lilith's blood, since she was an original that helped the others. The simplest answer had been right there in front of his face the entire time, and he couldn't help laughing out loud from where he stood behind the bar pouring himself a drink. After he was done with his first glass, he poured himself another before walking over to the couch, seemingly way more at ease than he probably should be, the magic of his drink pouring over him. He may not have access to Lilith's blood anymore, but he had the next closest thing within arm's reach: he had Lilith's daughter, Desdemona Starr. It may not be an exact match, but he felt, with absolute confidence, that it would still work and his plan could go on.

As he slept, no amount of liquor could have prevented Lilith infiltrating his dream and saying something Kione would never forget: *I forgive you.* Kione wept in his sleep for the things he had done in the past, but most importantly, he wept for the things yet to come.

* * * *

A Morning Star Institute Novel continues with **Ruthless**

Preface

Hundreds of eyes looked up at me, all hungry for one thing. My blood.

I stared without breathing across the expanse of the warehouse filled with enough warm bodies that my skin began to bead up with sweat. Some stared at me with open curiosity, others with hatred toward my position as Hell's Dark Princess, and the powers that go with it. I knew what they were thinking. *Why shouldn't they kill me when it was my blood that could set them free from their prison of a life?* Looking past the fevered eyes of the half-human creatures, there was only one set of moss-green eyes I searched for. The boy who always came first in everything, including stealing my heart. Ace.

A grisly snarl deafened the silence of the room. It encouraged others to curl their lips up at me in distaste as I began making my way down the rusty set of stairs. My legs felt like wood with each determined step I took. Many of the angry mob reached out and scratched at my arms with talon hands, causing thin lines of blood to trickle down. Ace was here somewhere. I'd been promised that he was. In the back of my mind I always knew that this could be a trap. It was a risk to come, especially with the knowledge of what they wanted from me—something I was prepared to give if it meant saving the people that I love from spending one more second as pawns in *his* game.

As though the mere thought conjured him, I heard the grating voice of the one hunting me, "Are you really so willing to sacrifice your life for your hound you'd risk coming here?" he asked. I held my chin high, prepared to prove that I was. He smiled a beautiful golden smile and stepped forward to put an end to this chase that had gone on long enough.

About the Author

Sagittarius Alissa T. Hunter is the author of a Dark-Fantasy series for teens. Originally a Nevada born desert-rat, where she has lived most of her life, now resides in a small town she likes to call "The Heart of Wyoming." Wherever she goes, she is accompanied by her loving husband and their three small children. When Alissa is not writing, you can find her reading, exercising, shopping, playing the piano, doing mom things, or if you can't find her there, she's probably hiding somewhere with a good book in one hand, and a cup of coffee in the other. Self-proclaimed coffee addict, and fitness enthusiast, Alissa considered other careers before writing full-time, and has gone to school for early childhood education, and now holds a business degree because, well, you never know when one of those could be handy. As a lifelong reader, she has always held a fascination with mythology and all things that go bump in the night. But the one thing she expects as a reader, and hopes to deliver in all her writing, is a degree of romance. Alissa firmly believes that the words that touch the heart, are the ones that stay with us...

Did you enjoy Shameless?

*If so, please help us spread the word about
Alissa T. Hunter and MuseItUp Publishing.*

It's as easy as:

*•Recommend the book to your family and friends
•Post a review
•Tweet and Facebook about it*

Thank you

MuseItUp
PUBLISHING

CPSIA information can be obtained
at www.ICGtesting.com
Printed in the USA
LVOW12s2307040917
547547LV00001B/82/P